BITS
OF *Sky*

DISCARD

Other books by Marc Severson:

Novels —

"The Chaos Series"

<u>Chaos Territory</u>

<u>The Streets of Chaos</u>

<u>The Waters of Chaos</u>

<u>Chaos In Winter</u>

Children's Books —

<u>Coyote and Woodrat</u> (in prep)

BITS

OF *Sky*

Marc Severson

iUniverse®

BITS OF SKY

iUniverse books may be ordered through booksellers or by contacting:

iUniverse
1663 Liberty Drive
Bloomington, IN 47403
www.iuniverse.com
1-800-Authors (1-800-288-4677)

ISBN: 978-1-5320-4835-7 (sc)
ISBN: 978-1-5320-5550-8 (hc)
ISBN: 978-1-5320-4834-0 (e)

Library of Congress Control Number: 2018909175

Print information available on the last page.

iUniverse rev. date: 08/14/2018

Dedication

To Bob. You're in here buddy, did you notice? Rest easy.

PROLOGUE

—in the hills above Sky Valley—

Her wind-swept soul cried out for revenge. He heard her cry and felt called to act. But he worried about the consequences.

"What will the Great Spirit think of me?"

He asked the question out-loud as if expecting an answer. Then he saw movement in the sky.

The raven flew lazily and low along the scrubby bushes and short trees on the edge of a deep valley. Suddenly it swerved upward in an awkward motion and let out a soft 'caw' of surprise. He had spooked the bird.

The boy was crouched amid the brush, unseen to all who were not standing behind him, or flying above him.

He lay in wait, in ambush. A lanky youth, approaching adulthood, his face set in a determined look. He crouched there, hidden, squatting, his legs tiring. He hoped he had made the right choice of hiding places. This one seemed to be the most likely trail, high and seldom traveled, it was screened from below by junipers and oaks. If he was correct his enemy should be traveling along it soon.

He meant to avenge the wrong done his family and put his sister's soul at rest. He had taken a long time to discover who was responsible but if his luck held, he would soon have his revenge.

Watching the black bird veer up and away from his hiding place he hoped his trap hadn't been exposed to anyone approaching.

The wind whispered caution, and for once he listened. His quarry was a man, fully grown, a man of water, who had killed with impunity many times before. The boy might wish to face his enemy in full light, before the Great Spirit and with all his ancestors looking on. But that would be foolhardy. Instead, he hid in stubby bushes, tense — another shadow in the dimness at the edge of dawn.

Fear gripped him. What he intended meant he must shun everyone for four days. How would he explain his absence? What if he met someone by mistake? How would he ensure their safety? The innocent were put at risk by his actions too.

Then there was the fact of the act itself. He would kill a man! He had never done such a thing before. Would he even be able to succeed against a real warrior who had killed before?

The boy knew he must strike quickly, from concealment — maintain the advantage of surprise to overcome such an opponent. And overcome him he must! Much depended upon his success.

He sought not only revenge but also to save potential victims from suffering a similar fate to that of his sister. Thinking of her helped strengthen his resolve.

Hearing movement along the little-used trail, he tensed. Was this his adversary's approach? Hazarding a glimpse between the bushes he saw that it was! Though he wore a mask there was no mistaking that distinctive physique. Sliding back, the boy prepared himself to attack, listening to the steady approach.

The sounds were furtive. The man did not brashly stride along. He was alert as always. This would not be an easy task and the possibility of failure haunted the youth's thoughts. But his mind was made up —it was strike now or never!

A shadow fell upon where he hid and the boy sprang from concealment. Swinging his hardwood club in a downward arc he meant to club the man insensible. He had the advantage of height, for even in adolescence the youth was taller than most men of his valley.

But the man reacted with surprising speed and ducking away from the deadly blow, he was struck only a glancing crack against the side of his head. That was still enough to cause him to stumble backward. Though he wore a cloth mask, it did little to protect his face. Blood appeared on the fabric. The boy saw it trickling down into his enemy's left eye and he was heartened. He renewed his attack.

Shaking his head the man managed to grasp and raise up his own club to block the boy's next blow. His legs were wobbly as the youth pressed his advantage, swinging again and again at the man's head.

Somehow the man countered each stroke even through his partial blindness. Blood poured into one eye and he had obviously been sorely wounded by the boy's first strike.

The clack of their clubs striking each other resonated across the valley and the boy was worried that someone might come to the man's aid. He did not know if he had confederates nearby. This fear caused him to overstep his attack and leave the man an opening that he quickly seized.

With a sidestep the masked man brought his club down in a powerful stroke striking the boy's right shoulder, paralyzing his arm. The boy's club fell from his shaking hand.

With a cry of triumph, the man followed his devastating clout by striding forward to deliver a death blow to the youth's head. But his elation was short-lived. As he watched in surprise the boy deftly caught his falling club with his left hand and brought it up in the same movement to explode against the man's groin.

Pain flamed up through his body.

Stumbling backward the man was helpless to block the next blow, a sweeping slam against the left side of his head where he was already injured. He crumpled to his knees. Now it was the boy stepping up, just as the man had with him a moment before. Bleeding and nearly insensible he tilted his head up to look at his adversary. Blood poured off his chin and dripped from his mask onto his bare chest.

Though his right arm still hung limply at his side the boy brought his club back with his left arm and swept it forward hitting the man's right temple. The crack of the blow echoed across the valley. His head snapped to the side and he sagged forward then back. Blood gushing from his nose and mouth the masked man's body slumped to the ground.

Kneeling beside the body, the boy struck at the dead man's head over and over until the muscles of his arm were exhausted.

I

—at the Mine—

Fat Badger awoke early that day, soon after the first of the sun's approach. Later, he would recall that it was a day within the Gray moon, also known as the Moon of the Mating Odor.

Arriving at the mine just after work for the day began, Fat Badger inhaled the scents of split cedar and a tang of burning air from the striking of stone against stone. Here, just inside the mine, he felt the world was both shadowed and sacred. Here, they touched the old realms of creation.

He looked and saw Laughing Fox squatting in a corner over to the right. The old miner was sorting through shims of wood. He had not noticed the arrival of a visitor in the mine.

Fat Badger meant to address Fox when he heard a noise behind him. Both he and Laughing Fox looked to see a slight form standing outlined in the mine's opening. It was Lazy Tree, the other miner of the stones of sacred 'bits of sky'. Lazy Tree spoke, in a voice both shaky and troubled.

"A man fell from the sky."

Behind him, Fat Badger heard the sharp intake of breath and a clatter as Laughing Fox dropped his shims on the stone floor.

Laughing Fox stood up. Staring at his assistant standing backlit in the opening to the mine, he asked, "What?" with confusion laced in his voice.

"A man just fell from the sky. I saw him," he repeated.

"What are you talking about?" asked Fat Badger.

Lazy Tree shifted slightly so he was looking at Fat Badger.

"Answer your Winter Chief!" Laughing Fox snapped.

Lazy Tree looked down and then back at Fat Badger. "It's true! I am the one who actually saw the man, just a glimpse out of the corner of my eye but there is no denying that just now I witnessed the entirety of it — a very strange event."

"What were you doing?" asked Fat Badger.

Laughing Fox answered, "He was placing prayers. The morning was chilly just after we opened the mine for our day's work." He walked up to stand next to the winter chief. Laughing Fox continued, "We had struggled long the day before this one to remove a stubborn fragment of sky stone from the grasp of the mother rock that held it. I suggested that perhaps a song, duly offered with a new prayer stick, placed at the shrine there," he pointed toward the opening with his chin, "just outside the mine, might encourage the ancestors to release it to our care."

"While he was gone I was preparing to pry the piece out with a wood shim." Laughing Fox surveyed his hardwood shims on the floor as if trying to decide which would best fit in the narrow crack in the rock matrix that held the precious fragment. "It is there." He pointed to a bit of clear sky blue amid the dark rock wall. "I said to this one," he indicated Lazy Tree with his chin, "You could do something you know!" the old man said grumpily.

Fat Badger nodded and looked at the assistant miner. "So you went out to place a prayer?"

Lazy Tree said, "Yes, I located a piece of willow of appropriate size and width. I sat chanting a short prayer song, first carving and then painting the stick. When it was ready I attached two turkey breath feathers and one tail feather with some clean string. Walking to the shrine, I placed it there, all the time still singing. I did everything reverently! Then I went to find more paints to mix."

"Why?" asked the winter chief.

The young man hesitated. Then he replied, "I thought perhaps a painting on the stones of the mine exterior if offered with the prayer stick might sway the spirits to release their prize."

"That was a good idea," said Laughing Fox.

"But first I felt the need to relieve myself." Embarrassed, he looked at each man in turn. He continued, "Walking down toward the creek I untied my sash, lifted my mantle and pulled aside . . ."

"We don't need those details!" snapped Laughing Fox. He looked askance at Fat Badger.

The young man nodded, "I was nearly finished when out of the corner of my eye off to the left I caught sight of an unusual movement high in the sky. Turning my head quickly I had only a glimpse of what had attracted my attention, startling me so that I almost urinated on my boots!"

Laughing Fox expelled his breath – loud in the enclosed space – and turned to Fat Badger. "See what I must put up with? This one rambles on all day!"

Fat Badger nodded but he turned to the assistant and said, "Go on Lazy Tree."

"I saw it! A flailing thing fell from the sky. It landed with a 'thump' somewhere across the creek from the mine. I heard it!" He looked over his shoulder as if he might see it again. "At first I didn't recognize what it was. It was only after I thought about it for a moment that I realized what I had seen was a man." He turned back to look at them, "So I ran back here to the mine to alert Laughing Fox that something strange happened. We must go look into it!"

"What do you think, Laughing Fox?" asked Fat Badger.

The old man was not convinced. He stared at his assistant.

"What are you talking about? This makes no sense. Did you place all the prayers?"

"Yes, but then I saw a man fall from the sky!"

"You think!" Laughing Fox grumbled. "It is absurd. Men do not fall from the sky!"

"I saw him!"

The older man started to rebuke him for his foolishness further and then he looked into Lazy Tree's eyes. What he saw shocked him. He brought his hand up to cover his mouth. Fat Badger saw it too. He said, "We should go look."

They hurried from the mine.

Fat Badger noticed that Lazy Fox could not resist a glance back over his shoulder up toward the Forbidden Place high above the mine. He put that detail away in his mind as they made their way to the crossing stones that lay downstream from the mine.

—near the Mine—

He, Lazy Tree and Laughing Fox found the broken body lying amid the bushes halfway up the slope across the creek just opposite the mine, as Tree had said.

3

They looked at the oddly placed limbs and a head turned at an acute angle with eyes that stared in surprise at nothing.

It was a stranger, his dress was plain but better quality than most people in Sky Valley habitually wore. To Fat Badger, his tattoos suggested a Southern White Ant person. He wore no jewelry but Laughing Fox noticed a place on his upper arm where he might have recently had a constricting bracelet cut off. His ears were pierced but unadorned. Blue tattoos on his chin beneath his open mouth were the best clue that he belonged to the White Ant people of the south.

"This bodes ill!" said Fox shaking his shaggy old head. Looking up he spoke his thoughts, "He could not have jumped from the cliff above us. He lies at least two body lengths from the rim. His body lays too far out from the cliff edge!"

As if anticipating his thoughts Tree said, "Perhaps he ran and jumped?" not wanting to think of the alternatives.

Laughing Fox waved off his suggestion. "What do we do?" he asked as he looked at Fat Badger.

Fat Badger thought for a moment and then looking at Lazy Tree he said, "Go and fetch help, bring Thunderhead."

The young miner ran off leaving the other two keeping watch over the broken body.

Thunderhead was soon arrived to care for the body and the valley council was alerted. Gossip fueled by the strangeness of the happening soon had the news broadcast across the entire valley. The event attracted hundreds of people to the place where the body lay. People ringed the place. Speculation was rampant.

Most were baffled and many were frightened.

Like Fox, some argued that a man could not have fallen from the sky. Others pointed out that he lay just below the little-used track known as the Ogre's Trail and they said that was proof that ogres must have thrown the man to his death. This theory gained many adherents because so little was known about the Ogre's trail.

This, of course, was due to the fact that no one wanted to talk openly about ogres.

The Ogre's trail represented a great mystery. One of the least known and most feared places in Sky Valley — Ogre's trail generated new stories almost with every new moon. The only other place that scared everyone more than the trail was Dead Women Canyon.

The name of the canyon spoke to its reputation. It lay beyond the Forbidden Place and no one was allowed to visit there or the old village that lay near its spring.

Because of those reputations, such places were to be avoided.

Ogre's Trail lay beneath a deep draw filled with brush and debris known as The Ogre's Tangle. It was a cluster of broken trees and branches that filled the deep ravine from side to side on the northeast slopes below a dark peak. This peak could be seen from everywhere in the valley. It was the tallest point of the mountain range that loomed above Sky Valley.

People outside the valley had named the peak the Ogre's Tooth. Locals shunned that name.

Within the valley, it was commonly known as Sky Sweeping Mountain — a much less daunting title. As the highest peak dominating the sky above them it also provided for them. Fresh water in the form of trickles and seeps that contributed to a deep cool stream flowing down through their valley was sourced from its rugged slopes. Sky Sweeping Mountain nourished the life of the valley and the jutting peak was equally seen as a protector of the people of the valley as the giver of life.

Still, it was rumored that there were sites untrammeled by human feet on Sky Sweeping Mountain — rumors abounded about its dark places and rarely seen caves. Legends told around winter fires emphasized its dangers and stark mysteries. Stories of other-worldly creatures living in those caves amid its forested crags kept most visitors and intruders away.

"Witches dwell there!" warned the ancient storytellers sitting around their winter fires.

Favored by the old grandfathers sitting around those fires were the legends of hairy giants living on the peak. Many deeds were ascribed to those creatures. One of the explanations for the deaths of the three women that gave Dead Women Canyon its name was that these hairy giant people were responsible. In the story, the women somehow broke serious taboos and were punished with death by the spirits of the mountains.

Some reasoned that the creatures were immortals moving between all the various worlds within the universe. Shared history told of three worlds that the people had passed through on their way to this one and it also speculated that there were more.

Other people thought differently about the stories. Some believed that these creatures existed but they were giants, who lived in the woods of the mountain peaks. They said that these hairy giants lived as far away from man as possible. They only interacted with the people on rare occasions, mostly by accident.

No matter how they saw them, they referred to them as ogres, which suggested a spiritual source additionally implying they were sacred. And all said they were to be avoided. An area that was named for such creatures was likewise unvisited.

Tall Claw, the valley's warrior, was the only person who had intimate knowledge of the area around those dark valleys. He occasionally used the trail which led to the tree cluttered valley of Ogre's Tangle on his hunting trips. People marveled at his bravery. Though his hunts brought him great success, few souls ventured into that haunt of spirits and witches, let alone risked stepping into the supposed home of ogres.

There were rare exceptions. These included brazen youngsters who saw it as a challenge to their rights of passage as they neared adulthood.

Infrequent sorties into its dim recesses became the legends in the lives of youths who were approaching their recognition as mature individuals. Most of the boys of Sky Valley, and some of the girls, who yearned to be recognized as scouts or hunters, cautiously journeyed at least one time up into the brushy area, darkened as it was with many deep shadows and imagined terrors, as part of their right to advance into the adult world.

Standing on the trail just below the tangle of fallen trees and broken branches within the draw, they yelled their names, pounded their skinny chests and bid the ogres show themselves. Throwing rocks up into the tangle they sounded their chests with a loud slap one last time. They usually retreated at the first hint of any noise from within the gnarled branches. Later, on the long hike home, they congratulated each other on their bravery.

Few, if any, ever made a return trip. Stories of ogres kept most sensible people away.

Tall Claw scoffed at them, discounting the stories, saying only that in numerous trips up through Ogre's Tangle, he had yet to see an ogre or encounter a witch in the draw, let alone a giant hairy man. He was a skeptic.

Still, many of the people of Sky Valley who had gathered on this day in the Moon of the Mating Odor, and who now stood staring down at the broken body which lay beneath the haunted trail, espoused in favor of ogres as the likely culprits.

A few others intimated that the man could be a victim of an even greater force.

First Light, a well-respected leader of the Vulture society, opined that this strange man was a sacrifice from the sky and as such he delivered to them an important message.

"The Great Spirit dropped this one into our valley as a warning to all who dwell here that we are not following his wishes. This unfortunate sacrificed his poor life to alert us all to the grave danger we face. We must heed the warning!"

"What danger do you speak of?" asked Laughing Fox, though one could see by his eyes he had already guessed the answer.

Glancing up at the Forbidden Place, First Light continued, "Just as we were forced to abandon the village near the spring in that canyon." He said without naming the exact place. "This is a clear message. We must immediately halt our rape of sky stones from the previous world. What's more, it says we should abandon this valley altogether. The first warning we received years ago should have been sufficient but now, of this," he waved at the broken body, "there can be no argument!"

A murmur of angry voices accompanied several people moving away from him when he had finished. A few others protectively moved toward the seer. The divide was clear.

"That's foolish!" said Laughing Fox eyeing the people who were aligning themselves with First Light. "It's true that the sky stones are of the old place — the third world. Though we have left that world behind us," Fox continued, "it was ours to live in then and we still hold the claim."

"No, no! In this you are wrong!" answered First Light quickly. "We relinquished all rights to that land when we left. Besides you know as well as I, one cannot own a piece of any world! It belongs to the Great Spirit alone. Our ancestors were given it to live in and they were to protect it.

Many died there. We should not plunder the land in which our honored dead dwell."

Fat Badger moved forward as if to speak but he was interrupted.

"This argument resolves nothing!" spat Thunderhead striding into the space between the two camps. "Whether he was thrown from the sky by the Great Spirit, our Blessed ancestors, or," here he snorted, "tossed off the cliff by hallowed beings; we all must become more aware of what happens in the next few days before anyone can interpret why this occurred. This deserves careful study and reflection. We will call to counsel! The spirits of our ancestors will visit and they will impart to us their wisdom and wishes."

The old priest addressed the entirety of the crowd, "No outside fires are to be kindled the rest of this day! Your leaders will inform all as to their revelations. Hearken to their words! Now, all of you leave this place and allow us to prepare this body so its soul will find its way!"

"Yes please," said Flowers Wilting, "we want no more ghosts haunting our valley." She turned to look at the two prominent spires of rock standing northwest of them.

"You are haunted only in your mind old woman," answered Thunderhead. "There is much work still to be done in preparation for the coming winter. I suggest you all return to your labors and let us see to this unfortunate!"

Though it answered no one's fears or questions the old man's speech succeeded in dispersing the gossips and lookers-on. No one wanted the taint of death following them home.

Which still left many speculating, as Fat Badger did, on the strange occurrence: How and why had a man fallen from the sky?

—at Hill-All-Alone—

Reflection was habitual among the leaders of Sky Valley. Old men sat and thought as much as they did anything. One ancient seer had been famous for his measured thinking. Fat Badger recalled that he had voiced those thoughts just a few moons earlier.

It was his grandfather, Loping Animal.

Sitting cross-legged on a small woven mat in the middle of the room in his wife's house, he watched, listened and thought much. Piled all about him were stacks of blankets and nested baskets that had seen much use. It was as if Fat Badger could still see him and hear his words.

The old man pulled a worn rabbit skin robe tighter about his shoulders and fed three twigs into the banked coals in the shallow hearth. His wife had made the blanket for him many years before and, though it was worn through much use, it remained his favorite — especially since his wife's spirit had departed this world two years before.

"Our ancestors gather in many numbers," he said.

"When do they come grandfather?" Fat Badger had asked, sitting across from him. One who observed the two closely might catch a hint of familial resemblance in the two faces — one old and lined, the other an adult but younger and displaying a worried frown.

"Soon, they come soon and they bring snow."

His worry intensified, "Much snow?"

"Very much, more than you have ever seen."

"More than you have ever seen grandfather?"

"I don't know. I fear I shall not live to see it."

And he didn't. Loping Animal, the trader of the people of Sky Valley and grandfather of Fat Badger, the current Winter Chief of Sky Valley, died in his sleep two nights later.

Four days after the old man's passing his grandson, Fat Badger laid Loping Animal to rest in the earth near his mother's house, close to the grave of his wife, Sparkling. "He goes to join Sparkling, his devoted wife," said his great-grandnephew, Angry Cloud, as they laid his body down on his final bed of earth. "He said she would wait patiently for his passing. She has waited on him long enough. Now they may journey west."

Many still clearly remembered when she began her last journey two years earlier also in a freezing time but Fat Badger agreed with his nephew. His grandfather, Loping Animal had stood by her fresh grave at that time and predicted, "She does not go far. She will pause in this world a bit. Just until I join her".

He often repeated that belief over the next years as if stating it helped make it true.

"She will be waiting for me, I am certain," the old man had repeated one last time the night of his death. "We will walk together again." Fat Badger nodded and the old man passed on — comforted by his beliefs.

Four times four days later Great Council was called and Fat Badger was acclaimed by the council as the trader for the valley.

So much was placed upon his shoulders. He could not recall a time when he felt more confused. Here he was in charge and yet nothing seemed within his control. It all began the day the man fell from the sky until then he thought he might be able to cope. Now —

It wasn't that he was naïve. He had seen the weight of leadership and the toll it took on his grandfather. He knew it was not an easy job.

While he expected as much, this honor also worried him. The timing was poor. If Loping Animal could have remained with the living one more year things would have simplified for Fat Badger.

Already serving as Winter Chief, with his wife Fire Star as Summer Matron, the implication of possible collusion between them – the centering of power and prestige, was worrisome. Too much power focused on one family would lead to jealousy and rancor. And as the trader, he supervised the selling and barter of the sky stones; more power. Fat Badger did not tell anyone but he would have been just as happy to not have been chosen Winter Chief.

His trusted counsel was gone. He was alone as the leader and all the responsibility was his.

And now a man had fallen from the sky.

II

The Sun rose on four more days of the Gray Moon, bringing life.

Crawling into the sky he smiled redly, pouring happy rays upon his world. Dawn brings joy to all things living. The rising of the Sun also brings — coyotes!

They gather nightly to hunt within the dark and afterward they huddle to await the dawn. At the first hint of his mirth glowing in the east, the coyotes begin to rouse and stretch. They lick the bits of flesh and blood from their whiskers and nip and play. They roll in the dust and scamper up the brushy hills into the approaching warmth.

Chortling, they can hardly believe their luck. It looks as if another day will truly dawn! Another promise kept! Time to go drink of the cold rushing waters, rest and play!

First, they must get past a danger. Cautiously they approach the rock-piles of man. Sniffing about the pieces of old wood that man has tied together with yucca twine they hear the muffled growls of their small brothers trapped within. Coyotes feel sorry for the dog. He knows not what he has relinquished in service.

Coyotes curl their lips and snarl in silent disdain at the dog's chosen life then trot off to the valley below. They rush to the rapidly flowing waters and drink deeply of the chilling cold. Their day begins anew! It will be another lazy one as they nap and watch in the daylight world. They are blessed! They sound their pleasure.

Coyotes laugh at sunrise. Their yips of laughter resound through the valley.

Some men say they laugh because they are happy that a new day of mischief is dawning. Others say they are simply glad to see each other. Priests suggest that they laugh because the sun has returned to its place in the sky once more and they laugh from relief.

Deep in their winter houses the oldest of the old men sitting in their warm cloaks, close to their clay-lined hearths and warmed by the glowing coals, pull their thick furs around scarred thin shoulders and gently disagree. They have the wealth of knowledge left to them by their ancestors. Gathered there, reflecting, comfortable and proof against another winter, they sip warm tea and say the coyotes laugh because they think their cousins, the men, are so foolish.

Men fight over thoughts and dig ground they will never live in and they argue over raging emotions! They fight and run about aimlessly. It seems absurd. Coyotes understand what life is all about.

Life is eating and sleeping, playing and mating. Life is raising their young to follow in their footprints and then dying.

Then the old men chuckle amongst themselves mimicking their cousins, the coyote's mirth, because they know in this belief, the coyotes are correct.

—at the house of Tall Claw—

Tall Claw, War Chief of Sky Valley woke as always, at the wild, frenetic, warbling cries of the coyotes as they gathered at the stream to celebrate the new day.

Slowly he unwound his great body from his sleeping robes. Standing, Tall Claw was the tallest man in the valley, full nineteen hands breadth high. He rubbed his shoulder. An old wound it always ached in winter.

Four days ago he had investigated a most remarkable event. A man who fell from the sky. As instructed by his winter chief, Fat Badger, Tall Claw traveled up onto the high cliffs above the spot to see if there were any clues as to the mystery. He had found no solutions to the problem of how it happened. It remained an unsolved problem — causing much speculation. The council continued to talk. No one was certain of anything, except Tall Claw. Tall Claw did not think much more about it.

Tall Claw did not hesitate or waste sunlight musing over his being, his soul, or past events. It was his habit to rise with the cries of the coyotes and face each day anew. At dawn they sang him awake; daring in their mockery and daunting in their intelligence. Even nestled deep within the womb of his house he always clearly heard them singing. He was a man alert even in sleep.

Yet even as meticulous as he was, he had not heard their passage close to his sheltered home as dawn first broke.

Walking close to where he slept, just beyond his walls, nearly silent and slinking along the compound, just a handful of breaths ago, his dogs knew the coyotes were there, but he had slept on.

He knew that if he went out now and looked, their tracks would be in the dusting of frost just outside his stout walls. Though they were able to slink past him in silence, still he was as comfortable in their habits as he was in his own.

Once as a test of his skill he kept watch at his gate all night – listening for their approach. Finally hearing them pawing about in the last of the gray sky preceding dawn, he was satisfied. He understood their habits then as he knew all the creatures of the valley. These were his certainties.

He knew nothing of ogres or men who fell from the sky.

He knew too, that the pack loped cautiously up the hill from the Blue Stream Valley to the low ridge where he lived. They came daily, just before sunrise. They would sniff and paw around the woven stick gate that blocked the entrance, listen to his dogs whining, then growling in low tones they ran off to Sky Creek to drink the cold water and celebrate at the coming of dawn.

The whole time this charade was played out the two dogs of Tall Claw stood frustrated just inside the gate. Sisters from one litter, they stood exactly the same height at the shoulder, just taller than a man's knee. Each dog had a mere stub of a tail and they had the same bright curiosity in their eyes, but there the resemblance ended. One dog was long-haired, mostly black with brown markings and she was husky in her build. The other was short haired, white with brown markings and she tended to be slender.

Long ago, Tall Claw trained his dogs never to bark at the approach of their wild brothers and sisters. All they would do is stand at the gate and nearly soundless, curl their lips; helpless to respond to the coyotes' bravado.

As the dogs' master, Tall Claw was a man of discipline and he demanded the same from others that lived in his walled compound. No coyote was going to tempt his dogs to bark if he didn't want them to. His sleep was not to be disturbed by such nonsense. He had seen to that.

When he wanted them to warn him of something, they would, but coyotes didn't bother Tall Claw. A few of these wild ones were no danger to him or to his dogs.

Their larger cousins, the wolves were a different matter; their packs could take down a warrior even one as great as Tall Claw, but wolves were rarely seen this close to the villages in Sky Valley. Should they appear, the dogs would know to raise the alarm.

But this morning he wasn't mindful of wolves or coyotes. Other matters held his full attention. Four days before this the man had fallen from the sky. It was a puzzle. He was told to investigate. The council met and still discussed the matter. Tall Claw was sent up into the Ogre's trail region but all he found was a place where a tree might have fallen. His terse report to Fat Badger had not satisfied the curiosity of the council.

All that was not his problem today.

Something else had happened — something that might be related to the falling man. He reported it and once again Fat Badger said he must investigate further.

He rolled out of his robes, shivering at the chill even in this, his well-built house. He laboriously excavated the foundations deep into the hill himself four years before, salvaging the many rocks to add to his compound's wall. Built an arm's length down into the rocky soil Tall Claw additionally roofed his house with extra layers of cedar bark and split juniper to keep it warm in winter and cool and fragrant in the heat of summer. It was a good house.

Stretching, he shuffled to the middle of a room that was barely lit by dawn's thin light slanting through the roof entrance. Crouching down over a rough clay-lined bowl sunken into the floor — that served as his house's fire hearth — he held his palm over the ashes and felt some heat. Good, he didn't want to have to make a new fire this morning — he was in a hurry.

A deliberate man, Tall Claw in a hurry was like most other people going about things normally.

Pushing a bunch of dry grass down into the ashes in the hearth he bent low and blew lightly at the base of the grass. Rewarded by a wisp of smoke, several breaths later a tiny flame flared up. He got to his feet and walked across to a low dirt bench where several pots sat. Selecting a rough jar, shaped somewhat like a headless duck, he brought it over to the fire and added some water. He waited while the contents heated, occasionally stirring them with a flat piece of wood. He passed the time thinking about his day's task.

Scraping gruel out of the jar into a shallow bowl he ate quickly using a gourd fragment to scoop the mixture of ground corn and wild grains into his mouth and chewing very carefully. Old Wolf Woman had assured him that she had meticulously picked through the cereal after she had ground it on her stone but he couldn't afford another broken tooth. Removal of the last one had been a ferocious battle.

Then too, he was a man who was familiar with ferocious battles.

Taking a gourd scoop down from where it hung from the rafters he dipped it into the water jar hanging by his ladder. He drank deep knowing that he would be traveling far above the creek today. Water might be scarce. He filled a second gourd that he used as his canteen and corked it with a carefully shaped piece of wood. Tipping the water jar he wet a piece of cloth and wiped his face and hands. He sighed. Throwing the cloth down he shook his head.

"Ogres!" He expelled the word as if an epithet, it exploded into the silence; strange, angry and harsh. He coughed and spat phlegm on his hard-packed clay floor in disgust.

Reaching down he picked up his bedding furs and hung them to air out on a rack set near the rough-hewn ladder.

Taking his quiver from where it stood against the wall, he examined the string on his bow and pulled it taut. Throwing a thin robe over his left shoulder he gathered it under his right arm and buttoned it closed with a carved bone peg, leaving his right arm free. Pulling the quiver strap over his head he drew the bow over his right arm. Picking up his war club he hung it from his girdle on the piece of deer antler woven into the belt for that purpose. He threw his shield over his head to hang down on his back. Reaching into his pouch he withdrew his bow guard and pulled onto his hand over his fingers.

He looked up.

Across the dim room, a bear stared at him with dead eyes. He considered the heavy bearskin robe laying beneath it and shook his head. Though its warmth would be welcome if snow came, he had to be mobile today. His movement would warm him. He could stand the chill. It would encourage him to keep moving.

Approaching the ladder he paused and bent to pick up a long-handled agave knife from where it was leaning against the wall. It would be useful as a walking stick as well as providing another weapon if needed. Scrambling up three rungs he raised the long handle quickly out of the square opening above his head before emerging. As the valley's warrior it was his job to be careful. People depended on him. When his dogs barked their eager greeting at his signal he continued up and out onto the roof.

Emerging from his personal door into the underworld he noticed his rabbit stick lying near the ladder on the roof of the house and cursing his negligence, picked it up and slid it into the girdle. He spat again.

"A woman would have seen to that." He allowed himself a thin smile.

Jumping down from the low roof — four hands above the ground, he saw that the dogs had caught another wood rat in the night. Only the tail was left and it had been well worked over by the two terrier sized beasts. The black one came up to Tall Claw, wagging its stub of a tail but hissing "Shah!" he kicked at it in annoyance. Dodging the blow it slunk off to gnaw on a bone.

No time for dogs this day!

He had important tasks to do. First was the most important: the ritual that he followed whenever he was leaving the walled compound.

Tall Claw raised his hands while gripping the haft of his agave blade, he signaled a salute to the southwest corner of his compound and growled his war chant four times. Punching the air with the stick, he smiled grimly. Lowering the weapon and his eyes, he chanted a long-practiced ancient prayer that his uncle had taught him. Reaching in his pouch he pulled out a bit of turkey fluff. He released it and watched it carefully as the brisk wind took hold of the feather and carried it helplessly off. It sailed up and over the walls and out of sight. A happy sign. Smiling he looked back at the same southwest corner and spat again.

Stopping by a large pot set in the ground as a cistern he noted that there was sufficient water for the dogs until his return. His ruined face looked back up at him from the water.

He had not always been so fearsome looking.

Some years before he had killed a bear, the same whose fearsome face had stared back at him. The same one whose skin now sat within his house.

It had been while hunting an elk up in the Ogre's Tangle. Tall Claw was the only man in Sky Valley who would set out to hunt an elk alone. No one else could manage to bring back so much meat. And he was the only one who would do so in the Ogre's Tangle! Such was his power!

He came upon a large buck just below the draw. Drawing his bow he strode forward and stepped in mud unexpectedly. His foot slipped when he let the arrow fly.

As a result, Tall Claw had wounded the buck in the rear haunch. Injured but alerted the buck ran off with Tall Claw in pursuit through the wooded tangle. Wounded, the elk was easy to follow.

Suddenly he came upon the fearsome apparition that was the other hunter: a great humped-back bear.

Surprised by each other they had joined in conflict upon an instant without forethought. It was an epic battle. One swipe of the bear's claws at his hairline caught the left side of his face, barely missing his eye; exposing two teeth and leaving a scar that made it look as if he was always half smiling. It was not a friendly sight and he felt the scar heightened the grimness of his visage. He liked that. After the battle, he had been given the new name Tall Warrior Who Killed the Bear that Clawed Him. Most people simply called him Tall Claw.

It was this person he saw in the water.

He looked away from the ruined face reflected there. Purposefully he strode over to the rough gate and unlashed it from the wall. Walking out he didn't bother to take note of the coyote tracks on the ground but instead looked at the distant ridge that was his day's goal. Turning back he re-lashed the gate — the dogs making no move to come with him. When they were wanted he would let them know. He had long ago made that clear — if left behind, until his return, they were to guard his compound.

Sitting on a large rock outside the walls he put his thickest sandals on over coarse weave socks. His feet would need all the protection he could give them today. He also wrapped heavy skins around his shins and tied them tightly to give him some additional padding against the sharp spines of yucca and agave. A thick bear-hide sleeve covered his right forearm. The sleeve was also made from the skin of the bear that had scarred him.

Rising off the rock he walked quickly down the trail toward the south.

He pulled a hood up over his coiled hair braid. Inside the hood were sewn pieces of the skull case of the bear he had killed.

That bear had left him scarred for life but it was a great kill that had solidified his reputation as a hunter and the skull of the bear was thick and strong. And despite fearsome wounds, he had returned to his village after the fight with the bear's head and it's skin. After stripping it he had cut the skull into fragments, drilled holes in them and tied them together with sinew to make a flexible armored helmet. It neatly covered the top of his head. The bits of his ferocious opponent's skull would work to protect Tall Claw. It was big with medicine. He thus ensured would not easily fall prey to the blow from an enemy's club.

The memory of that bear never left him.

The day was deeply cool, threatening cold and there was a breeze in his face. There could be more snow coming. The summer matron was doing her job well but he was ready. On his hip, he carried a pouch where he stored supplies. He kept the pouch well stocked. In it were: hardwood for making fire, his favorite snare, a length of yarn and several obsidian blades with leather wrapped around them as handles. If he was caught out in bad weather overnight or even a few days he would survive. He turned off onto a little-used trail that would take him well along toward his destination.

Not being a man subject to irrational fears, Tall Claw was unimaginative, careful and methodical. He was also humorless even though some people called him Smiling Bear behind his back. This was not because of any humor on his part but because of the scar that ran up from the left side of his mouth. Tall Claw knew of the nickname and tolerated it because it was the bear whose skull bones were sewn into his hood that had solidified his reputation forever.

He often thought of the power of that day and drew strength from it.

Running through the thick underbrush high above the valley to catch up with the wounded elk his mind was distracted. That was his fault. As he released his arrow his foot slid in some wet muddy leaves. That was his mistake. He should've checked his footing more carefully. Tall Claw hated mistakes and because of this one his shot had gone awry, only wounding the beast. He chastised himself for such carelessness as he ran in pursuit.

Wounded, the elk fled. With the smell of blood upon the wind, the bear apparently followed the same quarry.

Tall Claw did not think of this possibility. His mind was occupied with his own anger.

They almost collided in a small opening surrounded by pines. The initial swipe from the surprised bear threw him back against a tree. The bear rose up on hind legs and roared. Standing there each stared into the eyes of the other trying to gain a measure of their opponent.

Tall Claw acted. He held two arrows in his bow hand and he quickly notched them and let fly. At that range, he couldn't miss. After shooting the bear twice with arrows he had driven his handled blade into the chest of the beast as it charged and wrestled with him. Worn over his head behind him, his shield along with his thick robe had helped lessen the wounds to his ribs caused by the bear's scrabbling claws. He twisted the long knife and plunged it again and again. Suddenly, the bear seemed to hesitate. It claws stopped.

His snout was inches from Tall Claw's face. Each could smell the other's labored breath. The bear's eyes clouded over — blood trickled from its mouth.

Pushing away from the gravely wounded beast, Tall Claw ducked as the bear feebly swiped at him one last time with its great claws – as it fell back into a sitting position. For his part, Tall Claw had slumped back against a tree, equally exhausted. He glared at the massive bear in defiance.

Staring back at the man, his brown eyes dimming, slowly, one eye closed and then the other. Blood bubbling from its mouth, the great bear fell to the ground on his side and breathed its last.

Seeing it was over at last, Tall Claw collapsed. His eyes rolled back and he drifted off until fully unconscious. He was out for half the day; his dreams populated by roars of battle. When he finally regained his senses the body of the great bear lay before him, still and cold.

After eating the liver of the bear raw that night at the site of the struggle Tall Claw slept beside his kill.

The battle of the bear became an epic tale around hearths for many seasons afterward. Tall Claw himself rarely participated in the storytelling.

He let the evidence tell the story and he merely basked in the adoration of the youngsters who sought to emulate so great a warrior.

Hearing the story, no one doubted Tall Claw's bravery. Still, he was uneasy about his current mission and had been since he began planning for it. It was not just his world he was looking into. People whispered of portals into other realms. There was a hint of witches about the incidents that annoyed and troubled him. Tall Claw was a man of direct action. He hated gossip and supernatural gossip was, even more, to be avoided.

First, it was the falling man.

Now it was "Ogres!"

III

It had all started anew several days before, only two days after the man had fallen from the sky.

Tall Claw stood watching a dozen or so people talking in a clearing beneath him at the gathering for distribution of elk meat that the hunters had brought back. His job that day was to see order was maintained. Nothing ever happened to disrupt the process while he was standing watch. Tall Claw was bored.

Laughing Fox's wife, Flowers Wilting, sidled up to Tall Claw. Laughing Fox as the miner of 'bits of sky' from the earth, commanded great respect. His wife hoped to be given a choice piece of meat. Most people were involved with haggling over how much of the meat they would receive when the woman appeared next to Tall Claw. He pretended not to see her. Flowers Wilting was a known gossip and Tall Claw hoped she would simply go away.

He gave a sidelong glance at Flowers Wilting. She continued to stand next to him. He wondered what this woman wanted.

Finally, she spoke. "War Chief may I talk to you?" she pointed her chin to the right, away from the others. He nodded and motioned her to one side of the clearing above the high spring and out of hearing of the rest of the people and their contentious bargaining. He noticed her husband, Laughing Fox glance in their direction but read nothing into it.

He stood waiting for her to talk.

She began slowly, looking down as if at something in the dirt, "My husband is a good worker," she said.

He did not acknowledge the obvious statement but waited to see where she took it. "He has toiled, extracting the 'bits of sky' from the Earth-mother for many years. We have all prospered from his work, his good fortune and leadership." At this, she looked up at him briefly and he nodded to show agreement. "My husband respects Earth-mother. He performs all the necessary rites and prayers thanking her. He never fails to thank the third world people for their blessings."

Where was this going? he wondered.

She bit her lip and paused. "It is about the Forbidden place." Looking around to be sure no one stood close enough to hear her she continued, "The noises have come back." When she spoke it was only a bit above a whisper, "The noises are closer to the mine, much closer."

For a moment he allowed surprise to show on his face. "Is that all?"

She shook her head, 'no'. "Rocks were thrown at my husband and Lazy Tree. It happened just yesterday. Not many," she added hurriedly as if to downplay the seriousness, "two or three rocks, about the size of a deer's head."

He turned away, thinking. When he spoke he did not turn back to face her and his words were cautiously chosen, "Thrown or perhaps falling from a landslide high above them?"

He looked back at her then. Her face betrayed no indecision.

"My husband said 'thrown', they could not have just fallen. And they heard no falling rocks." She paused again, uncertain, "And they heard grunts and coughs."

Tall Claw stood for a long breath lost in thought, nodded at her and then walked away to gaze up at the mountain summits to the southwest. Dark peaks rose up against the sky. Sky Sweeping Mountain was largely unknown territory, no trails lead up there. Few if any hunters ventured far into its deep forests. Many whispered stories told of what mysteries lay amid the black cloaked peaks. In the dark of winter nights, old men delighted in scaring children with such stories. He knew them from his own youth. He grunted derisively at his remembered thoughts – the chills that those stories gave rise to as he lay in his blankets. These were just witch stories, meant to encourage the young to listen to their elders.

Weren't they?

There was always that lingering doubt. As a child, he had understood it as magic. Now it was more of legend. Such as the passage of the people through three previous worlds to arrive in this one. It was a belief in parallel realities: the world of spirits, witches, demons, and ogres. It was said that their world could be visited by witches from elsewhere. Some holy men said they were linked: previous worlds and this world — the fourth world. Somewhere, they hinted, there were hatchways where one could pass between the two worlds if they dared.

He did not credit such things. His world was stone and wood, bone and blood. But he knew of the stories.

Some years before, it was said, there had been incidents of rocks being thrown at hunters who ventured too far into the mountains. It was for that reason that he had been alone in the Ogre's Draw that day that he fought the bear. No other hunters would venture up there. It was his private place to hunt.

Never had any rocks been thrown at him. But there were stories.

Twice he had heard rumors of rocks falling near the mine. It was said that the ogres threw them as a warning. He had never given the stories much credence. There were those who argued that the spirits were angry at the mining of the bits of sky. It was meant to be a warning the storytellers said. In his mind there was surely another explanation, he would just have to find it.

The miners increased their prayers and the rock incidents stopped. At least that's what people said.

Flowers Wilting waited. When he did not turn back to her, she sighed and after another long moment of waiting, she walked back toward the groups of people who were wrapping haunches and ribs in netting to carry them home. Tall Claw watched Laughing Fox approach his wife and speak to her with a cross look on his face. She straightened up and replied in kind.

Tall Claw knew he would have to go talk to Fat Badger about this. But first, he needed more information. He looked beyond the people to where a slight youth stood apart leaning against a rocky outcrop. Tall Claw walked slowly around the group, eventually ending up slightly behind the young man.

"Lazy Tree . . ."

The youth jumped as if struck. Tall Claw almost allowed himself a smile.

"Warrior Chief, you surprised me. I am sorry. I didn't know you were standing there.

"Much has happened. You have thought long about the occurrence of the falling man of four days ago."

"Yes. It still bothers me."

Tall Claw went on ". . . tell me about yesterday."

He looked sideways at Tall Claw, "What did you say? Tell you about yesterday?"

"Yes."

"Eh-uh," the young man paused. "Well, we were at work."

"And something happened?"

"Did Laughing Fox speak to you?"

Tall Claw shook his head.

"Maybe he should tell you about it . . ."

Tall Claw interrupted him impatiently, "I'm asking you."

The youth looked around to make sure no one was watching them. He shuffled his feet and looked off into the distance. Tall Claw waited. He could see his discomfort.

At last, he began to speak, looking down at his feet as he did, once he started it all came out. "Laughing Fox and I were working, there is a fine bit of sky stone we are extracting from our mother's grasp – we made the correct prayers, we made offerings of prayer sticks . . . still, later it was, we heard noises."

He paused as if thinking, "They were above us, not too far. Rocks hitting the ground, hard and more than once. It was the same noise as it always had been but closer and more of them. We were surprised, it had been many moons since we had heard them." He paused again, kicking at sticks on the ground, "Then rocks came down near us."

"Were they on the same side of the creek as where you found the man who fell?"

"No, no they were close, on our side."

"Did they come from 'that' place?"

Lazy Tree looked around. He nodded.

If this surprised Tall Claw he did not show it. "How many rocks?"

"Three I think."

"All at a time?"

"No, one, then another then the last one. We heard trees being struck. Far away, up in the hills above us. From 'that' place. After what happened to the man who came from the sky we worried what it might mean."

Tall Claw ignored the reference. "These rocks were thrown at you?"

Lazy Tree nodded. "It looked like they were thrown from far away, up in that place, to land close to us. They made big marks in the dirt and rolled a long way."

"How big were these rocks?"

The youth looked up at the sky and then he stared off to the distant mountain peaks. "A deer's head," he glanced at the hunters, "an elk's head - maybe - one was bigger - like a bear's head."

Suddenly embarrassed he again looked sideways quickly at the War Chief but there was no acknowledgment of the allusion to a bear.

"Anything else?"

The youth relaxed. "Ee-uh, like I said, there sounded a noise like trees hit by clubs but no rocks banging against rocks. Then the rocks hitting the ground stopped — there were no howls or cries of any kind." He thought some more then continued, "Just what I told you. Eh-uh, wait, I heard a grunting sound like someone straining to lift something heavy."

"Someone?"

He paused still remembering, "Yes, someone."

"Have any other things happened before yesterday?"

"It's like I said." The young man glanced around. He looked at Laughing Fox and his wife pointedly for a few heartbeats. Planting his feet apart he gazed beyond Tall Claw as if scanning the distant mountains for movement and swallowed hard. He continued.

"Two days before this happened Laughing Fox was gone for the day. I went to work alone. It was just after the man fell. That was when I first heard the noises move closer. Not as close as yesterday but I could hear them clearly." He looked down again. "Sticks hitting trees and rocks banging against rocks. And I think a rock was thrown across the river. Maybe it rolled down the hill. And I heard a big splash. In the creek." He glanced at Tall Claw who nodded.

"I talked to Laughing Fox about it but he told me to keep quiet, even when we heard them together a day later. Laughing Fox said we should just do our work and not mind the noises. But then yesterday the rocks came."

Tall Claw also looked at the ground in front of him for a moment then said, "This will be looked into, I will see to it personally. Tell no one else!" It seemed to him that the youth stiffened then relaxed and nodded his head. "I will talk to the Winter Chief," Tall Claw added.

Lazy Tree looked alarmed.

"Laughing Fox will not mind you telling me. You did the right thing." Tall Claw added. Relief showing openly on his face, Lazy Tree walked away.

People were leaving with their elk meat carried in their bags and nets, discussing how well they did or how badly they had been insulted. Fortunately, there had been no trouble. For the sun's movement over the breadth of a hand, Tall Claw had been busy with other duties.

Finished then, he consulted with the new Winter Chief, Fat Badger.

His meeting with Fat Badger had been brief, their conversation terse as it often was. The Winter Chief gave his assent to the investigation and reluctantly he authorized Tall Claw to enter the Forbidden place. Tall Claw could see this worried him. Though Fat Badger cautioned him he asked the warrior to go alone and say nothing to anyone else so as not to arouse suspicion or unwarranted fears. He added that he did not want Tall Claw exposing himself to possible danger while alone.

"The falling man may have been a warning." Fat Badger said, "If you find any evidence of something unusual return to report to me immediately."

Tall Claw had gone then to the Bow Priest and been sanctified. The priest smoked him with sage and waved eagle feather wands up and down his body. Tying a pouch containing a stone shaped like a mountain lion, a warrior's fetish, about Tall Claw's neck the priest signified his mission was possibly deadly or one of a warlike nature. Tall Claw did not reveal the exact purpose. The spirits would understand his intent. The priest did not need details.

Still, the Warrior had been nervous about the priest's preparations. He wasn't sure it was warranted by what he knew — or that the correct prayers were said. But he had given the priest only vague instructions about what he had planned and after that, it was up to the old wise man to decide what was needed.

He hoped it would serve.

He gave his word he would look into this and he would. No matter if he felt it justified or not, it was not his place to judge. It was his duty. He was true to his word. He would climb the high trail above the mine and look for a sign that someone or something had been there. He would look for a place where rocks at least the size of a deer's head had been removed.

He would enter the area where no one from their valley had been allowed to go for nearly ten years.

Then he promised himself he would go back up the Ogre trail and see what he could. It was his duty. He would report back to Fat Badger and let him decide how to act next. He knew how to handle this.

Except that he had never been asked to investigate actual ogres before.

Tall Claw did not necessarily believe the stories that had been told on winter nights around the evening fire for years. In all his experiences he never saw anything to make him believe in "the rock breakers". Some thought they were spirits that were invisible. Tall Claw disagreed and thought them nonsense — or perhaps at best children's stories. He considered them fantasy, tales of ogres, 'witch tales' calculated to make the children behave their parents.

Not that he doubted ogres existence. He would not admit to being that fool-hardy. But why would such beings have anything to do with man or this world? Not in this world.

He remembered the stories from long ago as all people did. When he was young he had listened in awe to the elders and their characterizations of noise-making hairy monsters that lived in their connected, parallel worlds, high in the mountains. He recalled shivering when the storyteller said they could step into our reality and grab up children who wandered too far from home.

In those dark houses, lit only by meager coals, the old storytellers had pointed at the children with their chins and opened wide their rheumy eyes, "If you don't listen to us and go too far away they will get you. If you don't come at dusk when your mother calls, they will get you. They will hit you with rocks, and bash you with their clubs. They know you are supposed to be home at dark." Then they added, just for effect, "You know, what they do, don't you? Yes! They eat those children who don't listen to their elders!"

Later, as he grew older, he and his young playmates would venture up to the steep, narrow defile that pointed up the mountain, directing them toward the sky. If one credited the stories, the tangle of fallen trees and boulders supposedly lead straight to the lair of the magical beasts. It was the place of emergence from the Ogre world.

Thus it had become variously known as the Ogre Tangle, Ogre's Doorway or the Tangle of the Ogres.

It certainly looked the part. Shadows and darkness haunted the brush-choked gully. Advancing with clubs flourished and arrows notched, the boys retreated at the first sound of a falling rock or crack of a branch and later congratulated each other on their great bravery.

But he was no longer a child, he had grown up and performed an important job. As the Warrior for Sky Valley, it was his responsibility to quell rumors by investigation if necessary into possibly dangerous situations, whether he gave them credence or not. He would expose them for what they were. Tall Claw was unimaginative but he was dedicated to his position. He would fulfill his duties.

Including investigating the falling man whether they wanted him to or not.

He had gone up onto the Ogre's trail and found nothing to suggest how the man had fallen from the sky. That had been four days ago, now he had ogres to investigate again!

Other than the miners and Flowers Wilting, only Fat Badger knew he was investigating this.

Some would approve, others did not. It had become much worse since the man fell from the sky.

It caused a panic in the villages. He heard many whispers that the spirits of the underworld were angry with the people of Sky Valley for mining their stones.

Since the falling man, old arguments about where the bits of sky originated were revived and argued around campfires and in dim lit rooms.

One version of the origin story said that Sky Sweeping mountain was the source of the beautiful blue stone.

According to some when the winds blew strong enough on the mountaintop the tall pines swept across the sky scraping the beautiful blue color to fall on the valley below. If that was true then they weren't stealing from the third world. They traded in the wealth of this world. It worked for many as a good rationalization.

Others countered that they were mining the sky of the Third World, the one beneath theirs that they had climbed up from generations ago.

They argued that the people of the Third World, and the ogres who also lived there would be angry at them for taking bits of their sky.

Tall Claw didn't care which argument won.

Some things had occurred in his world and he had been directed by the chief, Fat Badger, to discover their sources. Tall Claw would do what his chief said.

IV

—near the Forbidden Place—

It took him the better part of the day to make his way to the high trail far above the mine where the 'bits of sky' came from the ground. He stayed alert, careful watching for a sign that others had passed this way. Even in years past the ancient trail was little used – it branched into a pair of lesser trails that took brave hunters up the deep mountains to the west. Long ago, it was said, people from the White Ant lands to the west had arrived by this route but no one could remember seeing them come from this way for more than a generation.

The other branch led to Dead Women Canyon, the place that was shunned by all. This was where the Forbidden place began. Some years before the bodies of three women were found in the canyon and it had been closed to visitation ever since. Despite the fact that there was a good spring at the head of the canyon that fed a small stream of sweet water emerging from its mouth, women chose to go upstream from that place to fill their water jars.

Even a small village that had existed in the canyon near the spring had been abandoned. All was taboo. No one took water within or north of Dead Women Canyon. And no one ventured there. Tall Claw included. His older sister had been one of the women victimized. It remained a place of dark memories for him.

But he was not one to brood on such things. He would perform the task Fat Badger had assigned him.

Tall Claw was glad he had brought the handled agave knife, it helped him clear brush from the trail more than once as he worked his way uphill. This trail was not easy to see. There were places where it had been washed out by rains or landslides. After most of the day spent struggling against the overgrowth, finally he was approaching the spot he was after for today. It would give him a view of the valley and he could crouch there and look out for any movement in the thickly wooded gullies that ran just above the mine or anything that spoke of recent disturbance. He hoped to have time to plan how to proceed from what he could see from such a vantage point.

He could also look across the valley to where the Ogre's trail led up into the tangle and the spot nearest where the man had fallen from the sky.

Stopping, he noticed that some manzanita branches were freshly broken. Sliding his large frame between them as carefully as he could he came upon a cleared, level space. Something had moved about here recently. It might have been a deer. All about him, on the ground, were signs of digging, as if some large animal had been pulling up paws full of dirt, and yet there was no sign as to why this had been done.

This was no burrowing, done to escape winter cold, nor scrambling to uncover an animal hiding in its nest for food. Neither were there sweet plants growing here that could be used for food. He looked about him. This space was relatively flat and looked to have been recently cleared of brush. Was it a sleeping place of some sort? Had a bear stopped there? He doubted it.

He searched the area looking for droppings from any animal to give him a clue as to what was digging up the ground in such an odd fashion. He found nothing. He scanned the diggings again.

Most likely manmade, he thought. *And it had to be recent!* The holes were too shallow for post holes, too small to climb into or to be of use to cut the bitter night wind. Who had been here and why? He stared at them. Tall Claw was puzzled.

Walking slowly about his eyes caught sight of something else and he crouched down to look closer. It was a large chunk of pinkish rock; the facing edge all fresh break. The fragment was thin, almost a blade but of grainy stone, useless for cutting tools. This kind of rock was more often used as a hammering stone. The piece showed no sign of having been struck forcibly from a larger rock. It seemed to be a natural break along fracture lines. Could it be a heat spall from a rock placed in a fire-ring?

He looked around one more time, but there was no sign of a fire.

His head shot up as a branch broke somewhere behind him then he crouched down instinctively, listening to try and catch the exact direction and distance if it happened again. It didn't. All was silent as if the very entirety of their Fourth World held it's breath.

Tall Claw felt a trembling in his stomach. *What feeling was this? What had he gotten himself into? Was this a spiritual experience? How would he explain that to Fat Badger?*

Being spooked was a strange feeling for Tall Claw.

After what seemed an eternity he slowly stood and turning, he surveyed all around him. Above and to his left, a fist-sized stone's throw away, a branch moved slightly, but that might have been a bird taking flight or a whisper of wind. He put his hand with the hafted blade against his chest and gripped his club handle with his left. His right foot was forward and his weight was back. It was his favorite battle position and more than one enemy had fallen as he shifted his weight, slashed up with the knife blade in his right hand and followed with a crushing blow from his hardwood club with his left. Enemies rarely expected to be attacked by both hands.

Slowly he sidled toward the movement of the branch.

Looking up instead of where he was going Tall Claw slid on some loose stones. He cursed his negligence as he nearly slipped off the trail. A fall here would be dangerous, possibly even deadly. It was steep and rough below him for several hundred paces. Using the agave knife handle like a cane he pushed his way back up to get both feet on the trail. Shaking his head in annoyance he edged around a sharp curve and stopped.

His senses told him there was something or someone here but he saw nothing. There was a bitter, unfamiliar taste in the back of his mouth. Was it danger he tasted? Or was this what fear tasted like?

From off to one side, at some distance, he heard a cough — a deep sound, almost akin to a growl or animal's grunt.

It might be a bear.

He shook his head and allowed himself a wicked, ugly smile. A bear would be fine with him. He could deal with bears. He noticed the taste was gone.

Though Tall Claw was not a man of great intelligence, he was phlegmatic and decisive. Little could be gained by standing here waiting for an attack. He was alert, if they came he was ready. Pondering what he had seen, the disturbed earth, the broken branches, the rock fragment, maybe there was something to it after all. Someone or something was amiss on the high trail in the Forbidden Place.

Finally, he decided. He knew his course of action — it was time to go. Someone was up to mischief. He was convinced of it.

Now, as he had been ordered by the Winter Chief he needed to return and report to Fat Badger what he had found. If they sat and talked maybe some sense could be made of the strange signs. Further investigation seemed warranted. Maybe he would return with a scouting party. Reaching down he slipped the fragment of rock in his pouch on his sash. Moving through the scrub oak and manzanita cover, he started down the trail carefully but quickly back the way he had come.

Not being a common passageway from place to place anymore, this trail was not for rushing. There were several areas where a steep fall waited as a reward for the distracted. But he was in command of his emotions now. Tall Claw did not need to consider this danger as he broke into a slow sustained lope.

He was no longer concerned with thinking over the strange clearing he had found but rather he tried to commit to memory every detail he had seen. However, as he ran he glanced down to the left and he realized with a clear moment of recognition that the cleared spot he had found was almost directly above the mine where they took 'bits of sky' from the earth. That might mean something.

While he was trying to decide if that was significant, something moved ahead of him. He stopped. Bringing his feet to a secure position he hefted the agave knife up to a protective position in his hand and gripped his club.

Tall Claw watched and waited.

Ahead of him on the trail, a slim figure emerged from the brushy area. The figure was backing toward him. He saw it was a young woman who moved as if frightened of something pursuing her. She was looking away from Tall Claw but as if suddenly sensing his presence she turned to face him.

His face showed his surprise.

He lowered the agave knife, removed his hand from the club on his girdle and raised his right hand in greeting. Smiling with pleasure for the first time that day, he took a step forward and then stopped again, frowning. Too late he recognized the look on the face of the other as one of warning.

Before he could react or even exhale Tall Claw was simultaneously struck by several large rocks that came flying down through the bushes from his right. He heard a scream and the rumble of more rocks beneath him and just had time to grab at a yucca plant fruitlessly before his body was swept over the edge into the valley below.

V

—at Hill-All-Alone—

Like Tall Claw, Fat Badger had also heard the coyotes cries early that morning. Unlike Tall Claw, he thought they did it just to annoy him.

Roused from deep in sleep, far above the valley's floor, Fat Badger heard them insistent at the edge of his consciousness, like the memories of his grandmother tickling his feet with her broom to get him out of bed each morning. She always warned him against being lazy. Today he awoke on his own, alone in her house. His grandmother was dead two winters since and his grandfather too had gone on, beginning his last journey with her not long ago. He hoped his grandfather had been able to find the spirit of his grandmother. Loping Animal so valued her companionship and counsel.

In his mind, he could see her still: a small, round woman, her hawkish nose and bright eyes dominating a friendly face, full of mischief. His grandfather was her twin in shape but not in temperament. He was business and tradition, dedicated to satisfying the ancestral spirits, his thoughts were always solemn and directed toward the future. He had served as the trading leader for their valley. He supervised the storage of items for trade, calculated their worth and made deals with the travelers who came to Sky Valley.

The ones who arrived eager to trade for sky stones.

Fat Badger came to live with his grandparents while still a young man. They raised him in this, a dichotomous world — one of the spiritual and one of the secular. These forces were always pulling him in both directions at once. Even in sleep, he knew they would never be far from his thoughts or prayers.

But thanks to the chortling coyotes, that was decided now.

Realizing sleep was now hopeless, Fat Badger threw off his blankets and shivering, stood up. Reaching for a peg set in a wall he grabbed a rabbit skin robe and pulled around him. His body slowly shook sleep's otherworld visits from his troubled mind. He coughed, spat in the corner and with his fist broke the thin ice on the surface of his water jar to get a drink.

Gradually the distant peals of coyote humor were dying off as the full winter sun revealed itself above the mountains. They too had had their drinks and were creeping back into the shadows to rest and plot the coming night's mischief.

Fat Badger sat on his haunches in front of his grandmother's house. His grandfather built it for her more than thirty summers before when Fat Badger was a young boy. She told the boy then that it would be his house someday.

"You will live here," she leaned on him as they walked up the trail of the steep little hill. "With or without your own family this will always be your house too." They stopped at the edge of the small, flat space where Fat Badger's father Dark Warrior was piling stones that he had carried up from the valley below to form the wall foundations.

Fat Badger had turned then to look out across Sky Valley. "It's high here Grandmother."

"I call it 'Hill-All-Alone'. It is high. I love it. That is why I chose this place for you, Fat Badger. You have far-seeing eyes, and you will watch for our people."

"Watch for what Grandmother?"

She had smiled dotingly.

"Watch the canyons, watch the hills, watch the sun rise and fall; watch for visitors. Your grandfather has chosen you to be the next Trader. And maybe more than that."

"Visitors are coming?" There was a note of excitement in Fat Badger's tone as he ignored her prediction for his future, "we are expecting visitors?"

His grandmother's eyes crinkled, "There will be many visitors over the coming years, my noisy little one. Someday you will be the one to see them and judge them welcome or not."

"Why wouldn't they be welcome?"

"Most will I think. They will bring the things we want: fresh meat, cloth, shells, stones, salt, and thus most will be welcome."

He had not known then precisely what she meant at the time, but over the years he had come to understand. This house, his grandmother's house, looked out upon the valley. From here he could see the hills, the springs, the creek itself as it drew waters down to the White Salty River, a long day's walk away. And from the back of his house, he could look upon the place where anyone coming to Sky Valley would want to stop: Cloud Spring.

Cloud Spring was the highest source of water in the valley. It was also situated on the main trail into Sky Valley from the east and south. In that direction lived the southern White ant people who came to trade with Sky Valley.

And they would come for the 'bits of sky' that the miners could break loose from the rocks deep in the valley below. It was their destiny, and his. His people, the Brown Ants, believed that they had climbed up from a series of worlds beneath the one they now lived in just for the mining of the precious stones.

The origins of the stones was a matter of conjecture.

He believed the story told by his grandfather. Deep in the canyon, there was a place where the blue sky peeked out from the Third World below. Fragments of that sky could be broken off and pried from Earthmother's grasp. And the White Ant traders that came would want to have those fragments, those 'bits of sky'. Theirs was the most valued stone in the whole of the known Fourth world.

Traders came from all the White Ant villages. Wealthy men, those from far to the south were especially welcome because though they were haughty and spoke in a stilted, formal manner, they brought the yarn and cloth made from the 'cloud plants'. These plants grew rank in the White Ants' large, well-irrigated fields. Fat Badger's people, could grow some of this magic plant but not nearly enough for all the needs they had, so they were happy to trade their sky stones for more spun yarn and woven cloth.

But others came too.

White Ants from the northeastern villages brought salt, another valuable commodity and those from the west and north traded their pottery, tool making stone and good grinding stone as well as corn and beans that would not grow in the mountains of Fat Badger's valley. These imports helped keep their diet varied and interesting. The sweet blue corn of the White Ants to the north, delivered dried on its little cobs, was especially prized by the people when they tired of their red kernel corn.

So Fat Badger, like his grandfather before him, watched the valley.

It was Fat Badger's job to alert the people that traders were at the campsite at the high watering place, named Cloud Spring by the elders. The visitors announced themselves by raising a long pole with bright pennants streaming from the end. Fat Badger could see it easily from his Grandmother's house at 'Hill-all-alone'. He would then go to the village criers to instruct them to make the announcements. Depending on the colors of the pennants he could predict what type of items would be available for trade. Everyone would bring things they had made and collected over the past weeks and hope they could strike a bargain to their advantage.

His job was more complicated in that he must negotiate the shared goods, offering their most precious item for trade – the 'bits of sky' stone that the mine produced. As the head trader for the valley, he kept track of what was needed by everyone in his charge and how much of the stone was available. He made the best deals possible, and as long as he was successful, he would keep his job.

This half of the current trading season had been short, winter storms came, and many traders avoided exposure to inclement weather with their burden baskets full of goods. Still, Fat Badger had been busy.

Now was the time when he would meet with the village leaders, and they would negotiate the distribution of the stored goods he had received in barter. Mostly it involved the cloth from the south or salt from the northeast. Most everything else the people needed they were able to get for themselves in their trading. If not they would tell their village leader and the leader would see if there was any available through the goods Fat Badger had acquired. Any surpluses he stored at his home village, the largest in the valley, downstream on the banks of Sky Creek.

Sky Creek Town, also called "The Place of the Two Round Rocks", served as home to nearly seven score inhabitants and was where Fat Badger's wife Fire Star, lived. As Summer Matron for the valley, she controlled the religious calendar for the summer half of the year. She assumed control of the valley at the beginning of planting and relinquished it to the Winter Chief after the crops lay in storage. Leaders and various persons, including her husband, continued to seek her counsel throughout the year. Her voice set the agenda for the whole of the valley.

Born to power through her mother's family, she grew up watching others direct and prepare the people for continued progress, eventually assuming the position of leadership.

Fire Star lived with her middle daughter in several comfortable rooms on a small raised earthen platform in the central plaza of the village. Formerly four ground floor rooms belonging to her family, over the years, her mother remodeled the rooms, filling them in with debris and clean trash to provide the raised area.

The compacted platform provided a cool place in summer as it rose slightly above the surrounding landscape and caught the breezes.

So far Fire Star's family weathered the insinuations of a few who, having seen the ceremonial platforms of White Ant villages intimated that her family somehow felt they earned their ranking through time and were thus better than the average person.

Fire Star disarmed her few critics with the ingenious expedient of offering to help any of the various matrons who were interested in similarly remodeling their homes. She proudly stated to Fat Badger on more than one occasion that plans were in place to build several elevated houses the following summer under her direction.

Fat Badger helped his wife build her home a full score of years before when they first took up joint living arrangements, and he served the tribe as a mere hunter. Adding two more rooms over time as their family grew provided the impetus for the resulting suite of rooms she now occupied.

Upon assuming the role of valley headman as Winter Chief Fat Badger moved most of his personal items to his grandmother's old house, abandoned as it had been, fulfilling her prediction for him. He planned to live there for the winter while he was responsible for leadership in the valley.

He felt the move necessary and expedient so he could separate his responsibilities from his home life. His wife disagreed but left the decision up to him.

Fat Badger's duties were now much more complicated than merely organizing trading. In addition to being the Cloud Spring watcher, he served as Snow Priest. That meant he was the Winter Chief - his annual term being from the end of harvest to the beginning of planting. As such he had to arrange the proper obeisance to the ancestors of the people to ensure adequate snowfall and female rains while preparing for the ceremonies that would enhance the male or summer rains. Complicated in scope and preparation he was lucky that little trading occurred in winter so he might focus his work to ensure summer rain would come.

Coordination with the Summer matron was crucial to this success. As such it kept him busy and made his longtime marriage suddenly problematic.

When he and Fire Star had joined together, there had been much gossip. Loping Animal had chosen his grandson as his successor, and as a leader, Fat Badger immediately became a potential Winter Chief. Having the Winter Chief married to the Summer Matron was unheard of in the remembered history of the valley. Fat Badger's solution had been to fulfill his grandmother's planned move to her house. During his time as Winter Chief, he maintained a separate home from his wife, and yet spoke with her daily as to religious matters.

Having trained for his jobs by watching his grandfather, Fat Badger assumed each with confidence. Loping Animal was elected winter headman for most of his adult life. Also, his trading was careful, and the valley prospered under both his winter leadership and his trading acumen. He organized the prayers and ceremonies to ensure that the summer rains would be plentiful and the fields productive and dealt with sly traders nimbly.

At least he did until Sparkling had passed.

Having no daughters, after his wife died and he soon became too crippled to walk up and down the steep hill, he went to live with his daughter-in-law, Fat Badger's wife at Sky Creek Town. Because there was no real familial connection between them and no clan association, few had thought anything of the expedient arrangement.

Though there was always gossip, Loping Animal chose to ignore it.

When traders came to their valley, he would be carried on a litter by his nephews to the campsite so he could use all his energies to negotiate. Having always known him as a shrewd leader and a careful man who thought long before speaking, Fat Badger sorrowed to see that after Sparkling left this world, he began to decline in health and energy rapidly.

Fat Badger had studied with his grandfather since he was twelve summers old. That was when he came to live with the venerable couple.

His father had disappeared on a hunt two winters before. After a proper term of mourning his mother found a new mate among the traders that came from the south. His brother, Drinking Bird, six years older than Fat Badger, left with his mother, Deermouse, and her new husband, but because of the duties, he was slated to assume, Fat Badger decided to stay with his grandparents. As his grandmother's favorite it was not a hard decision.

Fat Badger had never understood why Loping Animal had chosen him over his brother. Already by his seventeenth summer, Drinking Bird was a warrior of some renown. He seemed a logical choice. He once overheard his grandfather talking to his mother lamenting the flashes of anger and apparent avarice displayed by his brother Drinking Bird, so maybe that was it.

From all accounts brought to him by White Ant traders his brother, Drinking Bird did well in his new home. He went on to become an experienced scout and warrior for his step-father's people, the southern White Ants. Twice he even accompanied trading missions to Sky Valley, but his visits with his brother had been strained and brief.

Two years ago, during the winter before he had started assisting his grandfather, Fat Badger received word that his brother had been killed in a raid by Red Ants on a village on the Salty River west of Sky Valley. Fat Badger mourned briefly, and in private for the brother he would now never really know.

It was just another loss in a series that had become the markers of his life. His father, his brother and others. All these losses took their toll. But the hardest was that of his grandmother, Sparkling that same winter.

Winter had arrived early and severe. She continued her gathering of herbs and other resources despite the weather. One night his grandmother had lain down and did not get up again. Becoming feverish she grew steadily weaker over a moon, finally succumbing late one savagely cold night.

With the death of his grandmother, Fat Badger took to walking from his wife's village up to his grandmother's house almost daily. He saw to it that his grandfather had all he needed. He kept watch in this way for the pennants announcing the arrival of traders and the habit also allowed him to take care of the house against the day when it would belong to him.

As another benefit, the long daily walk gave him one of the things he valued most: time alone to think. As a child Fat Badger often played by himself in the extensive woods and rocky hills of Sky Valley. His grandmother had long encouraged him to preserve his lonely habits. "You must have time to think, unbothered," she had told him. The walk gave him that.

When he arrived each day, his grandfather continued his training.

Then the time came when his grandfather also passed at the inception of another cold winter. The village headmen had gathered four times four days later and after two full sun cycles of discussion they had named Fat Badger by acclamation to take his grandfather's place as Trader; the job he trained for all his life was finally his.

Sometimes, as he sat outside his grandmother's house, he imagined he could see his grandparents hand in hand on their way to the spirit world. It was one of the few thoughts that never failed to make him happy.

Today, however, Fat Badger squatted in front of the house and brooded on the many things that troubled him.

A man fell from the sky! That alone was troubling.

He had thought of almost nothing else over the last few days until Tall Claw had visited him the day before.

This nonsense about noises at the mine told to Tall Claw. Then the rocks came. Was there anything behind any of it? He didn't want to think that it was a real problem. But just in case he had authorized his War Chief to enter the Forbidden place. Some would not be pleased about that. He hoped no one would ever find out.

Fat Badger hoped that Tall Claw would find nothing except a place where stones had loosened from the cliff and fallen down toward the mine. Then he could forget this in its entirety and focus on other problems.

On the other hand, if he did find something, then Fat Badger was wondering if there existed a relationship with the strange man who fell from the sky. Somewhere he harbored a belief there might be a connection between the two.

Unfortunately, everyone knew about the 'falling man'. And everyone had an opinion as to what it meant.

There were those like First Light who warned that this portended great evil.

Fat Badger wondered, could First Light be correct in asserting that it was a warning? Should he stop all mining of the sky stones at least until more was known? But from where would such knowledge come? Tall Claw had looked and found nothing that could suggest what had happened. Should Fat Badger establish a council tasked solely with discussing the man who fell from the sky?

Hearing an owl scream the night before, down by the creek, only added to his worries. Was it a warning of more death coming? Would it be his people who fell prey this time?

He did not like the feeling of loss of control.

His lack of confidence spilled over into the job he felt most competent at doing. He greatly enjoyed trading. Fat Badger reveled in the 'give and take' of trading and the acquisition of rare goods for his people. Being Winter chief took away from that enjoyment.

The Southern White Ant people had been extremely contentious at their last trading session even with his grandfather sitting there observing. He felt that they were contemptuous of him as a leader. Now he alone possessed the job. Perhaps they thought they could cheat him.

But then he recalled his grandfather had told him once that they made everyone feel that way.

Winter, now there was the real problem. A dusting of snow had come early, and though it was not deep, it implied they would need to make sure they had supplies to last them a long cold spell. Fat Badger knew only too well from experience that the cold would be hard on the old people. Some should move in with relatives now.

All these things were on his mind when he heard someone coming up the hill.

Two cactus wrens squawked at being disturbed and flew from their cholla perch across the trail into a thicket of manzanita. Seeing Lazy Tree emerge from the chaparral that covered the lower part of the hill, Fat Badger thought to himself, *Why is he not at work?* He quickly noticed a worried look on the other's face. "What now?" the Winter Chief said quietly to himself.

Recalling the war chief's mission as he watched him hurry towards him Fat Badger relaxed momentarily. *Perhaps it is about what the War Chief has found*, he thought. Tall Claw went up into the hills above the mine to see about the disturbances, into the Forbidden Place. Maybe he had found something and had sent Lazy Fox to tell Fat Badger.

But that was not right, he argued with himself. It was not Tall Claw's place to direct the young miner! He should come himself, knowing it was part of his job to keep Fat Badger apprised of what he discovered, especially in light of where he was.

So many thoughts ran through his seething mind as he watched the miner approach. He noticed that the young man was perspiring heavily — his shirt drenched in sweat — yet the day was chilly. He had hurried, something was amiss! Fat Badger rose and walked downslope to meet the messenger.

Could something be wrong at the mine? He hoped not; it was hard enough to keep up with the demand for 'bits of sky' now without a crisis of some kind.

He took a few steps to meet him and stopped. There was something dreadfully wrong, he could see it on the face of Lazy Fox

"My pardons Winter chief." he began, obviously flustered, "Are you very busy F-F-Fat Badger?" he stammered, "c-c-c-an you come to the mine?"

"What has happened?"

The young man looked back over his shoulder toward the valley. "Eh-uh we are not sure but there was a d-disturbance above the mine, many rocks fell, there was noise and . . ."

More rocks! he thought. Fat Badger did not interrupt. He merely waited for the nervous young man to elaborate.

". . . we heard a yell as of . . . as of someone in pain."

"Who cried out?"

"I do not know."

"You did not go to see what it was?"

"Tall Claw had told us not to go up the hill. He would see what was there, he said, it was not for us. He gave the command in your name."

Fat Badger looked away for a moment. He understood about Tall Claw's order. After all, it was he who had told the warrior to keep this action a secret. "Let us go then." He took a robe to wrap around his shoulders and picked up his walking stick. He chose the hardwood one as opposed to something lighter.

It took them about a quarter sun to reach the mine, so the daylight was dying. They talked about little on their way and nothing about what they might find. For his part Fat Badger became lost in his swirling thoughts while Lazy Tree seemed too flustered for much conversation.

Laughing Fox had packed up the day's rough-hewn ore in a large open weave bag. He would have Lazy Tree carry it back to the Mine village where the 'bits of sky' would be carefully separated.

Fat Badger saw the mine had been closed for the day with the knot on the rough wood gate. As usual, Laughing Fox had tied a complicated knot that could not be tampered with without his notice. Four jay feathers protruded in different directions from the knot.

The older man sat waiting for their return off to one side of the gate, his small ax on his lap and a hafted maul leaning against his leg. He appeared calm.

"Welcome Winter Chief — I hope you are well."

Fat Badger nodded and looked upslope.

"There have been no noises since this one left —" he pointed at Lazy Tree with his chin, "all is quiet."

"You will show me where the disturbance was," Fat Badger said indicating Laughing Fox then he nodded in Lazy Tree's direction, "let him carry the day's work back."

It was clear that Laughing Fox did not agree. "He will go alone?"

"He has gone alone before." Fat Badger allowed impatience into his voice, "Has he not?"

"But Tall Claw said we should not go up there."

"And that was by my suggestion to Tall Claw, so now I am saying we will go!"

Laughing Fox sighed, nodded and pointed with his chin, "Come then, it was this way."

VI

Breaking a trail through the chaparral was not easy, even in leafless early winter. They made their way up the rocky slopes carefully but quickly — there was little daylight left. They managed about a hundred steps in a quarter of the light they had remaining, even with their necessity of often stopping to look around. Fat Badger sighed with impatience.

Laughing Fox led and deftly swung the long handled maul to knock branches out of their way. Even so, he was careless with one swing in the dim light and took an agave needle in his thumb. Fox extracted all but the tip from his painful wound. Shaking his head, he cursed his negligence saying, "I am getting too old to break trails. The poisonous spirits of the needles have entered. This wound will fester," he said dourly.

"Go see Grandfather Scorpion tomorrow — I hear he has a poultice that can stop the infection and relieve the pain."

"Yes, one poison for another . . ." Laughing Fox stopped speaking abruptly and looked at something behind Fat Badger.

Turning to follow the old man's gaze in the last purple light of day he noticed a hand protruding from under a bush. Hurrying over, they found that the hand continued to an arm on the other side of the bush and that arm was attached to the lifeless body of Tall Claw. He was dead — there could be no doubt. Tall Claw's sightless eyes stared blankly up at the sky, and his body lay askew, one leg bent so that the foot pointed back at his head. Rocks of varying sizes, some smeared with blood, were scattered around and upon him.

Looking back up at where the body had apparently fallen from Fat Badger saw that there was a sheer cliff a hundred and a half paces high above them with fresh dirt scarring the slope from the avalanche of falling rocks. It led back to the Forbidden Place.

Laughing Fox broke the silence. "Not another one! What do we do now? These deaths are unbelievable! What have we done?" His face was a mask of horror.

Turning as if he had forgotten that the other man was there Fat Badger looked through him for several heartbeats then, regaining himself, he took charge.

"What do you mean by saying that?"

"Another is man thrown from the sky and this time we know who it is!"

"And we know what happened!" said Fat Badger roughly.

"What do you mean?" asked Laughing Fox, his voice trembling.

"Compose yourself!" Fat Badger commanded, "Look at the slope; you can see where he fell." Fat Badger thought for a few moments, "Go to your village — send a runner to the Vulture Priest, then another to inform the town criers but make certain you warn him to tell them not to announce before morning."

Laughing Fox nodded, turned to go and then stopped as the Winter Chief added, "And send a runner to my second daughter telling her to bring her cousin Angry Cloud and come here to me." Laughing Fox was surprised at this, but his face did not betray the feeling as he turned and hurried off.

Fat Badger stood gazing at the broken form.

For his part, he too hid his feelings. If he was worried about being left alone with the body of his dead War Chief Fat Badger did not demonstrate it. His face displayed nothing of what he felt.

Sitting down on a rock, he sighed. He needed to think. No one had been more careful than Tall Claw; he knew his job so well. What could have happened? He tried to sort through the possibilities. He was a man that could not be surprised, for him to fall off the side of a mountain trail, even on a little-used path was hard to imagine. Had he been hurrying? And Lazy Fox had said something about a yell or scream. That made no sense. Fat Badger had seen his wife work at sewing up wounds on Tall Claw from various battles and all manner of injury, and he never uttered a sound. He was not a man to scream in pain or even when faced with death.

Following so quickly upon the incident of the man who fell from the sky made this look like it was not an isolated occurrence. He looked up at the cliff edge looming above him even though he could see nothing in the deepening dusk.

"What is happening in our world?" he asked aloud.

He stood again. Staring at the body, Fat Badger started to clear the debris from around the dead man. He rearranged the awkward limbs and attempted to close the sightless eyes. They would not close at first, so kneeling down next to the body he forced them to shut one at a time. Keeping his own eyes open meanwhile he looked over all the wounds, focusing on the cold, broken flesh that had been the valley's hero.

Unlike the man who fell from the sky, Tall Claw's wounds were numerous: deep cuts, abrasions, and many bruises. He was only wearing one of his shin covers, and his shield was missing. There were three arrows left in his quiver, but two of those broke during the fall. His right hand closed around something. Forcing it open, Fat Badger found it held a fragment of yucca leaf.

The retreating Sun was nearly gone. Fat Badger rummaged around in the dead man's pouches and found fire making tools. He apologized self consciously to the spirit of his dead companion for the intrusion. Clearing brush from a small patch of ground, he dug a shallow hole. Fat Badger lined the edge of the hole with stones - most of which were the ones he had taken from around the body. He broke dry branches from a tree that lay on its side.

Gathering dry brush and grass, he placed it in his little fire-pit. He worked to make fire. Inhaling the smoke, Fat Badger realized the winter chief should do something for Tall Claw's spirit. Though it was not his place, he wandered about looking carefully for bits of fragrant cedar wood bark until he gathered enough. He added them to the small fire and breathing in the smoke; he intoned a short prayer for the safety of Tall Claw's spirit within the darkness of the coming night. He hoped the man's soul would not get lost. He did not want the night wind to carry his essence off to become a wind wraith. Imaging Tall Claw as a lost wind spirit screaming in the night made him shiver involuntarily.

He intoned another short prayer: a blessing for warriors everywhere.

Talking to his ancestors was easy for Fat Badger — it was part of his morning ritual — but in this case, he must alert those who would know Tall Claw. They would guide his spirit and welcome him to his new home.

He must carefully consider his audience and his words in his invocation. He had heard such songs being sung before but, he had never attempted them himself. This kind of singing was the job of the Vulture Priest. He hoped his prayers would be well received. He finished with a blessing for the people of the valley.

While looking for the fire tools, Fat Badger came across a large piece of pinkish rock that was in one of the dead man's pouches. He sat now looking at it more closely. It was a spall, a heat spall or a broken fragment. He laid it down close to the flame leaning against the other rocks that were outlining the fire.

The night about him lay now in full darkness. The sky held some clouds and no moon, so the little circle of light from the flame was his only solace. Tall Claw's body lay opposite him beside the meager flame while Fat Badger leaned against a fallen tree. Though it was not the first time he had kept watch over a dead person, he could not fail to note the strangeness of the present circumstances.

Bathed in the orange glow of the flickering blaze, the half of Tall Claw's face he could see looked serene. He hoped it was so.

Was he responsible for this death? Was it because he had sent him into 'that' place?

A whisper of wind enticed the smoke into drifting downslope toward the mine and the creek. Though phlegmatic, Fat Badger again shivered slightly with the night and the company he kept. He thought about borrowing the dead man's hooded robe to wear over his own but rejected the idea. Concentrating on calming his breathing, he closed his eyes. Having composed his thoughts, the chief leaned forward on his knees to begin his evening prayers.

The clack of rock against rock was distant, far up the draw leading to the shadowed peaks. It caused him to stop — jerking his head in the direction the sound had come. But he saw nothing in the gloom. Scanning the darkness for some clue as to what had made the noise he decided it was merely a loose rock falling. Perhaps it had been loosened when Tall Claw fell.

He heard it again, this time somewhat closer and he stood and peered off into the murk. After holding his breath for some time, he exhaled and then he jumped. He thought he heard a distant noise of wood striking on wood. It all added to the unreal nature of the night.

He tried telling himself that these were typical night sounds. Feeling his own heart quicken its beating he found himself listening to the darkness expectantly.

Realizing the little fire backlighted him he moved off to one side and knelt down. Without warning a loud "crack" just to his right made him jump and bring his stick up into a defensive position. Looking into the makeshift fire-pit, he saw the pink rock had split; spalling from the heat into two wedge-shaped fragments. *Well, at least that mystery was solved* he thought, *it was a heat spall.*

He laughed nervously at himself for the irrational fear. He did not fully believe in ogres that came after you or the other stories – monsters and cannibalistic creatures in the woods living high on the mountain tops; they were only witch tales. Stories to scare children. Foolishness! He was a man of water, a leader of his people he didn't have time for old women's stories. And yet.

Again he heard a distant crack of rock against rock, faint, high above him. Keeping silent, not even daring to breathe, he stood in the gathered silence of the night. Though he listened intently for many heartbeats, there was nothing more to be heard from above. His heart calmed. Finally, he exhaled and returned to his devotions.

Finishing his prayers and those for Tall Claw's spirit, he sat back on his haunches to wait. He must have dozed.

The night grew quiet for a long while before he awoke, hearing voices approaching from below him.

"I am here," he called to them in his calmest voice. Two figures came through the brush. It was his daughter Pale Falcon and her cousin, Angry Cloud. The girl was nearly as tall as the youth and a finger's width taller than her father. The young man beside her tended toward a square, burly build. His face split into a broad grin when he saw his uncle and then just as quickly changed as he caught a glimpse of the highlighted body.

Falcon spoke first, "Father what has happened?" Decisive and quick of speech; though some thought her manner brusque, Fat Badger liked that about her.

He sat down ponderously and exhaling said, "Listen now, my children, and I will tell you," When they were seated he continued, "There has been an accident, and this one is gone." He pointed at Tall Claw's body with his chin. "I called on you because I knew I could trust your discretion. You must make a litter so we can take this one back to his mother's village."

He saw questions form on Angry Cloud's face, but quietly the boy nodded and moved off in the dark. Falcon hesitated, Fat Badger saw the girl open her mouth as if to question his decision so he gave her a look. "Not now daughter – I will tell you more later. Go with your cousin, find two strong agave stalks, we will use his — we will use the robe. Hurry, the dawn approaches and it will be light soon. Be careful though. Stay with Angry Cloud."

This last admonition gave her pause as if she caught a warning inherent in his tone, but she obeyed. Besides being his daughter, Pale Falcon served as one of the valley's warriors and scouts, the only woman currently serving thus. He was proud of this, but as the Winter Chief, she must follow his orders, especially now in mid-winter.

He heard the sounds of another moving below them near the mine. He thought for a moment and then realized who it must be. "Here," he called again. The newcomers were already on their way up. It was Laughing Fox and Thunderhead, the Vulture Priest.

"Good, you are here," he said to the thin little old man with Laughing Fox.

"Of course we came!" said the old man sharply.

Badger ignored the touch of rebuke in his voice.

"We came as soon as we could." said the miner, Fat Badger saw the old priest's face throw a scowl at him.

The priest looked at the body. Then he looked up into the darkness, "He fell from up there?" He asked.

"Yes," said Fat Badger.

"What was he doing up there?" he asked pointedly.

"I sent him."

The Vulture priest looked at him, "You!"

"The rocks thrown at us came from up there," said Laughing Fox quickly.

Fat Badger saw Thunderhead turn toward the miner and even in the dim orange light the little campfire offered; he could tell the old priest wanted to hear no more from him. Thunderhead grunted and looked at the body.

"It has been a busy moon," said the Vulture priest sourly.

Fat Badger nodded toward the body, "My daughter and her cousin will make a litter to bring this one who has gone. I have kept watch and am tired. I will go now."

"Who?" said the old man quick and short.

Fat Badger sighed, "My daughter, Pale Falcon and Angry Cloud her cousin." Fat Badger allowed himself a little temper in his voice. "they gather materials to transport the body."

Satisfied the old man nodded and moved to the dead man.

Laughing Fox shrugged, and Fat Badger began to walk down the rough trail they had cut.

Thunderhead stopped him with a question, "What has been done?"

Taking two steps back Fat Badger answered, "Only the initial invocation to let the ancestors know that this one approaches. I did not feel qualified to do any more than that." "Fine," the old man spat out, "it is little enough but will have to do until we get his body back to his mother's village."

Hiding his irritation, Fat Badger left to begin the long walk back to his grandmother's house on 'Hill-all-alone'. He thought about staying to talk to his daughter but did not want to risk an argument with the old priest.

Nearly back home he stopped and looked at the east as the flower-petal-colored light grew slowly brighter. It calmed his heart. He trudged on trying not to overthink about what he still must do. So much, too much! He must convene the council. A search for a replacement war priest was imperative. First, though, he needed some rest.

A noise in the brush ahead of him made him stop and then think again about the strangeness of his vigil the previous night. It had left him jumpy.

Starting up the hill Fat Badger could smell smoke from someone's fire. "They're burning the stew." he thought to himself, chuckling and simultaneously realizing he was famished. Then he looked up. A plume of dense smoke rose at the top of the hill. "Oh no!" He shouted angrily, "No!" and he ran up the trail.

Coming through the clearing at the top of the hill, he saw his worst fears realized. Smoke poured out of the door of his grandmother's house, the layered roof smoldered, and as he watched it flamed up, fully engulfed. Running up to the doorway he held his hands up before his face; he could feel the heat blasting out in waves from the opening. There was no way he could get into the rooms. In one corner he caught sight of a stack of his grandmother's best baskets blazing. The smell of pine pitch burning engulfed him.

What caused this? Had he left a basket or his arrow making kit near the hearth?

Running around the building, dodging in and out he grabbed what he could from outside the fire's grasp. Breaking through the wall on the north side only fed the fire. He made a little pile of his belongings that he had managed to salvage to one side of the flames and then sat on a rock upwind of the smoke to watch the completion of the latest tragedy.

Examining his clothing and the skin of his arms and hands he found several raw burns. The pain seemed distant; someone else's, not his.

Had he left coals in the hearth? No, he was sure he had scraped it out completely. He looked up. The sky was overcast, but he had heard no thunder, no flash of lightning. Had he left a bowl of pine pitch in the house near the hearth? He was too tired to remember. The night had been cold; the day was going to be cool, what could have happened?

He suspected a deeper meaning might produce the answer. Were the spirits angry with him? Had he somehow affronted the ancestors of Tall Claw, so they sought revenge?

He just didn't understand.

VII

Sometime later he awoke in confusion. *Where was he?* Then he remembered. He slept in Tall Claw's house. Fat Badger shivered involuntarily. Was that only from the chill?

More than just brisk he could tell it was going to be cold all day again. By looking up through the entry, he knew that the sun moved in and out of clouds and lay muted in the sky. That sky clothed itself in heavy gray. It looked like snow.

Snow!

Thinking of his grandfather then he remembered the old man predicted such on his deathbed. Less than two score days previous he saw a winter full of much snow. It was his last prediction just before he passed. Snow engendered still another need he must see to: the old ones required protection in this, the killing time of the year. He would have to contact the criers to remind each village to prepare appropriately.

Fat Badger had risen early in the afternoon; he felt uncomfortable about sleeping so long in Tall Claw's house. Yet it was better than having to beg a hearth to sleep near. Though technically still belonging to the man who had owned it until he began his trip to the spirit world in four days, Fat Badger felt that his intentions would manifest themselves as doing honor to Tall Claw.

In the state his daughter had discovered him he could think of no other solution. Before falling into restless sleep, he intoned prayers to the great Spirit and asked his protection for those who had passed. He hoped he had placated any negative spirits.

The idea of coming here had not been his. His daughter, Butterfly, had suggested it to him after she arrived on the scene of the fire about midmorning.

She found him leaning against a large rock, half asleep, his burns untreated. She hurried to gather salve and cloth to cover the wounds.

"Father, your grandmother's house," she said to him as he sat submitting to her care. "What happened?"

He shrugged spreading his hands.

"You look so tired; my sister told me about last night when she came to the village. You've suffered enough; now, you can't stay here, come to our house."

Smiling, he responded, "Thank you, my dear one, but that won't do. You and your family do not need to be awakened by an old man's snoring. Your husband needs his rest." Her husband was Wolf Runner, the second lead hunter of the valley. "And my grandson will be upset."

"He loves having you there."

"Yes, and I love being there but that's just it, I will give him too much attention and he won't listen to his mother."

"Nonsense, he's not even a full year old."

Fat Badger just shook his head. "I will not burden you." Privately he wanted to stay independent as long as he was winter chief.

She sat on the rock next to him and rested her hand on his shoulder. "Then you must go to my mother's house. She will welcome you."

As attractive as that sounded he again disagreed, "You know I try to maintain a separate household when I am Winter Chief – it is different when she is the matron, then I am just her mate."

She made a face, "Well you can't sleep out of doors like an old bear." Butterfly stood up. Suddenly, she had another idea.

"What about the walled compound of the warriors? You could stay there, just for now." It was the kind of sensible if unusual, idea Butterfly would think of to solve the problem. In his exhausted state he could think of none better.

Thus it was he woke in Tall Claw's house.

Thinking about the events of the last two days, he reviewed what he still had to do, who he had to contact, and what ancestors must be appeased by prayer. He had called a council. Now perhaps he could get them to take up the matter of the man who fell from the sky also. He stifled a yawn. He had not slept well, yet, there was so much to do.

While he worried about many things, right this moment his most pressing concern was how to get past Tall Claw's dogs.

Once he decided to come to the compound to sleep, he gathered up his few belongs and went. The instant he stepped up onto the ridge and undid the lashings of the gate the dogs raised the alarm. Stepping inside cautiously, they both charged at him, biting at his ankles despite his yells of "shah!" In desperation, he kicked each of them hard. They yelped in turn and ran off, but their growls followed him up onto the roof of the house. They feinted another charge as he stepped down the ladder, into the room below.

He slept fitfully on a mat that he found off to one side. Purposely, he did not select the thick sleeping mat that was airing on a rack by the ladder. He was sure that was Tall Claw's and couldn't risk any insult to his spirit. He hoped Tall Claw's relatives who had gone on would see his sleeping there as a mark of respect. Later he would gather up all the most personal possessions of Tall Claw and have them taken to the village where the body was being prepared.

But first, the dogs!

Climbing up out of the house, he carried two bones that he had found with scraps of dried meat on them. Making friends was better than having to fight to leave each morning. Standing on the roof, he scanned the compound. The dogs were nowhere to be seen. He whistled low, to try and draw them out. There was no sign of movement. He walked over to an edge and looked down; there was no trace of the beasts. Looking around, he saw the gate was unlatched. Could they be gone? He would check outside the compound for their tracks.

He relaxed and set the bones down on the edge of the roof; Fat Badger clambered down to the ground.

His first step down from the roof brought a cacophony of vicious growls and loud barks from his left. Both dogs appeared as if by magic out from behind a pile of wood stacked against the wall. He quickly snatched up the bones and tossed them, so they landed in the dirt just in front of the charging dogs. Ignoring his peace offerings completely, they continued toward him, only increasing their racket. Again, when he yelled, "Shah!" it did not affect them.

Grabbing a stick, he tried to fend off the beasts. They snapped and growled, worrying the wood and trying to get at his shins. Sweeping hard with one short swing he caught the white dog on the side. His reward was its yelp of pain. Unfortunately, his victory became short-lived; his yell followed close as the black dog latched onto his right calf. Swinging backward, with a vicious swipe at the blood-mad assailant, he caught her a glancing blow. Twirling about rapidly, he dislodged her by violently striking his body against one of the projecting house foundation rocks.

The black dog retreated to where its sister lay licking its wounds.

Reaching down he wiped the blood from his leg and saw that the two were evidently satisfied with their costly victory. Wandering off to the farthest corner from where Fat Badger stood they stopped only to pick up the bones as they went.

Fat Badger scowled at them; this would not be easy. Still, he needed a temporary place to live. Sitting down on the edge of the house roof the wounded winter chief used a cloth to wipe his leg. He poured water from a jar sitting on the roof and washed the wound. They watched his every move as they chewed the bones, continuously growling through their gnawing jaws.

He tensed as the two beasts suddenly jumped up, dropping their prizes, their hackles raised, deep growls coming low and vibrant.

"What now?" He too jumped up on the house preparing to meet their renewed assault.

Pounding erupted against the wood of the rough gate behind him. "Winter Chief are you there?" Someone had come on official business. "What now indeed!"

Turning he saw that Playing Cat, a runner from High Village stood at the open gate. The thin little man looked nervous.

Fat Badger took two steps toward the runner then whirled and yelled "Shah!" at the still barking dogs. Amazingly they instantly stopped their noise and slunk off to the woodpile. Fat Badger could barely resist covering his mouth in surprise. Resetting his bland Winter Chief face, he turned slowly back to face the young man.

Playing Cat nodded, "I am sorry to disturb you, Winter Chief, but my village council asks your presence."

"On what matter?" Fat Badger allowed a little annoyance into his voice — he was tired, his leg ached, and his mind was preoccupied with grave problems.

Catching the hint the young man continued, "They confess to being truly apologetic, we heard the announcement of the warrior's accident," he paused and looked down. Waiting for a beat he looked up and went on, "And I saw your grandmother's house. I looked for you there first, but your son-in-law told me you were here."

"My son-in-law?" Fat Badger asked, raising an eyebrow. He knew that Playing Cat had once hoped to become the husband of Butterfly, and his son-in-law, but Fire Star refused his suit.

"I saw Wolf Runner near the creek."

"The matter?" Fat Badger asked bluntly.

"Yes, Chief, it is the Immigrant's village, a girl has disappeared."

Only sixteen moons before a small group of White Ants from the southeast arrived and asked permission to settle in Sky Valley. They were allowed to build a small settlement just below High Village. Stating that they were farmers, they erected a few houses, a long wall and several standing shades in a cedar draw — a place that no one from Sky Valley would have thought of using. Planting many agaves they had brought with them, just upslope from the wall, the plants prospered immediately and were well on their way to grow to maturity. It had appeared that the plants would be ready to harvest in less time than usually needed. Of course, this also brought whispers of witchcraft among the other villagers. Because of the rumors, the immigrants remained as such, not fully accepted in the valley.

To still some of the gossips, Fat Badger had visited their settlement right after he took office that fall. His discussions with the head man of the little village had settled his concerns. The man, called Wind Killer, spoke a language that was not unlike their own. His people came from even farther south than the White Ants of the two rivers. He shared with Fat Badger that they had hoped to find a place just like this one where their plants would prosper.

Very bright but unassuming and friendly, Fat Badger had taken an immediate liking to the slightly-built older man. He increasingly found excuses to visit the hamlet more than once, and he was always warmly greeted by the man's wife, a White Ant of formal speech and strange accent. That she was from a distant place was evident to everyone – her manners and mode of expression were both exceedingly different from those of his people.

But she along with her husband welcomed his visits. Invariably she gave him refreshment while sending her daughter to find Wind Killer and let him know they had company.

Now a girl was missing.

Disturbed by this news brought by Playing Cat he hoped it was not Wind Killer's daughter that was missing. He also hoped they would not soon discover another body fallen from a high place. Or even worse, a renewal of the old evils that had led to the naming of The Forbidden Place.

"Go back and tell your council I will come after visiting Grandfather Scorpion yet today. It will be as the sun falls."

Nodding to his chief, the man turned and ran off. Watching him go he refused to allow his mind to speculate any more. It was to be a full winter. So much to be done.

A sharp pain just below his right buttock caused him to spin about just in time to see Tall Claw's white dog streak away from him. He could almost swear he heard the dog's laughter.

VIII

—on the trail to High Seat Village—

Fat Badger did not relish the thought of a visit to Grandfather Scorpion, but felt it was necessary.

Grandfather Scorpion who was neither a grandfather nor a scorpion, lived on a small spur of a hill set laterally to the high peak overlooking Low spring. It was a quarter of a day's walk from High Village. He had built his house just below the hilltop as was common for most small residences in the valley.

It was one of the few ordinary things he did.

Virtually all the houses in Sky Valley were located in one of two locations. Those nearest the water courses were on the second terrace above the floodplain. Most of these tended towards large villages, clusters of stone masonry and adobe houses numbering from twenty to forty households. They functioned as farming centers, with many fields of crops planted below them on the first terrace, close to water.

The other favored location for house building was a specific type of geographic feature common to deeply scarred, rugged canyons like Sky Valley. Between two high places, there would be a low spot; a sort of seat, nestled betwixt the peaks. Smaller than the valley towns and sheltered from winds and less visible from a distance high villages were nearly always located in these seats. Some were no more than one families' collecting station that was abandoned in the winter. Many families maintained two houses. During the colder weather, the lower villages gained population as small family groups moved back to their more substantial homes in the bigger towns.

Grandfather Scorpion had built his house in one of these sheltered seats between two high spots. A series of peaks rose to the west of his home, and a small rocky point was to the east. The eastern summit was known as Spider Hill. There was a legend that the rough pile of weathered stone was an ancient pile of bones belonging to disobedient children. They were victims of a creature known as Grandmother Spider. Another witch story to be shared around winter fires.

The ancient legends also said Grandmother Spider, in a more charitable moment, had given weaving to the people. She did so as an apology for her disgusting habit of eating children and other transgressions even more abhorrent. These were just a few of the many stories and legends told by old men to wide-eyed grandchildren sitting in their shadowed houses during the winter evenings.

But Grandfather Scorpion was no legend. Stories about him were often much more mundane or on occasion, tended to be even scarier than those of the witches.

One detailed how he had sold his eternal spirit in bondage to a demon who imbued him with his healing skills. Another said that if you removed the tattered cloaks, he invariably wore you would discover a monstrous body beneath. It might be the body of a vast insect, covered by a sturdy shell. Others argued that he was merely bones beneath the covering and he was also the great spirit of the dead. He did nothing to dispel these stories.

Dubbing himself Scorpion, the title Grandfather was added by others, seeking to make him sound more human.

Having never taken a woman to mate, he couldn't be a grandfather, so it was a bit of a joke.

But because stories about him spread, his presence was vital to all the people of Sky Valley. His renown continued all the way to the greatest of the White Ant villages. Over the years many visitors, as well as residents, sought his counsel. Medicine people throughout the known world learned their craft through his instruction. Although some were shocked when they met him for the first time because his appearance was less than imposing, it didn't seem to affect his fame.

Half a hand shorter than medium height, they saw a pale-skinned man approaching late middle age. Grandfather Scorpion appeared to be thin as a blade of grass beneath his soiled robes. His face was all sharp angles and looked somewhat hawkish. He rarely smiled and spoke softly with a harsh sounding, high-pitched, whispery voice.

These days, a young man called Climbs Hills invariably accompanied Grandfather Scorpion. This man was said to be a student of Grandfather Scorpion, and he often appeared at villages in advance to act as the medicine man's mouthpiece. While not obese, quite unlike his instructor, he tended toward excess fat around his middle and lower body. Rumors from the gossips branded him lazy. That these rumors arose from conversations with other acolytes, young men who came to study with Grandfather Scorpion, to learn his medicine and his philosophy, made them suspect. Fat Badger had always seen this as jealousy at Climbs Hills position of favor with his mentor. It naturally leads to the spreading of rumors.

Rumors were integral to the history of Grandfather Scorpion.

To the rest of Sky Valley the strange man existed as a person of mystery, a healer and something of a maker of potions; one who used herbs, liquids and minerals no one else understood. He would often be found far afield, collecting his weird and arcane ingredients. Carrying a kit with many odd stones and concretions, he applied poultices which smelled, some said, like death itself.

To Fat Badger, much of what was known about Grandfather Scorpion was just that — stories and rumors. No one knew the actual history of Grandfather Scorpion and his family, and he worked to keep it that way. Their sudden appearance in Sky Valley years before portrayed them as refugees of some sort. That story started the first series of rumors.

What was known was that he had come to the valley as a youngster with his mother and sister. They lived in the big village of Sky Creek Town for a time, but Grandfather Scorpion had left while still an adolescent. Then known as Vivid Sky, he moved to the place beneath the rocky point where he dwelt to this day.

Soon after building his house he disappeared.

At first thought dead, a rumor arose that for the days he was absent he was wandering into the northwestern mountain wilderness — a wild and terrible place. After having isolated himself for a full cycle of the Sun, he returned, far-eyed and thoughtful. Coming to the village plaza one morning, he proclaimed his new name to be Scorpion. He moved his mother, Antelope, into the comfortable two rooms he had built in the wooded seat between the hills.

Over the years he became Grandfather, some gossips argued it was his sister who began addressing him thus.

She stayed in the house in the village until managing to marry well. Her mate, a White Ant from a sizable northern settlement, took her away a few seasons later. As her arranged husband, part of an understanding made before the little family arrived in Sky Valley, they left to return to his home.

Though no one knew where they had come from, the fact that her mate was a water person from the north seemed to argue for that as their origination point.

Wherever they had been, it took little time for his mother to establish herself as a talented medicine woman. This skill put her in direct competition with the family of Fat Badger's wife, so the former's move to a more secluded location was politically smart, allowing Antelope to become the person that the outlying villages turned to for certain potions and specialized care. In that capacity, her son followed her footsteps.

His mother's death forced Grandfather Scorpion to assume her duties while he was still a young man. It was said that this was when his sister changed his name again so that he would seem more prestigious. It was a way to legitimize his ascendancy to 'healer'. The family reputation in no way suffered from the change as he proved to be as talented as his mother Antelope had been — maybe more so. His cures were precise if sometimes unusual. Demand remained strong for good healers in Sky Valley.

Burns such as he had on his hands were always a specialty for Grandfather Scorpion's poultices, but Fat Badger did not need his healing, he wanted to see him on a separate issue. Knowing Grandfather Scorpion ranged far and wide around the hills and canyons of Sky Valley to locate the materials for his cures, he hoped that he might have seen something that would help explain the disturbances Tall Claw was investigating or even something about the falling man.

Arriving just as the retreating sun was slipping behind the mountains, Fat Badger trotted up the hill, moving as fast as he could. He stopped only to fill his gourd with the sweet, cool water from the Low Spring. It was a bit of irony to Fat Badger that Low Spring's water seemed the sweetest in the valley while water from Sweet Spring, located at a point lower in the valley than Low Spring, produced a slightly bitter after-taste.

He hoped that Grandfather Scorpion would be at his house. As a courtesy, he 'hulloed' a greeting as he climbed the hill approaching the small pueblo of the medicine man.

It was a compact home — two low rooms of stone and adobe it featured a walled shade built up against a large boulder. The area around the residence was clear of all vegetation excepting one large cedar, but many other things crowded the space. All manner of bundles and nets, full of dried plants, hung from hooks and pegs in the walls; piles of bones and an array of antlers lay around the base of the patio walls. Large stones of strange shapes were interspersed with huge crystals. Fat Badger saw a group of brightly-colored angular rocks that looked like pieces of trees. He dodged the rain callers, woven structures, and wind bringers, hung in profusion from the lower branches of the cedar tree, just south of the house.

Along the top of the patio wall lay dried skulls of many animals of innumerable sizes. All were set facing inward, their empty eye sockets staring at the healer's doorway. Entry into the front enclosure was around the tree to the east side of the boulder. Two bear skulls on poles taller than any man flanked that boulder.

The entrance was meant to intimidate, and to any other visitor, especially the young men who arrived seeking knowledge, it probably worked. To them, it must seem as if they entered the lair of a great wizard. To Fat Badger, it appeared pretentious.

Coming up to the summit and around the hill, he found one of these aforementioned young men standing there waiting for him. Masking his surprise, he said to the youth, "Tell your master that the Winter Chief is here." Thin to the point of starvation and equally hawk-faced as the Scorpion, Fat Badger thought to himself, 'This young man could be Grandfather Scorpion's son'. He dismissed this thought as quickly - the medicine man had never fathered a child that anyone knew. The rumor was he was most likely a two-spirit who had no interest in laying with women.

The young man did not lower his gaze, but his voice was ingratiating, "Oh, Exalted one, my master is absent from his humble home. He is expected on the morrow."

Fat Badger masked his disappointment. He took the opportunity to examine the acolyte. That the young man was a southern White Ant was apparent by his accented flowery speech, this did not surprise Fat Badger as the many stories of Grandfather Scorpion attracted students from everywhere.

"Can this poor servant offer thee refreshment?" the young man asked.

Fat Badger shook his head, "Is Climbs Hills with him?"

"He is, oh lord of Sky Valley. Can this servant make up a place for thee to rest?"

Shaking his head again while purposefully looking annoyed, Fat Badger indicated the western hill with his chin. "I have other business, tell your master I will return tomorrow."

"Mayest this one inquire of my lord at what time of the day he is expected so my master will be prepared?" Fat Badger thought he detected a note of irony in the young man's honeyed voice.

"No," said the Winter Chief evenly.

"Mayhap my lord would deign to inform this lowly servant what the matter concerns so he might alert his master?"

"I will speak to him directly." He struggled to keep the annoyance from his voice, "That is all."

"As you wish." The young man bowed slightly and nodded. Fat Badger fixed him with a look and then turned to go.

Circling around the little house he was careful not to look back at the eager acolyte who he was certain had not moved from his spot. Stepping up onto the water carrier trail that led to High Village he glanced around. The water trail was used by the young women who went down to the Low spring several times each day to fill their jars. As such it was littered with many broken bits of clay jars. The day's retreating sun caused the polished pot fragments to glint of golden fire like the fading sunlight itself.

Emerging up onto the ridge above Grandfather Scorpion's he still resisted the urge to turn and see if the young man watched him in the gloom. Coming over a slight rise, he looked down upon High Village. Also known as 'the Place of the Giant's Seat' he remembered the story told to him as a boy about a giant who sat here throwing rocks down upon people who came to the spring below. In the story, the giant was vanquished by the grandsons of Grandmother Spider. They crushed his skull with their clubs as he slept. Then they buried him standing up. It was his skull forming the round hump of rock that loomed above the pueblo. Fat Badger saw it before him, lurking behind the village, shadowy and brooding.

IX

—at High Seat Village—

High Village was not large, but it was an old settlement. A shoulder height wall enclosed a score of houses arranged in several contiguous room-blocks scattered across the shallow seat below the scowling western peak. Smoke hung over the village and drifted northwest on the wind, the breath of the Great Spirit.

Fat Badger counted this as one of the more important of the outlying villages.

The village was placed in this spot to act as a watchpoint for the hostile lands to the west and north. Raids by Red Ant people were uncommon now because the warriors of this outpost always kept their watch.

Looking down, he saw there were few people out at this time of the evening and too, at this time of the year. He walked briskly down the path knowing he was expected.

Two scouts stood to watch. One, his rabbit skin cloak pulled close about his shoulders saw him coming. He marched out the two steps through the entrance and said, "Welcome Winter Chief, I will announce you. Please make yourself comfortable in the 'greeting house'." He indicated a square room just inside the compound walls with his pursed lips.

Passing the other guard with a nod Fat Badger entered "the Place of the Giant's Seat", High Village. He knew "the greeting house" was to his right.

Pushing aside a skin curtain, he ducked through a small doorway where he found a pile of glowing coals in the rock-lined hearth one step inside the room. They warmed the room nicely. Next to the hearth was a bowl of corn and meat soup and a pot of tea. He must have been seen approaching from below. Fat Badger washed his hands in a shallow water bowl to the left of the entryway and sat down on the floor mat opposite the doorway to eat.

Using thin cakes to scoop out some corn and meat, he set the first bite on a stone palette next to the hearth as an offering. Thanking the Great

Spirit, he ate the meal, first dipping corn cakes into the bowl using them as scoops then drinking the broth. Setting the bowl down, he lifted the pot of tea to his lips. It's faintly sweet taste told him it was ocotillo flower, a delicacy this time of year and a significant honor to his presence. When he finished, he put the first bite he had set aside into the fire for the spirits to consume.

He heard a cough outside the blanket covered doorway and then four men entered one by one. After nodding to him, they moved to arrange themselves around the little hearth each of them sitting on a mat. He knew three of the men. Directly across from him sat Dark Snake - the village rain priest, next to Dark Snake, to Fat Badger's right, was Two Eagles, the village headman. Sitting to Dark Snake's right was a person unknown to Fat Badger and to his left was Hungry Fly - the village warrior. He had known Hungry Fly the longest - since they were boys playing together, though they had not lived near each other since Fat Badger's mother had left the valley.

It was he who opened the meeting, indicating to the Winter Chief that he had taken charge of the situation.

"Thank you Winter Chief for honoring our village; we hope you are well."

"It is good to see my old friend again," replied Fat Badger.

"I agree, I rejoice to see you also. Were that it was a social visit, but we need to discuss some important matters."

The fact that Hungry Fly had gone directly to the issue surprised Fat Badger and indicated that he felt there was a significant problem needing immediate attention.

"Please continue."

Hungry Fly turned to the man who Fat Badger did not know. "This is Digging Squirrel. He is from the Brown Ants of Many Rocks Stacked Canyon." Many Rocks Stacked Canyon was west of Sky Valley on the other side of the low western peaks. "He came to our village three days ago. We have asked him to join our council."

Fat Badger did not ask why the stranger was there; he knew it would become clear to him later. Hungry Fly continued.

"The immigrants from the White Ant lands to the south are our wards." Fat Badger knew this; his predecessor had named them so. "They have worked hard, and already their labor shows results." He looked at Two Eagles who nodded his agreement. "They are welcome." He looked into the glowing fire as if hoping to see something there.

"Two days ago at dawn, one of their young women, Tree Cliff Sits went to the spring at dawn to get water. Several people saw her going down the trail, but she did not return. Her water jar was found at the spring, unfilled; just sitting there."

Then it wasn't his friend's daughter who was missing. He was relieved to hear that. He did not know this other girl beyond having seen her at the village. Waiting for several heartbeats, Fat Badger felt that Hungry Fly had left something unsaid.

"Was anything else found?" he asked.

The four men looked at each other; the village headman nodded at his warrior as if to permit him to speak.

"There is concern about this matter." Fat Badger felt some worry. *What now?* he thought. "We found tracks, eh-uh footprints, not many, but we found three or four." Hungry Fly said.

If invaders raided the valley, they would raise the alarm immediately. Runners should have been sent out. That was why High Village existed. Fat Badger thought there was something else as yet unsaid to this. His concern increased.

"Was there a pattern to their sandals?" Fat Badger asked. It was known that different groups of people wore distinctive sandals woven in styles according to regional tradition.

"They wore no sandals."

Fat Badger digested this information for a few moments. "They were barefoot?"

Hungry Fly nodded. "Yes, and something else. The prints were of big feet, bigger than mine, or yours."

Fat Badger looked confused, "Do you speak of the tracks of the gray bear?" The grizzled, humpbacked bears were always a worry. Massive and unpredictable fortunately they rarely ventured to the lands of men. As the largest bears known to the people, the gray bears were known to be found higher up, in the mountains, but down here in the valley would be unheard of in remembered history.

Two Eagles cleared his throat peremptorily, "It was no bear," Two

Eagles spoke quietly. "These tracks looked like a man's footprint, but they were larger, and . . . they were different." He paused for effect and grunted. "This man," he indicated the visitor from the west with a slight nod, "has a similar story."

They all looked at the stranger. He sat cross-legged, his forearms, resting on his thighs, were circled with many shell bracelets. Fat Badger noted that he must have worn some of them a long time, at least two were going to have to be cut off soon as they deeply constricted his flesh. He was also adorned with plugs in his cheeks and nose and wore three pairs of earrings. Tattoos ran up out of his robe along his neck and cheeks, as well as across his forehead. He wore his hair loose. Fat Badger decided he was evidently a man of some prestige or wealth with his people.

The man, Digging Squirrel, habitually exhaled as he spoke, making his words distant sounding. "In my village, two women have disappeared in the last moon, each when alone, one in the circumstances like this." He paused as if to gather his thoughts. "She went for water, her pot was found, broken, but not shattered and there was a scuffling of the dirt that may have been a footprint." He looked at Two Eagles, "I came here as one of four sent out to look for information about what might have become of her."

Two Eagles nodded. Fat Badger looked past the man as if seeing out the blanketed doorway into the night.

"The other?"

He paused and exhaling, spoke slowly, "The other was different, but she too is gone. We have found no trace," he exhaled, "of either of them since their disappearance."

Leaning forward, Hungry Fly continued, "The same is true of Cliff Sitting. We searched all up and down Blue Creek and found nothing else." Fat Badger was not surprised, the underbrush and woods around Low Spring were particularly dense. Few ventured off the trails.

The man Digging Squirrel added, "I came here to ask if they were seen by any of your people."

Fat Badger listened to his voice carefully, but he heard no implication in his story. He evidently did not feel that Sky Valley was somehow responsible for the missing women.

"Who saw the prints?" Fat Badger asked.

It was Hungry Fly who answered, "I was called to the scene by a boy from the Immigrant's village. I saw the marks, they looked like a man's foot but bigger. Unfortunately, the recent snowfall has covered them."

Each sat in thought for a time. Fat Badger was honestly concerned but was there enough to connect this mystery to what happened at the mine and to Tall Claw? It was hard for him to believe it was a coincidence.

"What do you make of these prints?" he asked Hungry Fly.

His friend did not answer immediately. He seemed to be weighing possible responses. "I am of two minds. It could be that we were seeing disturbed footprints that were not true to the actual size of a person's foot. In the mud this is possible."

Fat Badger waited.

"Or something strange walks in our valley. Something as yet unidentified." He seemed to hesitate then continued, "We have heard the rumors from your village."

This answer then was what Fat Badger was afraid of hearing. Two Eagles took in a sharp intake of breath. The old man whispered only one word, "Ogres?" They sat then in silence each lost in thought.

Finally, Fat Badger spoke, "Is there anything else I should know?" He addressed Hungry Fly directly. His friend shook his head. Fat Badger looked at all of the men who sAT ACROss from him. "We are still investigating things that have occurred in the valley. As we know, more I will send runners. In the meantime, you have given me much to think on. Tomorrow I will go talk to Wind Killer; please send a runner to let him know I am coming."

X

—at High Seat Village—

Fat Badger woke in Sun's early light, shivering even under the feathered blanket. The village fire boy had come and put fresh coals in the hearth, so he squatted over it warming his hands. Placing the teapot at the edge of the coals and using a scoop added some water to the flowers and leaves in the bottom of the pot. He poured some more of near-freezing water into the shallow wash bowl. Using a square of cloth he found hanging on a peg, he washed his face and arms, shivering as he did so. Covering his shaky shoulders with a robe Fat Badger sat back against a post. He lifted the pot to poured tea into a small drinking bowl.

He sloshed the tea around his mouth and drank it, chewing the dregs in the bottom of the bowl. Rising, he left the greeting house and looked out over the shadowed plaza of High Village. Clouds still commanded the sky. Muted light covered all. As high as the village was, a morning fog was common. It mixed with smoke and, clinging to the chill ground, lay above a fresh dusting of snow.

Few villagers were up this early, mostly young women and a few boys, preparing fires and the morning meal. Two young women left with open-weave frames on their backs. "Wood gatherers," said Fat Badger to himself as they moved toward the village entry and the trail to the valley below. A rangy young man, armed as a warrior, followed them. Fat Badger recognized him as a hunter named Coyote Alone.

Walking over to where the guard stood near the entry he watched then three of them walk down the hill. The guard looked at him nervously. He appeared to be about fourteen summers old, and asked, "Can I assist you in any way Winter Chief?"

"That man," he indicated the figures disappearing into the mist, "he guards the wood gatherers?"

"Yes, he walks with them since . . ." the youth paused.

Fat Badger saved him the embarrassment, "Yes. I know." Fat Badger turned toward him, "Tell anyone who asks that I have gone to see Wind Killer."

—on the trail to the Immigrant's village—

He walked down the trail a short distance then turned on a side path to the left. The way was steep but well used. In the chill, the mud ceased to be slippery which made him grateful for the cold. It was a quiet morning — sound seemed muffled in the mist. Fat Badger surprised they hadn't received more snow, looked up. Even through the fog, he could see the glowering sky was overcast and gray.

Making his way through a grove of junipers, he glimpsed distant, shadowed forms that were the neat houses of the Immigrant's village some distance below him. Crossing a flat area still encased in frost that crunched beneath his sandals, he started down the last slope into the basin where the immigrants lived. And then he stopped.

Far off, he heard the clack of rock against rock, once, twice. It was hard to know the exact direction, but it seemed to be to his left, toward the highest peak in the area, the Giant's skull. The noise sounded again, seemingly behind him and closer. He turned, squatted down and peered into the slowly brightening gloom. Gripping his walking stick in both hands, he stayed thus — alerted — for a long series of heartbeats. Realizing that he held his breath, he exhaled silently and slowly.

It could have been the echoes of a stonemason's work, amplified — the sound carried by the mist, he reasoned to himself.

He stood, gradually leaning vaguely toward the juniper tree nearest him. Hearing a noise behind him, he whirled to see Wind Killer standing there. For a moment the older man looked confused then he smiled at Fat Badger.

"My friend, how are you?" he held his hands out. "It is a chilly morning, and this mist makes it worse I am afraid."

Fat Badger took his left hand from his stick and stretched it out; grasping both of the other man's in his. Wind Killer brought a hand up to his mouth and breathed on it. "That should warm you some, though I'm afraid it isn't much."

Laughing, Fat Badger patted the man on his shoulder, saying, "You are who I came to see." He turned him to walk back down the trail toward his village. They trudged quietly through the misty morning, the older man in the lead until they reached the basin floor.

"Have you breakfasted, Winter Lord?"

"I am no lord, like those White Ants who claim their divinity," Fat Badger answered feigning anger, "I live on Mother Earth's natural mount, not on something massive, built on the backs of slaves."

"We can thank the Great Sun for that and pray for his continued blessings." Wind Killer looked skyward. "But more importantly," he grinned, "have you eaten?"

"No, my friend I came directly from your sponsors, shedding their hospitality and the warmth of their hearth in hopes of finding your good wife with a bowl of her stew waiting for me."

"Then I believe you are indeed blessed."

Fat Badger often felt blessed to be in the presence of the man called Wind Killer.

Clearing his throat, Fat Badger started to speak about the missing girl. Wind Killer surprised him by interrupting his discussion immediately. "Let us save other more serious matters until we have breakfasted," the older man said. Fat Badger complied but thought the request odd.

Referring to him as an unusual man did not sufficiently explain Wind Killer. He had lived many places, traveling all his life and was now a refugee, in search of a home again, an irony of fact not lost on him. He exemplified opposites. He arrived in Sky Valley bringing several displaced persons with him, Wind Killer acting as their leader and yet the ones he led were not his birth people.

"Are your people happy to have come to our valley?" Fat Badger asked.

"As a child, I often moved from place to place," Wind Killer responded, "I became used to moving. My parents brought us up believing it was important that we seek to educate ourselves and others to the truth of the world."

"You must have felt blessed to be possessed of parents who were privy to such knowledge." Fat Badger said allowing a slyness into his voice.

For his part Wind Killer responded by laughing long and hard. "Rest assured they told me as much many times over. They continued telling me so as we traveled from the little villages of the clam eaters all the way to the camps of the ferocious inhabitants at the mouth of Blood River."

"The Yellow Ants! You visited even them?" Fat Badger interjected, surprised. "I have heard they are not overly fond of strangers."

"Visited? We lived among them for a time!"

Fat Badger recalled dealings he had had with the Yellow Ant people on occasion. He knew that saying the people of Blood River were not fond of strangers was to speak an understatement.

Over the last few months, Fat Badger often wondered at the people who raised Wind Killer. Their unique passions made Wind Killer's parents remarkable, and it continued with their son.

"I was birthed in the village of White Ants far south of the two rivers land. They raised me with languages of varied peoples. I can converse easily with most people within ten days' travel of this spot." Fat Badger agreed that Wind Killer spoke their language well with only the slightest of accents and a good grasp of nuance.

Fat Badger knew this was no idle boast, Wind Killer knew stories of the great cities to the south, legends of the hairy ones to the north and prayers of towns across the land.

"Eventually after years of travel I returned to my birthplace, and I became a trader to the White Ants of the two rivers. It was a good living. I even knew a fraction of wealth for a time." He laughed — his tale implying that his life included a period of comfort and contentment.

"What happened?" asked Fat Badger.

Wind Killer walked on a way before answering. "Something occurred that sent me north."

Fat Badger, reaching this point in his friend's story before, knew Wind Killer ceased being talkative here. Every time he got to this subject, he stopped sharing. He never said what happened, but he hinted that someday he might confide the details of his departure from the land of the White Ants.

As usual, today, he changed the subject, "We must discuss that someday when we have the time, but for now we are here, to breakfast!"

This disarming misdirection made Wind Killer an enigma to Fat Badger.

Together they entered the little settlement through a gate at the west end of the long wall.

"Wife," Wind Killer called out, "look what I caught while out hunting — I think he is fat enough, but the meat may be spoiled." Both men chuckled at Fat Badger's expense, while Wind Killer's wife rose from her work next to a small hearth under a shade. Smiling, she offered her hands to the younger man. A tall woman — much like Fat Badger's wife, when she spoke her eastern White Ant accent sounded clear to Fat Badger in her voice.

"Perhaps if someone were to feed this poor catch of yours, his taste might improve considerably," answered Water Clouds, his wife. Wind Killer looked askance at Fat Badger and raised his eyebrows.

The couple shared their recent history with Fat Badger over many bowls of Wind Killer's wife's stew.

"Do you imply that your husband does not provide for you in a manner that befits the daughter of White Ant royalty?" joked Wind Killer.

"No one I know refers to the head man of a minor village, living near the great bend of Lost River, as royalty!" she countered.

"I do," said Wind Killer moving close to his wife accentuating the fact that she stood at least a finger taller than her husband. "And I treat his daughter as a such."

"What does that make me?" said Wind Killer's daughter as she joined the group.

"Ah, yes, we hear from yet another supplicant!" said Wind Killer. "You, my dear are the source of all my joy."

"Now you see, Fat Badger, the flowery words that allowed him to be the acclaimed leader of our little group of pilgrims." said Water Clouds. "Let us go inside out of the cold, and I will bring you breakfast."

Fat Badger nodded — they retreated through the area under the shade into the comfort of the attached room.

Water Clouds spread mats for them to sit upon and then went back outside to tend to her cooking pot. She returned with two steaming bowls.

"You seem unconcerned about the missing girl." Fat Badger said.

"Oh, that!" responded Water Clouds, "She will likely return soon."

"You are certain of this? The people I talked with in High Village were definitely concerned."

Wind Killer smiled, "You as well as anyone must know that when you have all the information, your decisions are more likely to bear fruit."

"Sometimes," responded, Fat Badger, "though the opposite may also occur."

Wind Killer looked at him, "Why do you say that?"

"I am a perfect example. Trained from birth to become Trader for our valley, I am confident in that position, and yet, first, this great responsibility of Winter Chief was thrust upon me. With my wife holding the Summer Matron title it casts scrutiny from every corner on all my decisions and keeps fanning the flames of gossip swirling across the valley. I must be deliberate in all things. I can not even go to my wife's house without setting tongues wagging as to whether I am there as Winter Chief or her husband. So much to think about."

"I do understand — to a point," responded Wind Killer.

Fat Badger waited to see if the man would elaborate before going on, "Now one of my three daughters will likely produce the next matron, leaving the Summer Matron and the current Winter Chief in a direct line to her. That creates a dangerous precedent." he said shaking his head. "To some of our more conservative Brown Ant People of Sky Valley, it borders on creating a royal family such as might occur farther south. That would be antithetical to the beliefs and precepts of our people that say that no one person should hold great power over others.

"When we settled into married life and became parents. I believed my future was secure at last." Wind Killer said. "I was wrong. Turmoil follows some people."

"You wanted to tell me about that," said Fat Badger hoping to get the story at last.

"Clouds of change threatened our lifestyle," he continued. "I saw issues arising even with the location of their village near Lost River; issues that persuaded me our people should relocate." He paused, and pain briefly crossed his face. "Few listen to my words, only those you see here. I led our little group north, and we arrived in this place, as refugees."

Fat Badger thought to himself that it was as likely his friend manufactured an excuse that some things happened. He spent his entire life roving. The current move reflected the inherent wandering so integral to Wind Killer's life. His dissatisfaction with settled existence led to his constant motion, including the one that brought them here. Fat Badger wondered how long his friend would stay in Sky Valley.

Fat Badger recalled his arrival more than a Sun's full passage and some moons ago. They came from the lands south of the two rivers, an area controlled by the southern White Ants. Explaining to the valley council only that they wished to relocate to Sky Canyon to continue to farm their crops, Wind Killer said nothing of turmoil.

Soon he met with representatives of the various villages of the valley requesting an opportunity to look for a place to raise their crops which included agave. Since Wind Killer's band numbered only ten people, the council agreed that it could not hurt to look, mainly in that the agave plant was one of the most profitable items grown in their valley. Increasing production of these valuable plants would only benefit them all.

With the help of two of the scouts from Sky Creek Town, they located their desired place. Much to the surprise of nearly everyone the place they chose lay in a sheltered, shallow basin, lined with cedars, between several small peaks just below High Village. It was an area traditionally used for wood collection — the cedar smoke was thought to be spiritually useful as well as being efficacious in keeping the summer gnats away.

Since High Village was the nearest settlement of any size, they were asked by Loping Animal to sponsor the immigrants for the next four years. Their village council met, and after two days discussion agreed to do so for a share of their future harvest.

The immigrants went to work.

Building a long stone wall at the low end of the basin while leaving a scattering of small rocks to the uphill side became the first act the immigrants undertook. They then planted some seedling agaves they had brought with them in amongst the debris and on the high side of the wall. Their intent proved immediately apparent as the first rain collected against the wall and soaked into the soil nourishing the young plants.

In addition to their water retaining wall, the group also installed another structure in the middle of their lower plaza area. Round in shape — with walls merely four hands high — it proved another mystery for those who observed it. They cut a shallow basin into the hard-pack floor of the soil within the walls. Upon seeing it for the first time Night Singer, the oldest of the traders for the valley exclaimed, "It's a water pond — I saw one in a White Ant village far south of here."

By keeping the wall to the south shorter than the rest water overflowing the south bank drained toward the agaves and the long wall. Seeding amaranth on the low side of the wall, they ensured yet another potential crop.

Next, the immigrants cut a channel to direct water flow from the hills above their village into the basin. Single course check dams slowed water flow even more.

These constructions completed, they begin to work on their houses which they located on the natural berms to the sides of the basin; two on the east and three on the west. All but one of the stone and puddled adobe houses had a shade or standing roof attached to the front. The single exception sat up high on the slope, and though low, it was of a stout build. Apparently, they meant to use it as a storage room for foodstuffs.

They supplemented their diet with available wild plant resources. Numerous patches of edible flat pad cactus, which also produced a sweet fruit between summer and fall, surrounded their basin.

Local wisdom among the collectors of agave said that in the wild the plants matured in six to ten years. The growth of the immigrant's plants seen in the first year seemed to suggest that the time needed to produce a viable crop would decrease significantly.

Talk of witchcraft arose among some who heard of this.

Fat Badger worked hard to quell such gossip, meeting with several of the men's and women's societies to point out the innovations that the immigrants had enacted to cause their plants to mature faster. The Corn Society meeting had been an overly divisive one as they were the most conservative in their philosophy. After several contentious arguments, Fat Badger felt he had gone a long way toward persuading the recalcitrant elders and hoped the rumors had largely dissipated. At least his informants in most of the significant villages said as much. It was in the process of defending the small group that he had become a regular visitor at their encampment and a good friend of their elder, Wind Killer.

He kept his people working at a frenetic pace. Their next project cleared stone and sand from in front of the wall face on the low side, and they built a vast mound slightly east of the basin center. It rose to a body length in height, four body lengths in diameter and lay twelve paces south of the wall.

Surprising most observers, they cut little or no wood in their basin for their use, preferring to go some distance away even to get the smoke-producing green cedar-wood used to relieve the annoying gnats of summer. Wind Killer requested that other villages follow their lead and restrict their wood gathering in the basin. If nothing else this suggested to many of the gossips that they were not true White Ants as their voracious hunger for wood of all kinds was legendary.

The inherent wisdom of Wind Killer's decisions resulted in a very stable life for their village site despite its apparent poor location on a downslope. Their reservoir stayed full long after rains had left and this water was used to keep the agaves and other crops, flourishing.

Collecting wild agaves and yuccas from nearby hills soon after all construction ended, the women of the group quickly made the use of the mound apparent. Stone-lined ovens insulated with sand produced sweetly roasted agave hearts which soon had mothers in all the villages of Sky Valley sending their daughters with items to trade for the treat. Additional byproducts included many leaves of agave that could be pulped to increase the availability of woven materials used for making mats, baskets, and sandals as well as the various repairs of the same. It was not long before the little village of the immigrants became a bustling community, busy with trade and commerce throughout their first summer.

It also hummed with those seeking relief for the ill, Wind Killer's wife; Water Cloud was talented in dealing with digestive ailments — an herbalist unrivaled except by Grandfather Scorpion, in that area. According to Fat Badger he heard from sufferers that her stomach medicines were the best in most cases.

Not prone to digestive troubles, it was her cooking that most interested Fat Badger this morning. He sat by the hearth, in the place of honor opposite the doorway watching her move about efficiently as the smell of savory soup made his mouth water. Wind Killer was a lucky man.

They seemed remarkably calm considering a woman was missing from their village. What did they know?

Served soup and corn cakes by Fluttering Dove, their young daughter, he could tell she would someday be tall like her mother.

As he sat down to eat Fat Badger removed the pink fragment he carried in his pouch and placed it on the floor. He didn't want to sit on a sharp edge.

Wind Killer looked at the piece. "Where did you get that?" he asked.

"I found it, why?"

"Nothing, it is just a type of stone like the ones we used to make weights for our canal gates."

"Eat, before your soup gets cold!" said Water Cloud. Wind Killer gave Fat Badger a knowing smile.

Finishing his meal - the best he had eaten in days, Fat Badger motioned for Wind Killer to join him outside. Then older man gently shook his head. "I think the counsel of women will be necessary to our discourse."

With a slight raising his eyebrows Fat Badger responded, "As you wish."

Wind Killer explained, "My wife has knowledge of this situation, and my daughter needs to learn the lesson it offers. I realize people are alarmed. I hope we have not caused undue problems for you as the Winter Chief." Wind Killer continued, "As my wife said earlier we are hopeful that the issue will resolve itself soon."

"You must possess more information than the council of High Village does?"

Wind Killer shrugged. "We shared our knowledge with them, but they may not have heard all we said."

"Or listened," added his wife.

Fat Badger looked at Wind Killer who motioned to his wife to continue. "Tree Cliff Sitting is the name of this girl. She is, as they say, headstrong, listens to wild spirits and goes her way, and . . ." she looked back at her husband, "what is even more significant, she has an admirer, a secret tryst mate."

Fat Badger raising his eyebrows again, waited.

"Through a friend of hers it was discovered she has been meeting someone, a young man, surreptitiously. It is a reasonable assumption that she has gone to him."

Nodding the Winter Chief asked, "So you think this missing girl problem may solve itself?"

"We hope that will be so, though I understand that our friends on the hill are distracted."

"They seem to feel that there is more to it."

It was Wind Killer's turn to raise an eyebrow.

"They have assigned a guard to the water carriers and wood gatherers," Fat Badger looked at his friends closely, "I would say they are worried." He decided not to talk of the other matter, the footprints the others had seen and the story of the visitor from the next valley. He needed more information before he said something that might alarm his friends. "I will talk to you soon. Thank you for the meal. Please send a runner immediately if Tree Cliff Sitting reappears."

Wind Killer nodded, "You can be certain of it. I will walk you to the trailhead."

XI

—at the house of Tall Claw—

Fat Badger woke the next morning back in Tall Claw's house, he sat up and shivered in the cold morning air. Remembering his conversation with Wind Killer, he shook his head at the last thing his friend had told him the day before as they parted.

They were walking up the trail, Fat Badger slightly ahead, "You say you hope for a resolution soon?"

"Yes, we have requested help in locating where the girl has gone."

"Who did you ask?"

"Kills Rabbits."

Fat Badger stopped suddenly and turned to look at the village chief. "Who?"

"The hunter, Kills Rabbits, you must know of him."

"He is a hunter?"

"What do you think he is?"

He turned back to keep walking while thinking about his experience with the man, Kills Rabbits. He had seen him of course, a tall, exceedingly thin man with ragged clothing and matted hair. The rumor was that he had come from the far distant lands to the west. There was even a story that he came from across the Great Salt Sea itself. Fat Badger figured he had personally started the story just as he told the tale of how he got his name one day.

"When my father took me out to introduce me to the Sun," the man said to anyone who would listen, "there was a small rabbit sitting just outside our house. Upon seeing me, even as a baby, that rabbit fell over dead from fright." He invariably paused the story at that point, then continued, "I've been a great hunter ever since."

Fat Badger's experience with him was that he was an inconsistent provider at best, but to his credit, he was often the one hunter who could

82

find some game when no one else did. Fat Badger thought him lazy and in need of hero worship to produce results.

"Kills Rabbits is not who I would have chosen . . . but if you trust the man," he shrugged, "I hope he can help."

"As do we. Good day, Winter Chief, travel with care." The older man patted the back of his friend who nodded in response.

On his way back he stopped first at Grandfather Scorpion's house, but to his surprise, no one was there. Annoyed, he continued down into the valley, changed onto another trail at the lower branch of Blue Stream and turned toward Sky Creek Town.

So much to be done. As Winter Chief he had to go to where people were to send out runners to announce the beginning of the selection process for a new War Chief for Sky Valley. The choice would be the responsibility of the Bow Society, but starting it in motion was his.

Arriving at the village near midday he first went to his wife's house, a group of three rooms near the central space. Climbing the ladder, his wife, and oldest daughter, Hummingbird greeted him warmly. Fire Star said to her husband the formal greeting, "Winter Chief, you are here." Sitting beneath the shade to the south of the house, Hummingbird coiled clay ropes onto a pot she was making. Her deft hands continued their work as she spoke to her father

"Father, you are well? It is good to see you."

"Thank you daughter, yes, I am well, what are you making there?"

"My mother requires another dying pot, to color the fibers of cloud plant." She added mock annoyance to her voice which caught a look from her mother.

Pointing at her with her chin, Fire Star said, "This one can make pots for all who ask, except her mother who must pursue her through the entire valley just to get her due."

Laughing, Hummingbird replied, "No, I don't think anyone saw my mother pursuing me through the valley! She sent my sister in pursuit while she sat watching the bluebirds flitting through the trees."

Fat Badger was used to their banter, and it pleased him that they were so relaxed. The events of the past few days notwithstanding it was refreshing. He needed to sit and listen to their idle wit for a time to help clear the dark clouds that crowded his thoughts.

"What brings you here, husband?" Fire Star asked while sewing new fur-lined socks that Fat Badger hoped were for him.

"The search for a new War Chief must begin." She nodded — her face darkened — losing its humor as he continued, "And other matters beg my attention."

She knew better than to pursue it any further; her time would come soon enough — she well understood that her husband needed time to think most of all, not to answer questions.

"We have a good stew cooking for our meal."

Smiling he nodded at her and sat down to lean against the wall of the house beneath the shade.

"Get your father a mat and a good blanket you lazy child," she snapped at her daughter.

"This lazy daughter is the one making your new pot for you to dye your yarn," she answered getting up and smiling at her father, "and she wonders why she must chase after me." Disappearing around the house, she returned with a thick fur mat that she arranged under Fat Badger as he sat forward on his knees. She spread a cloth blanket woven with turkey feathers over his shoulders. Settling back his face creased into a smile, "Do not heed your mother's chastisement too closely, I know you are a good daughter."

Fire Star spoke indignantly, "Oh, now I must suffer both of you?"

Laughing, Fat Badger put up his hands, "Do not drag this old man into your battle of wits; I am unarmed."

The women looked at each other smiling and went back to their jobs, continuing to spar verbally in subdued voices.

He slept.

He saw many people running. He could not see their legs or feet — they were all turned away from him as if running from him. Then one by one they turned around — with faces full of terror they pointed at something behind him. He could not turn around to see what it was that approached. He looked down. He had no feet! His legs ended in stumps — he balanced precariously upon them. Then he saw that his feet had been burned off. His legs terminated in charred flesh! He could feel the pain of the burns — he saw blackened stubs of bone extending from the bottom of his legs. Flailing in the air Fat Badger lost his balance — toppling over a high cliff.

He woke with a start. Sweating, though the day was chilly, he looked around. His daughter still worked on the pot. She smiled at him and said "Go back to sleep father, it has only been short time that you slept. You are tired." He nodded, he was tired.

He slept for a time without dreaming and woke to find Fire Star crouched next to him. She held a bowl of refreshing water out for him to drink. "Did your dreams help your decisions?"

"My decisions are made already."

"I have sent for runners."

This understanding of what must be done was one of the things Fat Badger liked most about sharing duties with his mate.

"Thank you for that."

"Butterfly told me of the fire at your house."

He did not immediately respond to her statement.

"What do you think happened?"

"I wish I knew," he sighed. "I do not have the time now to try and find out."

"Your grandmother's house was utterly destroyed." Her statement was more of a question.

Nodding, he added, "I will rebuild it."

"I thought as much."

"I can stay at the War Chief's compound for now."

She nodded vaguely looking at the ground, did he see a flash of disappointment in her eyes.

"Perhaps I could stay here if I need to?"

Looking past him, she rose, leaving his question unanswered.

"Here come the runners," she said, "we will eat when you are done." She went to the hearth and stirred the cooking pot. Rising, he noticed that his second daughter Pale Falcon was approaching her mother's house from the other side of the valley.

Fat Badger dusted off the front of his robe. A group of warriors stood waiting on the ground below him. Climbing down the ladder, he spoke to the four young men, giving them explicit instructions what to say in each village. Taking the eldest one aside, he added extra instructions to his task.

"Go to Thunder Village, where the Bow Priest lives. Say to him the Winter Chief requests that he assemble his council at the warrior compound two days hence. Return to me then at that place tomorrow with reports from all your runners."

Pale Falcon, walking up to her mother's house as the runners left, greeted her father. Carrying a brace of rabbits over her shoulder, she went up to sit by her sister where they talked, giggling frequently. After a while, she looked up.

"Where do the runners go, father?"

"To announce the selection of a new War Chief."

She slowly nodded as if having known the answer already and turned back to her sister to speak to her. The young women lowered their voices. Fat Badger moved away, knowing they engaged in more sisterly gossip.

He left the house of his wife in the early evening after a good dinner, bidding her and his two daughters goodbye and promising to visit more often.

"You know you are welcome to stay." his wife offered.

"Thank you," he answered, "but I must be at the compound when the runners return." He knew she understood.

He did not look back to see that Pale Falcon watched him go longer than the others as if she had something more to talk to him about yet.

The night was uneventful. He slept long, and thankfully without disturbance. The long rest was a blessed relief. Even the dogs did no more than growl at him as he opened the gate and entered the compound — maybe, he thought, their war was finally over.

It was well after dawn when he awoke. With a start, he realized he had not heard the coyotes' warbled cries at the sun's arrival. Leaping up from his bed, he drank from a water bowl and chewed a strip of dried meat folded in a cold corn cake from some his wife had given him. He pulled on his winter boots and grabbed his robe as he climbed the ladder to see what the new day would bring. The Sun was already well advanced in his travels.

He saw his two tormentors laying against the same woodpile where they had hidden the previous days. Giving him a cursory glance, he hoped he was correct in assessing that a truce was in effect. Good thing too, he thought, as his legs still ached from the wounds he had already sustained.

Hearing the sound of someone clearing his throat outside the gate he opened it. The lead runner was sitting on the ground outside the compound when he emerged.

Jumping up he reported, "The council has been informed of your message."

Fat Badger nodded to the young warrior. Deer Charging, was that his name? He couldn't be more than twenty summers old, but he was known for his responsibility in completing missions. "I may need you again later."

Nodding back at his chief, the youth turned and ran back along the trail toward his village; Fat Badger watched him until he was out of sight then turned and re-entered the compound.

He picked up his heavy stick and lashed his club to his sash. He grabbed a water bladder that hung from the crossbeam of the shade and looked back at the beasts. They eyed him with the disdain of a hawk watching a bug. He would have to start training them to respect him soon.

XII

Fat Badger climbed the hill to a spot below where his grandmother's house had stood to begin his task of rebuilding. Entering the clearing just below the crest, he stood for a moment to let sadness drain from him.

His grandmother's voice seemed to be whispering to him on the wind. "Do not grieve, Far Seeing, this will all pass."

She had always called him Far Seeing.

Halfway up the slope, the sounds of movement above him caused him to flinch and then hurry up to the charred ruins.

Out of breath as he attained the flat where the foundations stood, he allowed surprise to show on his face at finding Pale Falcon engaged in carrying debris from the ruins to the north side of the hill. He stopped to watch her.

She did not at first notice him as he stood watching from slightly behind her. Grunting, she lifted charred rubble, walked to the hilltop edge and dropped her load on the growing pile. Turning, she saw him.

Eyeing each other for a time, each smiling vaguely at the other, Fat Badger walked over, and with his breath back he began to help her gather debris from the burned house. They worked in silence for a quarter of the sun's movement through the sky. Almost simultaneously they stopped. With their loud breathing shattering the silence of the day in unison, they sat down to rest from their labors. Exhausted, both dropped awkwardly on two stones placed at the east edge of the clearing.

After a time Falcon spoke, "Father, isn't this where you sit to watch for visitors?"

"It is."

"And is that smoke at the place of the High Spring?"

Looking across the valley Fat Badger was surprised to see that she was right, thin smoke curled up from the area of the spring campsite. Smoke rising from this place usually meant traders but why now and why had they not used the pennants?

He left cloth pennants dyed various colors and attached to long poles at the trading site. Whenever he saw the colored pennants waving from the poles at the spring, he knew traders had come. However, he could never recall a trading expedition arriving at this time of the year before. It was nearly the moon of Owls Stealing Nests.

"I should see what they want."

"Do you want me to come with you?"

Fat Badger gazed at his daughter and saw she asked as a warrior. "No, I do not think that necessary."

"I have soap-root," his daughter said, reaching into a net bag. She knew he would want to wash before going to see who had come.

"Thank you daughter, if you leave it at the washing pool, I will use it when you finish at the creek."

"You go ahead of me; I can wait." He looked at her, as she drew out the root from her net bag, "You have your work to do."

Agreeing he took the proffered root and started down the trail.

Calling after him, she asked, "I can go for others. Do you want me to gather an escort, Winter Chief?" He shook his head and smiled, "No, Warrior, I doubt that there will be many waiting for me at the trading site. Have no concern." Winking at her, he added, "This time of year no one can afford to be contentious. Thank you."

Later he would, for a time, regret that decision.

While walking down to the washing pool below the hill, his thoughts swirled around like scattered snow flurries at dawn. He washed his tunic and hung it up to dry. Hanging it there signified that the wash pool was in use, keeping his bathing private. He scrubbed the ashes and dirt from his body and wondered at yet another strange occurrence in this season of strange happenings. Leaving the root on the flat rock placed there for that purpose, he took his cloth tunic down from the tree.

His clothes were not nearly dry. But he couldn't wait. He covered them with his winter robe. Fat Badger started up the trail to the High Spring.

Approaching the spring, he shivered in the breeze. He could hear voices as he got close, but he did not recognize the accents. They raised the pennants after all, and they were red — indicating meat available for trading. That ruled out the Southern White Ants of the Two Rivers; they never had enough meat for themselves let alone to trade.

Stopping just below the clearing he called out a loud greeting. Waiting for the reply at first there was silence and then several words spoken in muffled voices of conversation. Finally a loud "Come — friend!" in a strange, guttural accent sounded out from above him.

Straightening his robe and pulling his damp tunic down Fat Badger tightened his sash and stepped up the last few body lengths into the clearing where he instantly halted. His hand went to his club at his side, though he knew it was hopeless to resist.

Five Red Ant People stood before him, two women and three men. All were armed. Wild and strangely garbed, they eyed him like wolves seeing a fawn. Three of them were towards the back of the clearing, the other two, both men, stood just two body lengths away from him.

His first thought was to curse his nonchalance at dismissing Falcon's offer. He briefly considered fighting, but the odds against him were too high. Now he cast a look around him — thinking how best to escape.

For their part, the five Red Ant people merely looked at him. He thought it strange that they did not attempt to surround a lone man, in fact, he noticed that even though they were well-armed, they were not at the ready with their weapons. They eyed him with curiosity, but he sensed no real threat.

After what seemed an eternity of time, the one slightly in front and bulkier in build than the others laid his bow down on the ground in a very deliberate manner. He moved into the open space before the spring looking all the while at Fat Badger. Holding his hands open out before him, he spoke, to another man over his shoulder in a strange language.

The man he had spoken to moved to get something laying on the ground. He walked forward carrying a bundle with both arms. He dropped it in front of the tall man who nodded to him and the second man moved back. Fat Badger saw a deerskin wrapped package. The first man lifted his head and pointed at the bundle with his chin, motioning Fat Badger to look at it closely.

Tentatively he stepped forward and crouched down to look at the skin; he opened it. It was part of a fresh kill, four round shanks tied with sinew.

Motioning with his chin again the man seemed to want Fat Badger to take it. Looking up, he saw the man's face break into a smile.

"Good . . . meat," said the burly man, struggling with the words.

Did they mean to trade with him? Fat Badger nodded and held his hands open before him to ask the man what he wanted.

The other's face clouded over, and Fat Badger thought he might have made a mistake. Then the stout man shook his head as if to clear it.

Waving his hand toward his fellow Red Ants, he said, "Home, here?"

"Yes," answered the Winter Chief, "this is my home."

Looking puzzled the big man shook his head. Speaking over his shoulder again, he then pointed to himself and waved to the others behind him, "Home, here?"

Standing Fat Badger looked at the assembled people in confusion. "Your home is here?"

The other nodded and then looked confused again. "Your home here," he indicated Fat Badger, "we home here?"

Looking about him, Fat Badger struggled to understand the concept. Were these people living right under their noses without their scouts noticing? No, that wasn't possible. He was amazed Red Ants had gotten this far without someone raising the alarm. What did they want? Then an idea occurred to him.

"You," waving his arm he indicated the group, "want to live here," he pointed to the valley behind him, "with us?"

The man turned and looked at his companions saying a few words then he turned back and smiled, "Live here with us. Yes."

Fat Badger nodded while rising to his feet. He looked down at the bundle of meat, then he grasped their full meaning. "You hunt?" he said.

Nodding vigorously, the Red Ant leader said, "Hunt, yes!"

How stunning, thought Fat Badger. They were offering to hunt for the canyon or at least trade meat in return for a place to live.

Good hunters were always welcome, but these were Red Ants. If they wanted to live somewhere why didn't they go to the land of the White Ants? Many of the ant peoples of other regions found the lure of the White Ants irrigated fields along with their wealth too much to resist. Small bands of Red Ants went to live in their lands. Working as hunters and wood collectors, they found welcoming open arms if not total acceptance there.

White Ants tolerated their less fortunate neighbors when they weren't enslaving them. Their hunger for wood was legend and Brown or Red people in their opinion were suitable for the jobs they found distasteful. White Ants were always hiring Red Ants to do their hunting.

Everyone was welcome at a price.

Many immigrants; Brown, Red and even Black Ant people; sallied out from the sprawling White Ant villages to hunt animals, acquire wood, collect specialized stone for making corn-grinders and chipping sharp tools. They even chose them to gather the valuable shells from the Great Salt Sea. Workers were needed. The White Ants themselves spent all their efforts in the maintenance of their extensive canals that supplied water to their fields of corn and the Cloud plants. What little time they had left was eaten up in their many ceremonies that guaranteed those harvests.

White Ant children trapped rodents and shot birds near their fields. But these were diminishing through time. Starving for meat in the White Ant villages they welcomed Red Ants who were universally known as superior hunters. If they had killed game, why not take it south?

Why had they come here to seek to live with Brown Ants in Sky Canyon? Fat Badger shivered again. Another unprecedented occurrence.

Fat Badger's head was swimming. Everything that happened in the last few days was so strange — the world was turning upside down — things were happening too fast. There were too many changes, too many important decisions to be made.

He sighed. He must deal with first things first. He motioned to the leader, holding up four fingers and pointing at the sun: a dim circle of light barely visible behind thick clouds. The other looked where he indicated and then nodded. The leader understood Fat Badger to say he would return in four days with his decision. The Red Ant leader looked at the sun, then at his hand with the four fingers extended, and he spoke over his shoulder again to the man who must be his second.

Turning back to Fat Badger without waiting for a reply, he swept his hand across his chest indicating agreement. He held out his hand, and Fat Badger grasped his forearm just as the heavyset man grasped his. Fat Badger noted how warm the man's arm was to his touch. They brought their arms up and down once to seal the agreement. Leaving the bundle, the Red Ants melted into the chaparral and were gone. Fat Badger exhaled.

He had never negotiated with Red Ants before. He had fought them, he had hunted them but to rationally discuss living with them!

Looking up, Fat Badger directed a question to the sky. "Hu-eh! What are you telling me?"

While little direct contact between the Red and Brown Ant people happened, there existed a long history of occasional indirect trading. But there had been raiding too, sometimes for goods, at other times more harmful interactions when they took women and children. Now he stood here, next to their offering, considering extending an invitation to Red Ants to live in Sky Valley.

Some people would hold a grudge against any Red Ants no matter who they were or what they did.

He would need help to make a decision like this.

XIII

Returning to the compound with the haunches, he thought about the strange meeting much while he considered who he would ask to prepare the meat for smoking and drying. Thinking, always thinking! As had become habitual of late he also pondered many other things. So much to consider!

One mystery that involved mere fancy intrigued him.

After several days at the warrior compound, Fat Badger noticed something about the dogs. He had found a refuge from them. Walking to the southwest corner of the enclosure caused the dogs to slink away like there was a skunk that had just sprayed them. Watching them as they sidled away Fat Badger saw them looking back over their shoulders like he might be following them.

What magic possessed this corner?

Building a small rock-lined hearth in the corner ensured that he could cook his meals uninterrupted by canine attacks. While waiting for his fire to work down to coals so he could grill some meat, he distracted his poor mind further with the problem.

Surveying the area, he saw it as a corner, outwardly containing nothing special. Unroofed and not possessing a finished floor it appeared no different from the rest of the compound.

Or was it?

Looking back suddenly, hoping to catch the beasts slinking up for an attack, he found instead that they lay in the shade of the east wall apparently uninterested in him. Their heads lay down on their paws, their eyes closed.

They just did not come into this area of the compound. But why?

After eating and wanting to test his theory, Fat Badger sat down against the cold plaster of the wall. Closing his eyes, he allowed himself to sleep. It wasn't hard to do; he hadn't slept very well since the death of Tall Claw several days before. Waking from his nap sometime later, Fat Badger saw that the dogs still lay amid the shadows against the east wall.

"Hu-eh!" said Fat Badger aloud, surprised that he had been allowed to lay in full view unmolested by his tormentors. What was it about this corner?

Rising, he turned to look at the hard-packed dirt where he had slept. There was nothing unusual that he could detect. It was a used floor, dusty, unremarkable and even typical. Moving his eyes up to the walls, he traced the smooth adobe plaster, mixed with gray ashes which left a uniformly light colored surface. Imprints of Tall Claw's hands were the only thing which marred the uniformity.

Backing up three steps he looked over the entire area then turning he saw the beasts eying him hungrily, their muscles tense.

He took inventory. All around the edges of the compound, against the walls, there were things: piles of rocks for building, chunks of tool making rock, piles of wood, a stray deer antler, an old ax head made into a maul, fragments of broken vessels, all the usual debris.

Except here.

Looking back, he realized that this was the only place in the whole of the walled area where there was no clutter of any kind. For the length of a man's reclining body in each direction, nothing lay against the walls or on the ground in this corner.

All at once hearing their growls and rising barks, he spun about in a crouch, instantly on the defensive. But for once the beasts were not after him. They ran noisily toward the bound gate, raising the alarm.

Fat Badger was halfway to the opening when he heard the shout from without, "Winter Chief are you there?"

He recognized the voice of Dark Snake, a rain priest. He could tell he was not alone by the sound of others talking as they walked up the trail with him.

Taking hold of the bindings of the gate, he simultaneously kicked at the dogs who were worrying the wood in their zeal. Fat Badger shouted "Shah!" and he was immediately rewarded by the blessed sight of them creeping off — whimpering — to a distant corner of the compound.

Thunderhead was the first to enter, and he spat at the retreating curs, "I am glad to see that you have properly instructed those two as to their behavior. They were indulged over-much by their previous owner."

Fat Badger said nothing.

Following the old Vulture priest came Dark Snake, a few elders, an acolyte of the Vulture fraternity and four young men including Angry Cloud, his nephew. Between them, suspended on coarse ropes was a wrapped bundle - Tall Claw's body. It was his burial procession!

Under his breath, Fat Badger cursed his other preoccupations! He had forgotten that it had been four days. The time for final disposition of Tall Claw's body had arrived.

Under the bundling Tall Claw's remains had been washed in yucca soap. Clothed in new raiment with his hair combed and pulled back in a braid with a newly carved bone pin holding it in place. More importantly, by this time, his spirit had visited each of the cardinal directions: north, east, south, down, up and west over those days and now knew where to go to pass to the next state of being. All that remained was for them to bury his physical remains today. His spirit would then go west, to the land of the dead.

"You prepared the place for the burial?" Thunderhead barked out the question as he had spat at the retreating dogs.

Raising himself up to his full height and fixing the old man with his most disdainful glare, Fat Badger paused significantly while his mind raced. Then he smiled. This time he had him!

He bowed to those assembled. Then gazing above the old man as if looking to the spirits of the sky for his direction he intoned, "Though it is not the place of the Winter Chief to do so, I have prepared the area for the corporeal remains." Smiling inwardly at his good fortune, he turned and walked to the southwest corner of the compound and waving his arm as if sowing seeds in a scattering fashion, he indicated the cleared area.

From the corner of his eye, he detected the little slump of the Vulture priest's shoulders, indicating his disappointment that he had not caught the Winter Chief unprepared. In his mind, Fat Badger thanked the spirit of Tall Claw for having prepared his final resting place.

Looking at the area Thunderhead at first frowned and then smiled a thin and altogether unattractive smile. The priest cleared his throat, self-importantly while squaring his sagging shoulders.

Fixing Fat Badger with a stare he intoned, "While we all appreciate the Winter Chief's efforts in this matter," the old man's voice loud enough for all to hear, "it won't do to inter the body here." He waved off the proposed space as one would swat at a fly. Without noticing that Fat Badger raised his eyebrows to look at the old man with some surprise and shock, he continued, "As you well know," lecturing in his best voice to the Winter Chief, "Tall Claw was Summer people, Coyote clan."

Fat Badger knew what was coming next.

"As such he must be laid in the sacred line of the sun!" Swiveling with surprising agility the little old priest gestured toward the southeast corner of the compound, "There, closest to the rising sun or — " he swung his arm full in the other direction, to the west wall, "there at the sun's death. This 'location'" the word was spat out with contempt as he indicated the cleared southwest corner, "is a Winter person's place."

Expectantly the old man eyed him, triumph in his eyes.

"You are of course correct in this, Vulture Priest," Fat Badger conceded with a slight bow, "in this one's haste and seeking to honor the departed I erred in judgment. In the future, I will leave these tasks to those more knowledgeable in such matters."

Grudgingly nodding his agreement, Thunderhead continued, "I am willing to concede that your mistake was an honest one Winter Chief and we thank you for acknowledging it thus," he turned around, "Now, where do we begin?" He looked at the gate area and then to the southeast corner.

"Well it is obvious we must look at that place there," he pointed at the latter corner, "as the only suitable choice." He looked to all the assembled for agreement. "We do not want all who walk here to disturb the departed by walking on their resting spot, nor . . ." he paused significantly, "do we want the departed disturbing them, eh?" Not waiting for an answer, he chuckled at his wit and continued, "So lay down the bundle and begin clearing that area, now!"

Laying their load down gently on the ground, the attendants moved toward the southeast corner of the compound. Those workers had just started when the dogs again raised the alarm, though less raucous than usual at the approach of visitors. Walking to the gate Fat Badger saw Lazy Tree coming up the trail in great haste. "What now?" he thought.

Outside the gate hurrying toward him was Lazy Tree, his eyes wild with fear.

"Winter Chief, the stones came again, attacking Laughing Fox, even now he may be dead!"

XIV

Later, Fat Badger could not remember the running, scrambling trip to the mine. In his memory, one breath he was looking at Lazy Tree coming up the trail and the next he was at the mine bending over Laughing Fox.

The miner lay in the dust just before the mine entrance, his head in a pool of blood that clotted the dirt.

"What happened, did a rock fall within the mine?"

"No Winter Chief, a rock came flying down from the sky and struck him!"

Fat Badger stared at the man open-mouthed for a moment then someone moaned, breaking the spell. It was Laughing Fox. He lived!

Kneeling Fat Badger took the wounded man's head in his hands and lifted it gently up from the ground. The eyes fluttered, and a groan escaped his lips. His spirit had not left, not entirely, not yet thank the Creator! Lazy Tree stood looking down at them. Angry Cloud and another man came too — they stood at the watch, surveying the surrounding hills. Each held a bow at the ready with arrows nocked.

"Here is the rock, Winter Chief," Lazy Tree brought a stone over to where Fat Badger squatted. "This is the one that struck him."

"Not now," Fat Badger snapped, "later I will look at that. We need to make a litter and get him home to Mine Village right away."

Crestfallen, Lazy Tree dropped the rock as if it were on fire. He looked at the area surrounding, the mine. It was plain he was afraid to venture into the thick underbrush.

Regretting the shortness in his reply, Fat Badger looked up at him and said, "Stay here with your friend, I will gather what we need. Cradle his head like this."

It took a quarter of the retreating Sun, in these short days of winter, before they got the stricken miner to his village. Seeing them approach, his wife, Flowers Wilting ran out of the plaza screaming, "I knew this would happen, is he dead? Was it the Ogres? I knew this would happen! Oh, my husband!" More people quickly gathered.

"Quiet woman!" snapped Fat Badger, "he lives!" Leaning in and whispering sternly to her, he added, "Go send for Grandfather Scorpion. Tell him it is a head wound."

From the litter, a hoarse voice slowly added, "Yes, please you old woman, before you finish me with your screeching."

Fat Badger put his hand on the wounded man's shoulder, smiling he spoke softly, "Save yourself, my friend, do not talk." He looked at Flowers Wilting and smiled at her wanly, "See he lives to joke even at a time like this."

She calmed herself, "What happened, what happened to him?"

"Go send someone for Grandfather Scorpion," he spoke even more gently, "and I will tell you."

But in the end, he told her only that a rock had struck her husband, and he silenced Lazy Tree with a withering look that said further elaboration was unnecessary at this time. Just as he had with Wind Killer, he withheld information to prevent possibly rising fears and rumors. He hated this part of his position as Winter Chief.

He had stayed on at the village until the runner returned saying the healer was on his way. Stopping to talk to Lazy Tree, he ordered him to go with two of the village scouts, seal the gate at the mine and keep the mine closed until further notice and to talk to no one. Lazy Tree was reluctant. Fat Badger sensed that in him but, with two warriors as escorts, he went. Then taking Angry Cloud and the other young man with him, Fat Badger set out for the warrior's compound.

The Vulture Priest was waiting for him, agitated at the long delay in his rituals.

"So do I have another spirit to prepare for passage?"

Fat Badger shook his head, "Not yet at least." He walked in and sat down heavily on the raised edge of the house. "I had them send for Scorpion."

He chose not to reply to Thunderhead's "Humph!"

Exhausted, he hoped the ornery priest would go about his business and leave him alone. He was not to be so lucky on this.

His voice sounding accusing, Thunderhead said, "Winter Chief, we must have six participants to release this soul properly."

Reluctantly Fat Badger nodded and rose. He walked over to the elongated oval pit dug in the prescribed corner.

The two men left behind efficiently dug out the rocky fill of the grave. Fat Badger surveyed their work. The soil surrounding the numerous rocks and cobbles was a deep, reddish brown color. It mimicked the color of the bark on the bushes that grew around outside the compound.

A framework of thin sticks lay in the bottom of the pit. The small branches came from water trees: the tall ones with the mottled bark and light green leaves that died each fall and came back to life in the spring. Many of these trees lined the creek bed, their massive trunks greater around than two men could reach — their broad leaves waving bright green greetings to the warmth of spring. At this time of the year, their leaves lay crumbling and brown, littering the ground on either bank of Sky Creek. But if the leaves were ephemeral, the wood was not. A water person needed a bed of water tree wood to lay upon for their final rest.

Beside the grave the bundle containing the body of Tall Claw lay athwart two long cords of thickly twined yucca fibers. Fat Badger stood at one end of the pit and the Vulture priest stationed himself at the other with the four young men in pairs to either side.

Taking the ropes in their hands, the four lifted the wrapped body off the ground. The two on the west side of the bundle stepped forward as the two across the pit stepped back. Fat Badger watched solemnly — the air filled with the sacred words the Vulture priest intoned. Prayers of passage accompanied the body of Tall Claw as it was lowered slowly into the waiting soil.

Thunderhead passed out breath feathers to each of them and one by one they dropped the feathers into the hole. They watched them float down onto the bundle, one by one, where they lay still fluttering as if alive upon the wrappings.

Dropping the ropes to drape over the body, the men placed large, double-fist sized rocks neatly into the hole. When a complete layer of stone shrouded the body from view, they used their flat bladed digging sticks to push dirt in over the rocks.

As the hole filled, the Vulture priest kept a close watch. Then, signaling the diggers to halt by raising his hands, he stepped down into the shallow pit. Reaching up, one of the men gave him a square chunk of a pinkish stone matrix surrounding various water worn egg-shaped cobbles in numerous colors. He staggered under the weight of the substantial piece. It was a type of stone found commonly in Sky Canyon but unusual elsewhere. Fragments of this unique stone were often interred with the bodies of the honored dead to remind them of their former lives and as a substitute for the people they left behind. It helped ensure that prayers sent to those going on would be recognized as coming from Sky Canyon and therefore be welcome.

The priest hoped that by having a piece of their former home with them, the dead would not seek to return and worry the living. In this, the stone was seen as harboring magic and power.

Many believed that the peculiar pink stone formed from the pooling blood of a great monster slain by the legendary Warrior twins. After terrorizing the ancient world, the creature had its heart removed by the two heroes after they intentionally allowed themselves to be swallowed by the monster. Once inside they sliced the vessels bringing blood to the beast's heart. They cut their way out carrying the still beating heart. Blood had flowed all about, down into the washes in and amongst the stones laying on the ground. The blood hardened to become the pink stone, encompassing the various gravels and forming the sacred talisman now interned with Tall Claw.

From their shaded spot, the two dogs watched the whole procedure without stirring as if they too were cognizant of the solemnity of the occasion.

Climbing laboriously up out of the pit and standing away from the others Thunderhead drank from a small gourd and then handed it to one of the others. The priest poured the remaining water onto the grave.

The last of the dirt was scraped in to level the pit with the surface and cover the sacred stone. Walking deliberately across the damp clayey surface, first from east to west then south to north, the Vulture priest completed his prayers and sat down on the ground before Fat Badger. He or one of his priests would sit thus for two days without food or water overseeing the passage of the soul of Tall Claw.

Freed from obligation, at last, Fat Badger turned heel without a word and stalked off to the house of the recently interred man. Once inside he collapsed and slept — troubled and dream harried. Striding through his dreams were shadowy creatures. Ogres lurked in darkly tangled underbrush peering out at him as he ran by them. Red Ants raced at him screaming and brandishing war clubs threateningly. Then he stood on a cliff and watched as an entire village was consumed by fire.

He woke with a start, shaking and sweating. Looking up through the opening in the roof he saw stars in the sky and climbing up the ladder he peered across the compound to where the Vulture priest sat. Faintly he heard a low repetitive chant snaking its way through the chilly night. As his eyes accustomed to the dim light, he was surprised to see that the two small terriers lay quietly atop the mounded grave, just an arm's length behind the old man.

Sighing heavily he returned to the sleeping mat, and after a hundred or so heartbeats of troubled, crowded visions, he fell into a blessedly dreamless sleep.

XV

—on the trails near the Mine—

Not fearing local legends like so many others, Kills Rabbits went where he pleased. He even hunted in the Ogre's Tangle on occasion though not too often because, truth be told, like many others, he was more frightened of Tall Claw than of any ogres. But Tall Claw had died. Now he stood looking across the valley at a darkened portion of the forest that shrouded the slopes of Sky Sweeping Mountain.

He even went into the Forbidden Place, surreptitiously of course.

"Would she have dared venture up there?" he wondered aloud. Shaking his head, he answered his own question, "No, even as an immigrant she was smart enough to avoid that place as the local people do." He smiled to himself. "Only the greatest of warriors, Tall Claw; the dead man from the sky, whoever he was, and I, am foolish enough to tempt fate!" He laughed, pulling his robe closer, "And now there is only me."

He trudged up to the summit of the same little-used trail that Tall Claw had investigated the day of his death. He looked across the ridge and sighed, "Where are you hiding little dove?"

Often ranging out by himself, soliloquies were frequent for Kills Rabbits as was thinking aloud. It facilitated his reasoning. Today he hoped to kill two rabbits with a single throw of his stick! Wanting to see the place where Tall Bear fell and yet needing to visit one of the outlying villages to ascertain if his quarry found sanctuary there he was traveling the long way. It offered him much time for solitary conversations.

He also kept to the brush to make sure no one happened to see him from below.

Kills Rabbits knelt by the side of the high trail. He read to himself aloud what he saw, "See! He stopped here, he was on his toes though, tensed." He touched the dirt, "Then he planted his heel, something made him relax." Looking up, he examined the branches of the bushes at the edge of the cliff. "He might have broken these as he grabbed them for support – but then they would have fallen with him." He leaned far out to look over the side, "And what made him fall in the first place?"

Pushing through the bushes away from the cliff, he scanned the ground. It was disturbed, but no tracks were there. If he was correct, it had been swept or brushed to erase the signs. But why, and by who? It spanned more than the length of a man. Much more. It was flat and protected by surrounding vegetation. A sleeping place? Had large bodies laid in the cleared space? Further on he found more scattered broken branches. Was there one a shelter here, a brush house? To Kills Rabbits the litter looked like nesting material.

He couldn't think of any bird or any other animal that made a temporary nest this large.

"Do Ogres sleep in nests?" he asked aloud, startling himself with the sound of his own voice breaking the silence of the place.

He stood and carefully skirted the trail on the hillside, away from the cliff. "What happened to you, War Chief?" Looking at the ground near the trail he stopped and bent down. "Eh-uh! What do I see here?" He scooped up an object laying on a slight dirt berm beside the trail. It lay nearly hidden beneath a small yucca. "Oh, ho," he chortled, "so you were not alone," he smiled, "I begin to understand. Thank you blesséd spirits for this bit of luck you have given me." He frowned, "But then," he looked up and down the trail, "where did she go next?"

He found himself looking toward Dead Women Canyon. "No, I think not." he mused, "But I'll have a little look."

He trotted off down the trail as snow began to fall in soft flurries through the frosty air, looking very much like the breath feathers dropped into Tall Claw's grave.

—at the house of Tall Claw—

Fat Badger woke to more voices. Crawling up the ladder into the full morning light, he blinked and saw that the Vulture Priest's assistant and the pair of small furry acolytes still kept their vigil. Had the dogs even eaten since their master's death? Then the voices came again from just outside the gate of the compound. Turning, he saw the old Bow Priest, Sad Gopher stride purposefully into the open area of the warrior's plaza.

Behind him came several men dressed for war and then Fat Badger's jaw dropped. Trailing the group in full warrior array was his daughter Pale Falcon.

She looked neither left nor right, over her left shoulder was her bow, and her quiver was full of arrows. Her war club swung from her sash at her left hip, and she carried a small round shield on her right forearm.

"Now what?" he said to himself. Shaking off his surprise, Fat Badger hastily composed himself and scrambled up out of the opening. He fairly sprang to the ground. Hurrying over to the Bow Priest, he stopped in his path causing the old man to pull up short.

"Winter Chief . . ." he began.

"What is this Sad Gopher?" he inquired tersely.

Taken aback the elder licked his lips, looked at the entourage behind him and answered matter of factly in a strident whisper, "It is the selection of the new War Chief, of course, what did you think it was Winter Chief?"

Unfortunately, that was precisely what Fat Badger had thought it was.

Looking over the dozen or so warriors who followed the Bow Priest, Fat Badger motioned him to one side, away from earshot of the others. Looking surprised and somewhat exasperated, he nonetheless followed the younger man.

Keeping his voice low, Fat Badger asked, "How many candidates are there?"

Looking back at the group as if to assure himself that he was right he leaned forward conspiratorially and whispered, "Four, Winter Chief, four, of course."

Relieved for a moment, Fat Badger nodded. "Of course the rest are simply escorting."

"Yes," the old man continued somewhat louder than before, "and you can be sure that your daughter, Pale Falcon will not be given any special treatment."

"My daughter . . . my daughter is a candidate for War Chief?"

"Well, yes, isn't that what you were worried about, that I would show favoritism toward her?"

After standing still as a rock for unnumbered breaths, Fat Badger swiveled and strode off leaving the Bow Priest's question unanswered.

Walking past the gape-mouthed Bow Priest, Fat Badger stared at Pale

Falcon as he returned to the house. She did not turn her head to meet his stony gaze even when he passed within an arm's reach.

Reaching the house, he started to step up and then paused then thinking better of it he turned and approached his daughter's side.

"What are you doing, father?" she asked in the barest whisper of a voice.

"That is what I want to ask you."

"I am a candidate for War Chief."

His worst fears realized, he spoke too abruptly, without thinking, "No! I forbid it!"

She turned and fixed him with her dark eyes, "It is not up to you."

"Do you realize what a position you will put me in?" he hissed. "Or how it will affect your mother in the eyes of the rest of the valley's populace? If the Winter Chief, Summer Matron and War Chief are all of the same family?"

"This is not about our family. It is about my qualifications as a warrior and leader."

"Then you are defying your father?"

"It has nothing to do with you! I am a made person of water; I can decide this for myself."

He stared at her. She noticed his entire body fairly shook.

Sad Gopher spoke up, "Winter Chief, can I be of help to you?" His tone was neutral but, his eyes spoke of his confusion.

There was a long pause as Fat Badger continued to stare at his daughter. If she thought him rude, she did not choose to react. Then, as if suddenly hearing the question Gopher had asked, at last, he turned and looked at the Bow Priest rudely. Finally, spinning on his heels, Fat Badger took two steps and vaulted up onto the roof of the house and disappeared within.

Shaking his head, the Bow Priest led his group to the open area of the central plaza of the compound. Seated before the grave, the assistant Vulture priest took no notice of what was going on. Nor did the dogs look up as they continued to lay on the top of the grave as if keeping the same vigil.

Sometime later, when the sun was full in the sky, Fat Badger emerged from the house with a bundle over his shoulder. He did not even glance in the direction of the candidates for War Chief. Jumping to the ground, he walked briskly to the gate and passed through it without looking behind him. Outside two warriors stood guard to prevent any interruptions. As he went by the stern-faced guards, Fat Badger said tersely, "I go to keep watch at the mine."

The warriors looked surprised but said nothing.

Hearing a noise behind him, Fat Badger turned and was surprised to see that the mostly white dog stood at his heels. Looking back over his shoulder, he saw that the other, the black one, still lay on his old master's grave, behind the Vulture priest.

"May our ancestors always forbid that I should be allowed to leave without some tormenter!" he said softly to himself with an ironic laugh.

XVI

—on the trails to the Mine—

Traveling quickly, his anger fueling his leg muscles, Fat Badger worked his way down the familiar trail toward the canyon bottom and the mine. Staying ever close at his heels the dog trotted easily and seemed content to follow where he went.

Reaching the creek the two stopped to drink the icy water. Crouched down on bended knee Fat Badger brought one after another cupped hand up to his mouth. The dog lapped hungrily at the fast-moving water. Taking one last handful Fat Badger washed his face and shaking his head rose with a sigh. "So," he glanced at the dog, "now we're friends?" He shook his head more slowly. "I'm not even supposed to talk to you, you know."

Looking at the man the dog seemed to be listening.

"They say, if you talk to a dog and the dog answers, it means this world is about to end."

Cocking his head to one side, to Fat Badger the dog looked quizzical.

"You used to talk to us, you know," Fat Badger continued. "Long ago the animals used to talk, but you stopped after revolting against man and the Great Spirit. Now you won't talk until the world is about to end." He noticed his nose was running, "Out in this weather and talking to dogs," he sniffed. "I tempt fate."

The dog still looked at him.

"I can tell you're concerned about that." He looked across the creek. "This is the depth the Winter Chief of Sky Canyon has fallen to — wandering about having conversations with a dog." He looked down, "A rude dog who bit him several times!"

His small companion trotted off seemingly unconcerned. Shaking his head again, Fat Badger looked up at the sky. Clouds were gathering to the east and south. They were dark and deep gray. "Oh thanks to the Great Spirit," he said with sarcasm, "it looks as if it will snow again." He sighed,

"My wife must stop asking for our ancestors to come and bless us." He followed the dog with his eyes. "Not listening to me now, eh?"

Sniffing the area around the point at which several large stones had been laid to assist crossing the creek, the dog's hair bristled.

"You're looking for a new victim?" Fat Badger walked toward the dog, "I wonder who the lucky one is?"

Kneeling down, he pushed aside the wet leaves that lined a depression, over which the growling dog stood watch. His eyes went wide at what he saw. A large, foot-shaped print lay embedded in the wet soil along the bank. The heel end pointed back the way he had come, the toes across the creek. It was at least half again as large as the one left by his foot. The dog growled at this strange print.

Bending down, even more, he felt the edges. They were still wet — the clayey soil pliable — telling Fat Badger that the print was not old. He scanned the surrounding area, but the soft sod, many rocks, and mottled brown leaf debris offered him no clues as to how long ago it was formed. He saw the little white dog jerk his head up and look across the creek. The dog stopped growling, but his fur still bristled. Following his gaze, it seemed to Fat Badger as if the dog saw something in the brush beyond the opposite bank. The bushes there moved ever so slightly in the wind. Then, to his surprise, the dog whimpered and tucked her tail between her legs while backing off two steps to a place behind the crouching man, as if expecting Fat Badger's protection.

Staring intently, he saw nothing. Neither he nor the now silent dog moved for a hundred breaths. The creek flowed shallow but wide here, more than four body lengths across. Realizing his exposure to an enemy's arrow, Fat Badger crouched lower making himself as small a target as he could.

He felt a tickling sensation run down his spine. Then it was at his nostrils. Abruptly his body exploded with a violent sneeze, followed quickly by another.

The dog stared at him as if in reproach.

"I know what you are thinking. Good job hiding our location," Fat Badger wiped his nose, "That's why I am chief."

As abruptly as it started the dog stopped watching across the creek and relaxed. Sitting down, she scratched behind her ear with her foot and turned her attention back to Fat Badger seemingly asking with her eyes, "What do we do now?"

"Thanks for your confidence in my judgment." Fat Badger sniffed and looked back across the flowing water. If the dog was no longer concerned, neither was he. Shrugging off the worry he felt a moment before, Fat Badger said, "Let's go see what's there."

Standing, he led the dog onto the stepping stones and across the creek. Fat Badger figured if the senses of this beast, which were much keener than his, saw no danger, it must be safe. Not taking any chances, he had his club out in his right hand. A tickle came to his nose once more, and he tried to stifle the sneeze, but it was too late. His body, wracked by the shock of the sneeze, wobbled. He lost his balance.

Sliding off the rock he landed upright in the near-freezing water. It was all from snowmelt atop the mountains and nearly as cold. A chill shot through him like a fiery jolt of pure agony. His breath stopped as he sucked it in at the sudden shock. He staggered and saw the dog look back at as if confused by his actions. Pushing his stick down to brace himself he scrambled back up on to the stone almost sliding off the other side. His boots were dangerously slick with the icy water.

Finally steady, despite the shivers that passed through him, he carefully stepped ahead to the next stone. Reaching the other bank, he looked up and down along the creek for some sign like the print they had seen on the opposite side, but he found none. He sneezed twice more.

Two narrow trails lay ahead of them. The right hand one skirted the creek, the other rose up out of the creek bed area, toward the mine and eventually the dark, looming, Sky Sweeping Mountains. About halfway up to the first ridge a branch trail led off the way Tall Claw had gone and on to the Forbidden Place.

His thoughts turned again to stories. No one went up there into the lair of spirits, witches, and ogres. The tall, densely forested mountains, were where they lived, high up where people never ventured at least according to the stories he heard as a child. Witches might sometimes lurk near the edges of his people's world, gathering their forbidden tools. Spirits, bones of humans, ghosts of unburied dead wandering lost; these they coveted. The ogres though were different. They were said to only come down to the valley to look for misbehaving children. He knew all the stories. Witch tales created to scare those children. He half chuckled self-consciously: they used to stalk him in his nightmares, now here he was looking for them.

Taking the slightly ascending trail to the left, he walked briskly, keeping his eyes sweeping from left to right and back again. The wind picked up, bringing a chill and the cold scent of moisture to the air. Dark clouds crowded the sky. It was good weather for lost spirits. He shivered again. Trotting at his heels the dog took little notice of anything else keeping his eyes forward.

Fat Badger was glad the dog had accompanied him. His thoughts were muddled. Whenever he needed to think, he walked; walking to the mine was an excuse. He could allow the dog to attend to the possible dangers while he sorted his scattered ideas. At the mine, he would be alone, unbothered by all the furor surrounding the choosing of a new War Chief.

Would his daughter be selected? He could not imagine the outcry if another of his family took such a prestigious position, let alone a woman, as War Chief.

It wasn't that she was not qualified if anything she might be the most qualified, and yet some would see her selection as interference by him or his wife. They wouldn't look at the fact that she had proven herself in all three of the most necessary areas: war, scouting, and hunting. Nor would they see her innate intelligence, a cool head under pressure and skills of decision making. Physically she was tall and powerful, again, well qualified. But it didn't matter. All they would see is that she was the second daughter of the Winter Chief and the Summer Matron.

He almost stumbled over the dog. It had stopped again.

Gathering his senses while allowing the problem to drift off, for now, he scoured the surrounding brush with his eyes. Glancing down, he saw that the small animal had sat and was looking at him expectantly. A chill wind ran across his robe from behind bringing the strong scent of water. Looking up Fat Badger saw the sky was completely clouded over. He was so absorbed in his thoughts that he had not seen the rapid approach of storm clouds. Many were the ancestral spirits filling the sky. Eager to please they would soon release their blessings.

Speaking to the dog, he said, "My wife does her job much too well!" Clouds, the spirits of the best of their ancestors, came to nourish the people with life-giving rain and snow. The Summer Matron ensured that the winter rains and snow appeared when needed by initiating prayers and preparing shrines to call in the spirits of those ancestors as clouds. He hoped his efforts would be half as effective at luring summer rains, though he knew that job was more complicated and required the cooperation of many to be successful.

Snow flurries drifted down around him, dancing in the air.

"I am already wet and freezing; I suppose we should hunt cover, eh?" Fat Badger looked at the little white dog for a moment as if waiting for an answer. He shook his head, "There I go again, talking to dogs. What is wrong with me?" He stared at the dog, "Thank you for not replying."

Looking about, he saw they were nearer the mine than anywhere else so that was where he would seek shelter. His feet felt like ice in his soaked, wet boots.

Glancing up, he noted that above him to the left was the spot where they had recovered Tall Claw's body. He decided he would go back there first, see what he might have missed in the dark. Struggling up through the brush, he emerged into the scattered rocks and broken branches where he found the body. With the gathering of clouds, there was not that much more light at this time either. Snow lazily scattered their frozen bits of moisture upon the ground.

He stopped amid some bushes. Sheltered from the relentless wind, he bent down and scanned the area. After a few moments, he grunted. Where were the rocks, the fragments of Tall Claw's weapons, bits of clothing and other items that had lain scattered about the body? He was confident this was the spot where his body was.

Standing, he looked for the dog. Finally, he saw its wagging tail peeking out from behind a low bush. Walking over, he found the dog standing over a small pile of the missing items. Someone had gathered them and placed them together in this spot. Atop the collection, he saw a piece of shell that had been drilled to allow it to be strung on a necklace or as an earring. It was a valuable piece of the rainbow-colored shell from the Great Salt Water to the west. He did not recognize it as belonging to Tall Claw. "Where did this come from?" He reached down and picked up the shell.

He spoke aloud, seemingly to any spirits who might be watching, "I am simply borrowing it. I will look at this in a better light and . . ." he looked up, ". . . in better weather and then replace it later." He slid the shell into his waist pouch and then looked down at the dog, "Why do I feel I have to tell you this? Do I need to justify myself to a dog?"

The sudden harsh croak of a raven sounded like jeering laughter as if in answer to Fat Badger's question. He saw the enormous black bird sitting a few body lengths away amid the tangled bare branches of the water trees behind him. "And who asked your opinion?" he growled.

The bird swam in his vision. He shook his head and blinked.

"Hu-eh," he coughed the exclamation, "What is happening to me? Am I being witched?" Ravens were rarely a good sign. Was this one an omen? His mind would not let him recognize the significance of things if there was any. He seemed unable to gather his thoughts in any plausible fashion. What to do?

The raven snapped at a snowflake, its monstrous beak clacking in the hushed air. It flapped its wings and was gone.

Continuing their quest under the threat of snow might not be his best idea, but it was the best he could think of currently.

Even as he took a painful step in his near-freezing boots down toward the mine, the flakes began to fall faster becoming more numerous. One slid down his neck causing him to shiver again. Looking up, he shook his head.

He did not know that he was not alone in surveying the thick gray skies.

—at the house of Kills Rabbits—

Kills Rabbits stood at the entrance to his brush hut and chewed a piece of old dried venison. Slowly the smoky meat softened, and juices reformed from his saliva. He unconsciously pulled his thin robe up around his shoulders. The snow fell in large, loud clumps that sounded like the distant rattlings of shell tinklers on the legs of dancing priests. It whispered warnings of more flakes still to follow them in spiraling to the ground. "Oho, wouldn't you know it would snow? Guess I better get going," he muttered, "hope she's not on the move," but then he thought aloud, "though probably not in this weather."

Conscientious study over the last several days and no little luck had enabled him to piece together some idea what had happened to Tree Cliff Sitting. If he could locate her alive and return her to her family, his reputation would climb into the sky. Imaging the acclaim he would receive, he smiled showing a broken tooth grin. Then the prospect of failure occurred to him. He needed to prove himself to these farmers. They would learn that much of what Kills Rabbits said he could do was true.

Shouldering a pack made from a jackrabbit's skin and pulling his bow up onto his arm he took a gourd of water that hung from a peg at the shaded entrance.

He stepped out from under the overhang and opened his mouth to let several bits of the snow flurries fall upon his tongue. Adjusting the bulky, fully-stuffed bundle over his skinny shoulders, he moved down the trail, already made slippery by the snow. Grasping a small rock he had strung on thin twine tied around his neck, he fingered the smooth stone. It was a pebble of milky white quartz that resembled a wolf. It had taken him the better part of a day to cut a narrow groove around it to allow for stringing. Kills Rabbits ascribed much of his luck to the power of the stone.

Looking left, then right, he turned his eyes skyward, ignoring the snow. He recited a short singsong prayer in a strange tongue never heard before in Sky Valley.

Then looking neither right nor left, his thin form wrapped in his robe from neck to ankle and using a long pole to assist his cautious movement downslope toward the stream, he became a shadow and disappeared into the flurries amid sere bare bushes.

—at the Mine—

By the time he reached the mine Fat Badger was drenched in sweat, wet with melted snow and shivering constantly. Chiding himself for the rashness of his actions this day he slid his body into the shallow opening to the mine and looked for materials to build a fire. Sitting with his back against the rock wall did not help, and he began to shiver uncontrollably. Taking out his sleeping fur, he arranged it behind and under his body. At least it wasn't damp. If his whole body had gotten wet, he might be much worse off.

He stripped off his wet clothing and then wrapped the sleeping fur around himself. He lay out his clothes to dry.

The white dog moved closer.

"Ah so now we need each other." He patted his lap. Crawling up onto his legs the dog lay down against him and its warmth helped somewhat. Gathering bits of wood, he fashioned a small pit lined with rocks. With his hands shaking, he extracted his fire making kit and reached out of the shallow enclosure to pull up some tufts of brown grass. Wet with the snow he feared they wouldn't help much as kindling.

He briefly considered opening the mine gate and crawling farther back into the hole, but he discarded it as quickly as unnecessary. How long would the snow last? After a short passage of the sun across a part of the sky, he would crawl out and build a proper shelter.

Gently he moved the dog off his lap to a spot against his left thigh. Leaning forward, he began to move the little bow back and forth as rapidly as he could, spinning a hardwood stick against the flat piece of soft wood that already had several charred fire starter holes drilled into it.

His shaking fingers prevented him maintaining the wood in the proper position to maximize the effects of the friction. He kept resetting the spindle and starting over. His vision swam. Sometimes coughs interrupted the rhythm of his actions. Often, he stopped and spat phlegm to one side of the small enclosure.

He flinched as the sound of falling rock came from somewhere upslope, behind the mine. It clattered down with a muffled, far-off sound. He decided that it was likely the effects of the thick snow loosening a small boulder ready to fall might cause. He redoubled his shaky efforts at starting the fire, absently listening for more sounds. The dog left his side and went to growl at the snow shadowed entry.

"Shah!" Fat Badger whispered at the dog, and the little beast got quiet but stayed near the opening. Peering out through the driving wall of white, he could see nothing. He did not doubt that the dog's senses were much keener than his. What had the dog sensed?

He felt feverish. It affected his thinking. Was there a threat out there? He didn't relish the possibility of discovery in his weakened state. The falling snow sounded like whispering voices. It walled him off from the rest of the world like a curtain.

Fat Badger stopped and felt the wood beneath the spindle; it was barely warm. He picked up the pieces and threw them against the opposite wall of the mine in disgust. His head was spinning, and his chills and the shaking increased. Pushing himself to his feet, he walked over to the bits of wood and the spindle and picking them up he apologized to the fire spirits for his impatience. He looked down at the dog and said, "Coming here was a bad idea, I guess I should have listened to you."

XVII

—at Sky Creek Town—

Fire Star entered from behind the curtain of the entry into her comfortable home. Inside tea simmered on a stone next to the hearth, and the room was pleasantly scented and warm. She turned back and poked her head out. Calling out across the small family work yard, she looked for movement from the house opposite hers.

Pulling aside the curtain of her house Hummingbird looked out and then hurried across to her mother. She could tell at a moment's glance that something worried her.

"What is wrong, Mother?"

She beckoned her into the room, and they sat on thick furs near the glowing hearth before answering.

"I wish I knew Hummingbird."

"What do you think?"

Sighing, her mother reached for the teapot and filled two shallow bowls. "I sense turmoil. These storms become worse each time they appear. This one now approaching looks to have gathered all the ancestors in the entire sky world."

"Father said that grandfather warned him that this winter would be a severe one. He told him just before he went on."

Fire Star looked at her daughter. "He told you that?"

"Yes, he said it one evening when he was visiting."

Fire Star wondered why Fat Badger had not shared that information with her. Usually, they tried to help each other in all their various tasks. Perhaps he was concerned about affecting her prayers for snows? "Well he certainly seems to have been right about that!" she said thinking aloud.

"The snows will seed the springs Mother," replied Hummingbird, assuming she was talking to her. "They are always needed. The blood of the ancestors will nourish all of us."

Fire Star smiled at her, "This I know daughter but the winter storms

118

bring biting cold. Old ones suffer, some will die, no one can move, people may be trapped with not enough food."

"Perhaps the storm will not be so bad this time."

"This is what I hope." But her eyes betrayed her doubts. "But just in case I want to see your cousin Angry Cloud. I have a task that I need him to perform.'

Hummingbird knew that since Fire Star had only daughters, she often called upon her favorite nephew to perform tasks that her son would have done. He would do so readily, as was expected.

"If you will keep watch on the children, I will see if I can find him."

"Certainly," Fire Star said and smiled while looking back at the three who played within her home. "Go cautiously though; the snow is increasing!" Fire Star added.

—at the village of Grandma Acorns—

Kills Rabbits struggled too, but his problems were more of the physical nature. He stopped above the small seat on a flat-topped hill. Below him in an open area squatted a cluster of houses. The small village was seasonally lived in mostly by one extended family. A row of three houses, two rooms deep, were capped by two individual rooms set at a right angle at one end and two freestanding shades — roofs without walls, at either end of the houses.

Kills Rabbits had visited here previously, the family who had built the houses were collectors of local natural resources. They gathered useful plants and stone from the surrounding region and periodically trekked down into the canyon to trade.

He hoped they would welcome him. He carried a snared rabbit over his back. Knowing him as a hunter often made Kills Rabbits a much-appreciated guest at their hearths though he had not visited them in winter before.

This time of year he wondered who would be in the village. He expected few people to be home and no one to be out collecting in this weather. Several of the adults and older children would be gone, doing their collecting and trading in the lower deserts for the winter. He would only see the aged, the very young and their mothers left behind. Still, he hoped they had a warm dinner ready.

Sprinting and sliding the last few feet to the first shelter, a small shade roof attached to the outside of the first house, Kills Rabbits shook his shoulders trying to clear them of the snow that coated his robe. He stood for a few heartbeats, breathing heavily. Melting snow slid down his back like frozen fingers causing him to shiver involuntarily. Seeing a water jar beneath the overhanging roof, he struggled over to it, barely able to feel his nearly freezing feet with each step. Tipping the jug that hung from the rafters, he scowled. "Nearly empty and frozen too, of course." He knew better than to eat the ice that was in the bowl - the frozen hand of the winter spirits were already tickling his insides. He did not want to end up a 'snow haunt': an icy wraith howling outside the warm rooms of the living. "With any luck old Grandmother Acorns has a pot of tea simmering inside one of the rooms."

Looking about he tried to see which of the little rooms built around a small partially enclosed plaza might be occupied. Typical of people who made their living gathering wild plants such as acorns, yucca fruit, and pinyon nuts; some rooms were just for storage. He thought chiefly of the acorns. The old matron, Chattering Jay, was renown for her acorn soups and cakes. She had ways of processing the acorns, soaking the tannins out of the plentiful nuts and seasoning them just so. It made them amazingly sweet and flavorful. An ancient woman, her skin was the color of the acorns that brought her fame and her nickname, Grandmother Acorns.

The little village was far north of the more significant towns of Sky Valley. It commanded an excellent panoramic view of part of the valley. Situated on a high ridge half a day's walk from the valley floor, Kills Rabbits had hoped that he might be fortunate and maybe the missing girl had sought refuge here.

Unable to see any light or detect the smell of cooking he rushed through whispering snowfall and halting just outside one doorway, coughed loudly. Hearing no reply, he lifted the blanket and entered the dark room. Standing just inside the room he barely saw his breath before him in the dimness. Even without much light to see by he quickly determined no one was there. Bending down, he found the hearth by touch. It was cold but laying to the right, just beside it, he felt dry kindling ready to start flames anew.

In the time it takes for the moon to rise entirely above the horizon he had a small fire going. But this night there would be no moon to speak of, snow clouds commanded the sky. It would be darker than dark outside the room. His fire began to warm and Kills Rabbits surveyed the house. The dim light showed that while the room was empty of other inhabitants, everything was left in place for their return.

Finding a pot, he poured the last of his now thawed water into it and added a mix of dried cactus fruit, seeds, and grains from his bag. Setting three small cobbles as a trivet in the hearth he placed a flat stone atop them and set the pot there. While he waited for his gruel to cook, he decided to look in the other rooms. Rising stiffly, he pushed aside the curtain and went into the small back room. He searched the room by touch for a few moments, found what he was looking for and returning to the hearth. Kills Rabbits lit the torch that had been left by the inside door. "Ee-yah," he groaned, his joints echoing their groans in reply as he spoke to the empty room, "I better look around." He hung the rabbit from the rafters. Emerging reluctantly from the rapidly warming space and shielding the sputtering torch as best he could, he repeated the process of coughing outside at the other room's doorways.

After finding the other two-room houses equally deserted he was ready to give up and turn back. Then he thought he would check the farthest west single room.

Pulling aside the curtain, he pushed his torch into the room and gave a sharp involuntary intake of breath.

She lay on her left side her hands splayed out before her as if she had been warming them over the hearth when she fell over. The room was so cold that he shivered uncontrollably. Or, was it from his unwanted discovery? He strode over and crouched down. He surveyed the body. He could not tell how long she had been dead, but it looked as if some mice had been nibbling about the frozen fingers of her gnarled hands.

Grandmother Acorns would make no more stews for her family in this world.

Going back to the other rooms, he gathered up some old robes he had found there. He returned and wrapped the body tightly. He then set the body in a corner of the room where he had found her. He collected stones from all about and piled them upon her to form a cairn. Then working with freezing hands in the driving snow and near darkness, he walled up the entryway as best he could.

Returning to the first house, he hurriedly removed his dinner from the stone above glowing coals and yelped at the burn he got from the rim of the pot. Putting his fingers in his mouth, he muttered, "No one left alive here to hear me anyway." Abandoned and with its oldest and most celebrated citizen left behind, unburied, this little village was a strange mystery.

"I wonder where they all went and why they left Grandma Acorns?" In all his time in Sky Valley, he had never known this village to be deserted by the living particularly while leaving someone behind.

He resolved not to stay in this place of death. After he finished his meal, he would take his rabbit and push on, no matter the weather.

—at the Mine—

Fat Badger coughed and spat. He could not stop shaking with chills and sweating. He looked at the spittle on the snow. It was yellow and thick. "White dog, I think I am sick. Some evil spirit infects me." He looked out at the snow which fell more quickly now. "If we stay I may never leave." He pushed himself to a standing position. He grabbed his still damp clothing and redressed. The effort exhausted him. Feeling too weak even to bend down and retrieve the fur he had sat on he stumbled out into the wind. The falling snow seemed to whisper to him, "Go back, rest, all is well."

"I will not listen to the false advice of the snow!" he said. It occurred to him how strange everything was. It made him wonder.

Had he somehow entered a world of constant winter? Had he stumbled into another place? His muddled thoughts stumbled over each other. That was it! He was bewitched! The croaking raven tricked him into crossing over into this place of endless cold? Enemy witches were said to take the form of animals like ravens or coyotes to deceive people.

What of the strange visitors and their gifts? Were those Red Ants the witches? Was he a fool to have let them stay?

Using his stick as a cane he struggled down the trail. Oddly enough it seemed warmer outside the mine. Or was he becoming more feverish? The snow lay mounded on the ground, but beneath it, the trail was thick with mud. His rabbit-lined boots, still wet from his fall in the creek, slid back and forth on his feet. Only his grip on the stick kept him standing. This trip the dog became the leader. Fat Badger squinted and blinked in the driving snow and tried to keep the little dog in view. Stumbling and sliding with each step, he would stop to catch his breath as often as he dared. His legs moved woodenly.

Whenever he stopped, the dog would turn, and he imagined her anxiously urging him on. His breathing struggling as much as his legs, Fat Badger wondered if, in his fevered state, he had incorrectly made a fatal decision by leaving the mine. Maybe the counsel of the snow had been wise.

Reaching the stream, he eyed the rocks. Covered with snow as they now were, passage would be treacherous and another fall, well, that would solve everything. He would not survive the dousing in freezing water this time, let alone be able to extricate himself.

"One foot at a time," he was talking out-loud to himself now, his voice shivering with his chills. "Don't rush!" He stepped with one foot, then brought the other to stand with both on each rock. The wet soles of his boots slid, and he precariously balanced himself with his stick held horizontally in both hands. Waiting on the other bank, he could faintly see the white dog through the blanket of falling snow as it watched the sluggish progress from stone to stone.

After what seemed a lifetime, he felt his foot touch the soft bank of the other side. Almost immediately he nearly slid back into the creek. Only by jabbing his stick into the mud did he stop his fall.

Savage shivers wracked his body. His vision swam. He shook his head to try and clear the haze. It didn't help. Whimpering, the dog took two steps up the trail and looked back. Fat Badger put one foot ahead of the other and followed as best he could. Anyone observing from the other bank would have seen his shadowy, huddled form being slowly swallowed up by the falling snow.

XVIII

Shadows stirred in the plaza of the Warrior compound. The old man moved his stiff body slowly. He stretched his arms out and rubbed his knees with an aromatic salve from a small jar at his side. Shifting his shoulders, he grabbed a stout stick and shoved his body upward from the ground.

Finally finished with the four cycles of prayers of passage to the next world the old Vulture Priest groaned "Ee-huh!" as he stood up. He looked at the slight mound behind him. It lay thinly covered in snow. He stood alone. The black dog which had kept watch with him was nowhere to be seen.

Thunderhead watched as an assistant approached him. The young man's nervous eyes kept returning to the mound where Tall Claw's body lay.

His assistant handed him a small bowl of liquid which he drank. His midsection grumbled at the intrusion. The emetic worked quickly, and he heaved up the meager contents of his stomach on the snow-covered grave. Taking a swallow of water from another proffered bowl Thunderhead spat it on the ground. Then he parted his robe, lifted his skirt and urinated on the snow, and finally, he squatted and defecated on the place to let the spirit of Tall Claw know there was no return by this route to the living world.

Waving off assistance from another acolyte standing beside him waiting, he spoke in a low voice to him and then indicated the guards standing by the gate. The young priest started to argue, but Thunderhead cut him off with a slashing motion of his arm and a rebuke. Dropping his head, the man nodded and turned to go.

Watching him for a heartbeat, Thunderhead turned and shuffled toward the house. He heard his bones creak as he slid along the wet ground, seemingly unaware of the snow falling all around him. As he walked he chewed a root that would help settle his stomach and prepare it to accept food and water again. He climbed up onto the roof of the house and carefully worked his way down the ladder, pulling up the folds of his blanket. Hands reached up to assist him. He waved them off.

"I'm fine," he snapped the words out even while slipping on a wet rung and nearly falling. Reaching the floor, it took several breaths for his eyes to accustom to the dark. Snow falling through the roof opening sizzled in the firepit, keeping it from burning well. Still, the presence of other people in the well-insulated room served to keep it from getting too cold.

"Where did the Winter Chief go?" Thunderhead asked of no one in particular as he sat down amid the huddled men. Then, looking around him, his eyes went from face to face of the elders of Sky Valley. Some met his gaze, and others looked away.

After several heartbeats pause, Sad Gopher cleared his throat peremptorily and answered, "He told the guards he went to watch at the mine."

"Bah!" responded the Vulture Priest quickly, "That is no task for the Winter Chief. Any young pup of a warrior could have done that." He looked down and shook his head, "Thirty score people depend upon his decision-making skills, and this is how he decides to perform his valuable duty?"

A middle-aged man named Old Elk Eating, an elder from Mine Village, shifted in his seat and added, "It appeared to some that the Winter Chief was upset about the selection process of the new War Chief."

"That was none of his business," the old man spat the words, "he is only responsible for initiating the process, after that he has no say in what happens!"

The reproof brought an uncomfortable silence to the dim room; the only sound was the sizzle of snowflakes falling through the smoke-hole onto the fire. Noticing that they were increasing, Many Elk Eating leaned forward and placed a tall legged lattice of sticks above the fire to catch some of the flakes as they fell.

"Do not start a fire that will kill us all," warned Thunderhead half in jest, "we have much to discuss and decisions to make."

—near the Mine trail—

Snow also swirled about a tall, thin figure standing atop a hill.

Sheltered in the lea of a juniper, out of the wind and the rapidly increasing snowfall, Kills Rabbits tried to see around him. "This is useless," he thought, "no one could be out in this." He hoped he would be able to fight his way back to his shelter.

He had stayed no longer than necessary at the village, and now he was eager to return home before the real storm hit.

Before he left the little village, he had said a brief prayer for the safe passage of old Grandmother Acorns. He did so without mentioning her name, merely alluding to who she had been and that she had often offered him refuge in these rooms. Kills Rabbits avoided saying her name for two reasons. First, he was afraid that if her soul, currently journeying westward, heard someone calling her she might try to return to the land of the living and become permanently lost.

And second, he was afraid that if he spoke her name and she did return, she would follow him.

"I have enough troubles already," Kills Rabbits said trudging on.

Using an agave stave as extra support as he slipped and slid down the rocky slope, he had to watch for sharp-spined yucca leaves and nasty whitethorn bushes that could pierce flesh to a depth as thick as two fingers. Infection could follow quickly upon such wounds.

Snow was getting deeper in the open areas where there was less vegetation standing. The wind swirled it, and numerous bits flew at his exposed skin, stinging his face and lower calves.

"By nightfall, everything will be ice!" he lamented, regretting his decision to set out in the first place. Suddenly the air around him vibrated with light; each falling flake seemed on fire! Sound followed quickly, grasping everything in its massive claw.

He stopped as he heard the subsequent rumble. Was that thunder? Then it struck much closer. The sky was alight, and the flakes of snow briefly were aflame! Involuntarily he ducked. Laughing at himself, he stood back up. "That was indeed a surprise," he said speaking to the spirits of the sky. "Thunder and lightning in a snowstorm!"

He could not remember another time when he had heard of the great Thunderbird being abroad in a blizzard before.

Then he heard something else off to the left. It took him a couple of breaths to realize it was the distant bark of a dog.

—on the Mine trail—

Explosive waves of sounds and sudden light simultaneously assaulted Fat Badger's senses, as a snow-coated tree glowed like dawn. Stumbling back, he slid on the muddy trail and then lost his balance. "The world ends!" he said in a hoarse whisper. He looked up into the cloud-filled sky hoping to catch a glimpse of the Great Thunderbird before he died.

Looking up made him dizzy and he slipped!

Toppling over the edge he vainly grabbed at a manzanita! The bush offered little to no resistance, the frail branches coming off in his hands. He fell backward, striking his head against a tree trunk and yet managing somehow instinctively to wrap one arm around the solid feel of wood. As he was fighting against losing consciousness, his depleted energy quickly fading, he struggled to keep ahold.

Thorns of the green tree and even thornier canotia stabbed at him and pierced his fevered flesh. He heard the croak of the raven again close by. "You witch!" he croaked in kind, "leave me alone!"

Then a more welcome sound came to his ears.

Hearing the bark of the dog, he thought perhaps the little dog held a spirit that might yet save him.

"White Dog!" he cried, "where are you? Evil besets me!"

He feared that the dog, attacked by the raven, was driven off. That would leave him alone to fight against the forces of winter and death. After he passed, all would be lost. Death would stalk the villages. Many would die, and the ravens and vultures would feed on their unburied corpses. Their vengeful spirits would become howling wraiths, their freezing claws tearing at the flesh of the living just as they tore at him now.

All because he foolishly stalked out of the warriors compound in a fit of anger!

He closed his eyes against the pain and chills. His grip on the tree loosened and his feet slipped on the muddy side of the mountain.

Was the world truly at an end?

With his feet finally gaining purchase on the loose gravel, he caught a ragged breath. Looking up, he could barely see his companion leaning over the ledge looking down at him. The dog had beaten the raven! There was yet hope! He heard the dog's worried bark.

XIX

—in the house of Tall Claw—

Inside the house, each of the several men gathered there were started by the distant rumble of thunder. Faces clouded with concern.

"What would bring the Great Thunderbird out of his cave in such weather as this?" Striped Tail, the Keeper of Smoke asked rhetorically.

The Vulture priest leaned forward, signifying he would speak. "The same fate that brought us all here at this time. Momentous decisions are to be made, and the serpent-bird demonstrates that the Great Spirit agrees: it is time!" Thunderhead pushed himself to his feet and standing continued talking, "I have asked Him for direction, and He has answered with my sacred symbol!"

"Pah," said Striped Tail, "I have heard the sound of those great sacred wings thundering in snowstorms before!"

"True," answered Thunderhead raising one finger, "but not often. We should heed his counsel!"

Turning his body slowly, Fox Ear, the elder of Mine village, looked quizzically at the Vulture priest, "What counsel? I agree with Striped Tail. Sit down old man; this is no time for theatrics —" he was interrupted by the appearance of a set of legs descending the ladder.

"Ah, good, they have come," Thunderhead said smugly. He watched as three young men carrying wrapped bundles climbed down into the room, making quarters close. As they stomped the snow off their boots, he continued, "I asked the warriors here to gather these," taking one of the bundles he unwrapped it to reveal a long painted stick with a crooked handle.

A clamor arose from the men seated around the hearth as some of them rose to stand including Fox Ear "You presume too much. . .", "Under what authority?", "Who has requested sacred council . . . ?"

Raising his hands, Thunderhead made flapping motions asking all to sit, "I will explain." Gradually and with reluctance they sat. Turning to the warriors, he said, "Please distribute the sacred wands."

When each of the men was seated again with their canes of office in their laps, he continued, "You all see what has happened in the last days: first a man falls from the sky, then our War Chief's accidental death, if indeed it was an accident." He held up a hand to stop one of the others from interrupting. "The fire at Vision hill that destroyed a respected ancestor's house and now a storm of unparalleled force, much beyond what we have seen in as long as any of us can remember, even bringing the sacred feathered serpent out of slumber."

He looked at each man in turn and then went on, "You all remember that time when three died! The ones whose deaths led us to abandon the village near Ogre's spring and close off the canyon and the rest of the Forbidden place."

"What does that have to do with now?" asked Striped Tail.

Thunderhead looked at him. "A fair question. Perhaps nothing, except this! Each was a time of remarkable events requiring strong actions and decisions by this council. Just as we did then, we must do now!"

Pausing, he looked to each seated elder one by one. "We are charged by the Great Spirit with deciding purpose and leadership. I have something surprising to tell you."

"What now?" asked Fox Ear.

Thunderhead waited until the silence grew almost unbearable, then he answered, "Fat Badger sent Tall Claw up into the Forbidden place."

Shock registered on each face; Fox Ear started to rise again and, as if to mollify him, Thunderhead put out his hand while he closed his eyes and nodded his head knowingly. Slowly then he sat down. Fox Ear settled back down to the floor, his face shrouded with doubt.

—on the Mine trail—

In the time it takes to expel a breath Fat Badger slid further over the edge and only by instinct did he catch a second branch of the green tree that lay half buried below the cliff. His other arm found empty air. Kicking to try and gain a foothold only served to loosen his grip on the branch above, so he stayed quiet for a moment and surveyed his situation.

Looking up, he could just see the white dog peering over the edge at him through the stinging snow. It barked furiously at him as if to encourage him to hurry and get back up on the trail.

A thorn of the tree branch was piercing his wrist; his feet could gain no purchase; his other arm hung below him useless. "I am trying, dog!" he said in an exasperated fierce whisper. Once more he shifted his weight and tried to bring the arm up. The resulting slip of the precarious hold on the branch and the slide of the wood downward convinced him he was in big trouble.

He closed his eyes while he visualized just letting go.

His body would fall, roll down the hill and lay broken amid the debris and falling snow. Probably it would not be found until the winter had passed. Is that how he wanted his life to end?

He exhaled and tried to muster what little strength was left him.

He heard growling and barking. A hand with a strong grip latched onto his wrist slung around the green tree. He heard a voice yell, "Hey, stop that! I'm trying to help here!"

"Dog, is that you?" Fat Badger mumbled. He felt the strength drain from his body like water pouring over a fall of rocks.

"Give me your other hand," he heard the voice say from above as if at a great distance.

"Dog, do you speak? Is the world truly at an end then?" He swung his dangling hand up with what little energy he had left, "I am trying Dog. I am trying!"

The voice continued, "I am no dog! Ouch! I said stop that!"

Fat Badger felt another hand grip his dangling wrist. He felt himself pulled upward. "You are a strong, dog!" he muttered almost inaudibly, and he slumped back and heard no more.

—at Sky Creek Town—

Hummingbird looked at her mother, worry creasing her face. "This is madness, mother! You must not go out now. At least let me go and get Angry Cloud back to accompany you!"

"You said he was at the compound on duty."

"I'm sure he will come if I ask him."

"Daughter, I am the only one who can go, and I must go alone."

Hummingbird held the curtained doorway aside and looked out of the room. "But the storm is full; you will be swept away by the wind and snow." She held out her hand as if to demonstrate that it was an impossibility.

"It is not far; I will just go to the Twins' shrine, it is the closest, I should be able to change it there. We have left many wands at that place. I am sure I can undo this."

"Mother we cannot even see the Twins through this snow!" Hummingbird peered out in the direction she knew the rocks to be as if to prove her point.

"I have gone many times. I will have not trouble finding them, even in this." Answered her mother stubbornly.

Hummingbird tried one last argument, "Wait, just a little while! It is just a storm. It will end soon!"

Fire Star shook her head gently, "You heard the Thunderbird, he flies in the snow, that is proof this is not 'just a storm'! When before has he flown in the snow?"

"It has happened."

"Yes, that is true, I have heard of it, but it is so rare, and I believe the meaning is clear, this is a warning. I must go now!"

"I am afraid. I do not want you to become a snow wraith, seducing children from their warm hearths."

She ran her hand softly against her eldest daughter's cheek, stroking it fondly. "I will return as I am now, I promise you. If I am not back by nightfall," she paused to hoist the small burden basket onto the frame on her back, "have your sister, Pale Falcon come get me at the sheltering rock near the shrine of the Twins, she knows the place." She smiled, "I can set prayers to the ancestors, try to get them to stop this, it is my job! I must try."

—in Tall Claw's house—

Thunderhead was still arguing for action. He had cajoled, threatened and almost begged. Now his voice took a conciliatory tone.

"We happen here, just at this time, the elders necessary to enact a change of direction for our people. It is fated, and you are all to be honored for the decisions we make today. It will bring happiness and prosperity to our valley. Our people will be pleased. This action is ordained not by any man but by the Great Spirit himself."

"I do not seek Fat Badger's removal from all his duties," he continued, "he has been an effective trader, and I think he will continue to be so. It is just that serving as the trader for our sky stones, with all the increasing demands for them and also serving as Winter Chief has taxed his skills, as it would any man."

He paused finally satisfied that he had made his case. Sitting back down, he yielded the floor to see the effect his words would have.

Fox Ear lit a sliver of cedar and held it up to a stone tube. The aroma of smoldering native tobacco filled the small room. The room was close; each man sat with his knees against those of the men to either side of them.

Since they were in council, the warriors were dismissed, and they huddled together under a roof attached to the wall near the gate. Despite the fire they had kindled, they shivered with the chill. "What do you think is being discussed in the house?" a warrior named Horned Toad asked the other two.

Angry Cloud just shrugged. "It is not for us."

Rockfalls, a young warrior of fewer than sixteen summers spoke up, "I heard the old priest say that they needed to make a change in leadership -- well, the only council member not there is . . ."

Angry Cloud looked at him pointedly and held up his hand with one finger extended, nearly pointing at the younger man, "It is not for us to say!" He spoke quietly but firmly. Rockfalls lowered his gaze at the rebuke.

They sat in strained silence for several heartbeats. The snow whispered around them. Wind fiercely pulled at their robes.

Horned Toad peered out from under the shade, "This is a lot of snow."

"More than I have ever seen," agreed Rockfalls, "What about you Angry Cloud?"

"It is more than anyone has ever seen!" he observed.

—approaching the Twins—

Fire Star, tromped wearily through the deepening snow. She wore the woven basket shoes that helped her walk over the snow, but even with them, she struggled.

Though she had told Hummingbird she was convinced of her way forward; it did not take her long to begin to doubt the wisdom of her actions. "What a storm, our ancestors are munificent, they are working too hard to bless us." Fire Star looked up through the opening in her hood. Several flakes struck her, stinging, surprising in their force. One hit her eye. She lowered her face away from the onslaught. She had tried to get a look at her goal, known locally as "the Twins", a rock formation consisting of two large, lichen-coated boulders standing side by side, one slightly larger than the other.

Legend had it that in times of great need, the boulders would split open and two twin warriors would appear to help the people. Then, when all was well once more, they returned to their stony homes to await the next call.

They had no names; they were merely referred to as 'the older twin' and 'the younger twin'. The older one was serious and thoughtful, the younger, more playful and mischievous. They were said to appear to be typical boys, about twelve summers of age. "They probably don't age while within the rocks." she thought. She tried another peek. Her eyes watered at the exposure to the icy wind. No vision of gray-green boulders loomed into sight.

She visualized them in her mind. "I believe they're like eggs," she thought to herself, "able to hatch out the twins whenever needed over and over again." She repeatedly blinked to clear the melted snow from her eyes. "I know they're right ahead of me now, not too far." She looked up warily, with only one eye open, "I wish I could see better."

Almost upon her thought the snow slacked, and then gradually stopped altogether. "Thank you, ancestors," she said aloud. Ahead of her, out of the mist loomed the rounded twin spires of rock.

She stopped suddenly and cocked her head to one side. Did she hear voices? Or was the noise whispering echoes of the falling snow?

XX

—at the house of Kills Rabbits—

He laboriously opened crusted eyes. Blinking rapidly to clear his vision he started to rise and drew back. Staring him straight in the face were the decapitated heads of two vultures. They hung directly over him by long strings tied to the roof of a rude hut. Fat Badger started to roll to the side but his head throbbed, and he fell back.

"Not a good idea Winter Chief," said a voice across the room. Turning his head with some difficulty, he saw Kills Rabbits sitting against the brush wall.

"How long?" he asked, his voice sounding unfamiliar.

"How long have you slept? Two days."

"Where am I?" his voice croaked, his throat raw, it hurt him to speak.

"My house, I brought you here." he smiled, "It wasn't easy, you must weigh half again what I do, and that beast of yours," he gestured with his chin, "wouldn't leave me alone."

Turning back the other way elicited more shooting pain in his head, but he was able to see that the white dog lay at the threshold of the structure.

"Why do you keep such a disagreeable animal, he bit me three times as I was struggling to pull you up and once again when you moaned as I unloaded you from the sled. I would have gladly bashed his nasty skull, but it was his barking that saved you."

"She," said Badger. Smiling at the animal through his pain, he held out his hand toward the apparently sleeping dog. It raised its head and growled at him warily. Fat Badger smiled broader, which also hurt. Slowly turning his head back he looked at the two buzzard heads suspended above him.

"Grandfather Scorpion put those there, he has been feeding you a soup, I think he made from the bodies of those two." Kills Rabbits indicated the vulture heads with his pursed lips and shivered. Fat Badger could hear the question in his voice. "I haven't tried it myself, it smelled strange. It's in that bowl sitting over there," he nodded to his left, "if you want some."

Closing his eyes hurt nearly as much as keeping them open. Kills Rabbits continued, "He and his clown, what's his name? Climbs Hills, strange man but funny! He can tell a joke." He chuckled, "Know what the two vultures said when their best friend dropped dead?"

He paused as if waiting for Fat Badger to answer.

"'Too bad, I really liked him. Oh well, let's eat!'" His chortling filled the little room. "Funny man!"

Fat Badger drifted off to sleep listening to the man's laughter.

The doorway curtain was pulled aside, waking Fat Badger.

"Ah! Winter Chief you are awake." Grandfather Scorpion hunched down as he entered the shelter. Snow coated the thin robe covering his narrow shoulders. The white dog slinking off to one side looked back at the gaunt man. Behind the healer came a pleasant-faced younger man who smiled at Fat Badger and added, "Back from a visit to the underworld, does it snow there this much, too?"

Rising up on one elbow, Fat Badger looked at the two men and croaked, "I thank you for your care, Kills Rabbits says you are why I am still among the living."

Shrugging Grandfather Scorpion nodded in the direction of the dog who lay in the corner, "Perhaps. If that little one there had not alerted Kills Rabbits, who knows — ?" He bent down and felt Fat Badger's head, then placed his hand over his heart.

"When can I return home?" the Winter Chief asked him.

He took his time answering as he felt Fat Badger's heart pulses in several places.

"Tomorrow, no sooner and only if you are significantly better, and . . ." he looked at the open end of the shelter, "if the snow stops falling." He placed a pot that was set off to one side on the small hearth. Reaching up, he pulled down the two grisly heads. "These have done their work – keeping death away."

"Except for themselves," added the other man jocularly.

—at High Seat Village—

Dark Snake and Hungry Fly stood under the groaning rafters of the shade piled high with snow next to the latter's small house. It was set apart from the three-room blocks that formed most of the village. His home was nearest the gate opposite the welcoming room.

"This is amazing! The ancestors must have saved their snow for years to be able to produce such a storm." Hungry Fly marveled, worriedly eyeing the rough beams above him.

"We have had to keep the fires constantly going in the bean sprout house so as not to lose the young ones. Two men are keeping watch there all the time."

"I am not surprised that it has taken so much effort."

Peering into the dense wall of falling snow, Dark Snake turned back as if a thought had just occurred to him. "Has anyone been down to the immigrant's village recently?" the Rain Priest asked.

"In this weather? I would be worried that they would never make it." The War Chief shook his head, "Why?"

"I am worried also," he looked in the direction of the hollow where their village lay as if he could see the small village, "that they have not the resources to ride out this weather," he answered, "Do you think they are adequately prepared? They are Southern White Ants -- they know little of snow."

"No one knows anything of this much snow," Hungry Fly pulled his robe closer, "I know I don't." He looked down at his feet; his rabbit skin boots lay half buried in snow even beneath the roof. "I could send men to check."

"It might be wise. The Immigrants are our responsibility."

"Coyote Alone is a cautious, thoughtful warrior, he and another could go."

"He has not returned from the Warrior's compound as yet."

"In that case, I will have to see who I can find."

"What about Playing Cat?"

"Yes, perhaps, I'll see if he is available to go."

—in the house of Tall Claw—

The snow stopped falling and night fell almost simultaneously. Standing near the top of the ladder with his hooded head projecting out into the darkness Thunderhead called back into the room below, "It will be a bitterly cold night, it may be best to stay here until morning."

Some grumbled. A single figure rose from the floor.

"If you will move I think I will risk it," answered Fox Ear, "I wish to sleep in my own robes tonight. These days have been exhausting."

"Of course, I will send a warrior to act as escort." the Vulture Priest allowed as he climbed down the ladder.

"Hu-eh, you can afford to be magnanimous, Thunderhead, you have likely achieved your ends this day. You finally have your desire."

Thunderhead puffed up in resentment, "I achieve nothing by our decisions, it is for our people we met in council. There is no victory here." Then he paused, "Tell Angry Cloud I said to accompany you to your village."

"Isn't that the job of the Bow Priest?" asked Fox Ear.

"Thunderhead brought the three warriors with him, as part of the burial party, they are under his command," Sad Gopher replied. "I released the escort that accompanied us when I saw the storm approaching."

"Must you always defer to Thunderhead, Bow Priest?"

Sad Gopher bristled slightly, "Why do you say that?"

Fox Ear shook his head, "It is nothing, old friend, nothing, I am tired. Good night to you, stay warm." Fox Ear climbed the ladder and disappeared into the darkness beyond the opening in the roof.

Striped Tail moved the trivet from above the fire and added several dry twigs which caught fire quickly adding to the warmth within the room.

"Yes keep feeding that hearth," said Two Ravens, "there is not nearly enough body warmth among the wasted flesh and fragile bones of all these old men to keep us all from freezing before morning."

A few chuckles answered his jibe, and several of the men looked to find an adequate space for them to stretch out and still be near the hearth.

—outside the Warrior's compound—

Angry Cloud looked doubtfully at the old man who stood before him as the flakes still fell from the sky. "You want to go home? In this storm?"

"It is not far if we are careful."

The warrior looked up at the dark sky. No stars or moon were out. He thought that the ancestors were not done with their blessings yet.

"We must cross the stream near the mine to reach your village. It will be very treacherous."

"That is why I have you to make sure I do not fall."

Angry Cloud looked at the snow-covered ground.

The old man followed his gaze. "It is a good trail . . . clearly marked even in the snow."

"The trail will be slippery in the storm, Uncle."

"It has abated," he snapped. Fox Ear shuffled past the young warrior, "I weary of arguments, I have spent my entire day arguing with someone. Come!"

While shaking his head in resignation, the tall, burly youth pulled his robe tight about his shoulders and purposefully stepped past the elder to break the trail through the snow for the older man.

"Do not rush!" Fox Ear chided, "We have a better chance of getting there if we are cautious."

"Yes Uncle," Angry Cloud muttered. There was still doubt in his voice. "If we get there at all," he mumbled to himself.

"What was that?"

"Nothing, Uncle, it must have been the wind."

"I have had enough of foul winds too these last days, trapped in that house with all those old men."

Angry Cloud swallowed his laughter.

They were engulfed by night and disappeared from view.

XXI

—on the trail near Hill-All-Alone—

Pale Falcon sat under a woven mat tied between trees to keep off the snow. She pulled her robe close, warming as best as she could before a small flame. A stubborn girl, unwilling, as of yet, to return to her mother's house, her anger controlled her. "I wasn't even given a chance to become War Chief!" she snarled.

She shook her head, and her mood shifted. Holding wet leggings out to dry over the fire, she laughed at herself. "That's what I get! Believing I should be War Chief was foolish. What was I thinking?"

Not attending to where she was going she had punished the deep snow, striding with unabated force in each step. Though she told herself she was hunting there was no effort made to hide her movements or look for signs of game. She plodded unaware of her destination, only focusing on her anger. There was no hope that anything would be out and about in this weather or at this time and she knew it. In the process, she had drenched her leggings.

Finally, she had swept an area beneath two trees clean with a branch, tied up a mat to keep off the snow and settled down to make fire. It also allowed her anger to simmer.

It took a hand's breadth of time for her anger to completely subside. Sighing, she stood up. Kicking snow onto her meager flame, she untied her matting from the tree.

She pulled on the still damp leggings. It was time! She was ready to go home.

As she walked, struggling against the drifts her mood began to change further. It was her best medicine, getting away from people. In that, she was like her father. She liked doing things alone. No one would suspect she was upset; her disappearances were commonplace enough. Of course, that had an adverse effect too, if something happened to her no one would look for her for quite some time. Slowly she calmed and warmed to her task.

The snow drifted in places nearly as high as her thighs.

Looking about for the first time since she had stalked off, she realized she was east of her father's house; the hill where he had sat, and her great-grandfather before him; watching for visitors at the high spring.

A thin moon smiled down from behind the clouds, shedding meager light. Standing at the base of the hill, she could distinctly see the mounds of snow-coated debris that she and her father had moved after the fire. She would have to get back to the rebuilding as soon as the snow cleared. "If it clears!" she added with irony in her voice.

She walked until near dawn.

A muddy sun struggled to rise into the cloud crowded sky. It looked like more snow might come. Still, the storm must end eventually.

Turning, she looked around, how soon would that be? The snow coated everything, and the clouds were still shrouding the waking sun. Was it possible that they could be preparing to drop more snow? It seemed unbelievable to her that the ancestors were not exhausted from their labors in that area already. A maniacal wind whispered freezing words in her ears. Maybe being out at this time was not such a good idea even for someone as self-sufficient as she was.

She continued moving -- it was too cold to stand in one place for very long. As she did, she fell into her habit of scanning the ground for any sign. Any movement should leave visible marks in the snow. Large tracks such as deer or elk would show as regularly spaced shadows. But she did not expect to see anything of that size moving. Rabbits were more likely than deer. She fingered a long hardwood stick she carried in her left hand. With a broad hook at the end, it could be used to draw out little animals from their burrows. Maybe she could persuade a couple to return home with her.

That would provide a reasonable story for her long absence.

After locating their tracks in the snow, she would find a hiding spot where the rabbit waited. Pushing the stick into the hole when she encountered the soft, yielding fur with the end of the stick she would twist it, embedding the hook, and then pull out the animal. Three or four rabbits caught that way would make good stew for many people. Old ones might survive this winter yet if they received enough nourishment.

It was like the Huntress of her favorite story; the one her great-grandfather told her. Then she thought more about the tale. She recalled the twist. The huntress had almost been devoured by ogres! It had taken the intercession of the Warrior twins to save her. Hopefully, her story would not include an encounter with ogres.

Nervously she surveyed her location, wishing now that she had not thought of that story!

Fatigue was creeping up her legs. She should turn back soon. Or find a place to rest. She glanced around, then noticed something. Shadows lay amid the snows.

Was that anything? Looking closely, she saw that something had indeed moved through recently. In fact, it appeared that a small group of large animals had passed by just before the heavy snow began. The shadows were deep but hard to read in all the snow covering them.

—wounded and lost—

Fire Star woke. Her thoughts were jumbled. Where was she? How had she gotten here? It all seemed muddied like a stream after a heavy rain.

Had she fallen? Fire Star did not remember sitting down. And why would she sit it the snow? No, it was cold, but she sat on stone. What had happened?

Where had she been? It hurt to think. She reached up to feel her forehead and discovered blood crusted to her hair.

Huge shapes strode through her dream. It must be a dream! Was she at her home?

She looked around. No snow was falling around her. She was still outside, but no snow hit her.

She closed her eyes. That felt better. Had she been going somewhere? She had, she remembered that, but she couldn't think of where.

Her head swam. She opened her eyes tentatively. Fire Star tried to sit up but fell back, her head throbbing. All was dim. Was there light here? She closed her eyes again. What had happened to her? She smelled a faint perfume mixed in the cold air. The headache flower? That was foolish. There could be no flowers growing in this weather.

What was that? Was there noise? She opened her eyes tentatively. It still hurt, but she kept them open as long as she could. There was light flickering at her feet, beyond her, a glow in the dark. Her eyes closed. Maybe there was a fire. That would be good. She needed to get warm.

Her head throbbed. She reached her arm up and felt around her skull.

Her arm was only able to reach the front of her forehead. Something was limiting her arm's movement. She thought maybe she was dreaming. Sometimes in dreams, she had been so restricted in movement.

But the pain in her head said this was no dream.

Her hand found a lump under her scalp. Had she fallen and hit a rock? She didn't remember. Had she run into a branch? Or had she been struck? Trying to recall what had happened hurt. She relaxed, her breathing calmed, and she started to feel warmer. She was so tired though, why was that? Her breathing slowed and became regular, she rolled over on her side, and she slept.

—on the trail near Giant's Head—

Still another soul wandered lost amid the swirls of increasing snow this night. She looked up into the icy flecks that streaked towards her to see the landmark that marked her passage.

To anyone watching her movements would seem aimless, almost frantic. It was like she was running away from something but unsure of where to go or how to get there.

Her robe was inadequate to the cold. She shivered constantly.

Every few steps she turned and looked back the way she had come. Was there someone following her? Did that shadow move in the dim moonlight? Or was that just a tree its actual form indistinct through the falling snow? Her head swiveled quickly. Did that other shadow move?

Ever since Tall Claw's death and her lucky escape she remained terrified that her captors would find her again.

Her only protection was that they were trying to keep their presence a secret. That worked to her advantage. She, on the other hand, was trying to be found, if only she could figure out exactly where she was!

She stopped to catch her breath. How long had she been struggling through this world of frozen white? It seemed like she had been doing it forever. Step by painful step, keep going! Force one freezing foot to move out in front of the other.

She had eaten almost nothing for days. A few sprigs of grasses and old dried cactus fruits were all she had found. Her stomach rumbled in protest at having been ignored so long.

Ahead of her, she saw the Giant's Head looming gray through the falling snow. Finally! A place she knew! She stared at it as if willing herself to fly to its side by witchcraft. Engrossed at the welcome vision for a moment, her sandals slid out from under her, and she barely kept her feet by grabbing onto a clump of beargrass. A serrated leaf edge sliced shallow cuts into her arm and her palm. She hardly noticed, she focused her whole attention on escape and salvation!

If she could just reach the base of the hill below Giant's Head, she would finally feel free. Only then would she begin to believe she could actually make it back home.

Home! Once she got home, then the hard work would begin! She must persuade them all that they must flee yet again! Now!

XXII

—at the house of Kills Rabbits—

The day began with a dull gray sky. Fat Badger noticed his throat was not as sore as it had been the previous day. He sat up, leaning on one arm. The white dog still slept between him and the entry.

Shivering in the chill air he found a bowl of water and drank in small sips, it was flavored with willow bark and felt good on his raw flesh. He closed his eyes letting the cold liquid slide down his ravaged throat. Opening them again, he saw he was alone in the hut. Seeing a piece of the root that Grandfather Scorpion had given him the day before he put it in his mouth and began chewing experimentally. The taste was acrid and resinous, but he immediately noticed the soothing effect it had mixing with his saliva and taking the last of the soreness out of his throat.

He recalled part of the conversation with Grandfather Scorpion. "What had he called it?" he speculated aloud. His voice sounded odd. "Oh yes, bear root." He looked at the dog. "Speaking of a bear that's what I need! A good stew of bear meat to build strength would be welcome or even deer for that matter."

Deer! Suddenly a chilling thought came to him. The Red Ant people, they were waiting on his decision. They were still out in this weather. He must find them!

Standing cautiously, while leaning on the center post of the roof, his head swam for a breath or two, and then he seemed to gain some of his strength back. Eyeing him warily, the dog got up and stretched. Fat Badger reached out a hand toward the dog. It moved away from him with its familiar low growl. Fat Badger allowed himself a smile, "Ah there's the white dog I have come to know so well!"

Bending, he picked up his boots. They had been turned inside out to dry. Turning them back, he pulled them on then draped his robe over his shoulders. He selected a sturdy stick from several that leaned against the wall.

Pushing aside the curtain and walking out of the house he saw that a thick coating of snow still covered everything. How far could he go in this?

He decided he felt well enough to try and make it to his wife's village first. The trail from here was gradual, slightly downhill and it followed the stream.

The dog stayed close upon his heels.

He walked slowly and deliberately. Stopping often, he found that his breathing was labored and there was soreness in his right knee. "Probably I hit it when I fell." At one of his rest stops, he looked up to a saddle where one of the larger villages lay. It was located by one of the small springs, called Snow spring because the water was always cold. He noted with some surprise that there was no sign of smoke above the place. "There may be a wind up there, blowing it away." But he also noticed that there was no hint of wind down where he was. "Odd." he said looking at the dog, "don't you think so?" Then he laughed, "That's alright dog, you don't have to tell me what you think!" Fat Badger shook his head gently.

He continued walking. Since this trail trended mostly downhill and it lay beside the stream, it meant the snow was not piled so deep. He thanked his ancestors for that.

Arriving at the outskirts of the town where Fire Star lived he was again surprised. People scurried around the plaza, some with bundles, others looked as if they were preparing for battle. Young warriors were standing in groups talking. They were painted for war, shields slung over their backs and carrying clubs and bows. No one seemed to see him. He grasped the arm of one young warrior who was painted in red and black and carrying his weapons tightly to his chest.

"What is happening here?"

No more than fifteen summers in age the youngster stopped as if suddenly awakening from a dream. It took him two breaths to realize who had impeded him so brusquely.

"Winter Chief . . . ahhh, elder, I mean, yes sir, what can I tell you?"

"Tell me what is happening."

The young man looked confused. He said nothing but instead looked around as if hoping to see someone who could save him having to explain.

"Speak!" Fat Badger snapped at the nervous young man. At his heels the white dog growled menacingly, he didn't bother to look at who the little beast was threatening.

"Fat Badger!" a rough voice sounded at his shoulder. Turning, he found Thunderhead standing there. Growling lowly the dog slunk behind Fat

Badger's legs. Seeing his chance the young warrior took the opportunity to extricate himself and hurried on.

Moving surprisingly close the old man looked him up and down for a moment. When he spoke his voice was a whisper, "I heard you were ill. You are well now?" the old man asked.

Ignoring him, Fat Badger demanded answers, "Vulture Priest! What is happening here, what are these people doing? Who called for the martialling of warriors?"

"Here, Trader sit, I can see that you are weak still," the old man indicated a covered area next to a house.

"I asked you who is behind this?"

The old man just stood and eyed him, waiting.

Sighing, he moved to sit and answered, "Yes, I am better," he could not hide the exasperation in his voice, "Grandfather Scorpion has routed the evil that possessed me." He waved his hands to indicate the plaza as the old man joined him. "These people?"

The old man looked at the hustling individuals as if seeing them for the first time. He coughed into his hand. "Those there, and those," he indicated with his chin, "they are leaving the valley."

"At this time, in this weather? What reason — ?"

"It is because the weather has broken that the people hurry to leave. They hope to be far away before more snow comes!" Seeing Fat Badger about to protest further Thunderhead shushed him with a hand and continued, his voice conspiratorial, "The Great Spirit has sent a warning. They fear our valley is cursed! They fear the retribution of Ogres!"

Exasperation now appeared openly on Fat Badger's face. He was struggling with all that was happening. "You mean the attacks? Nonsense. They can be explained!"

"For you, in your mind maybe, you hold such knowledge and belief in your power but these people," he waved his hand at the scurrying groups around him. "They are simple farmers. They only know what they see and what they see scares them!" He shook his head. "Did you know another woman has gone missing? Yesterday she went to Snow spring and never came back! Too much has happened and now with the threat of sacred ogres angry and attacking — it is too much for them!"

"Humph!" Fat Badger made a rude noise deep in his throat and asked, "What proof is there that these are attacks by the Ogre people?"

The old man looked at him with feigned innocence, "Oh yes, I had forgotten you don't know what has occurred while you were ill!" He shook his head, "They have been seen."

This news gave Fat Badger pause. "What? What do you mean ogres have been seen? By who?"

The old man eyed him as if weighing his response.

"Who has seen ogres in the valley?" Fat Badger repeated his question.

"Your nephew."

That caused Fat Badger to catch his breath and lean back upon his cane. He did not immediately continue. The old man waited.

"When and where did he see them?"

"He saw them when they killed Fox Ear, and he rashly tried to attack them."

Fat Badger sat down hard and said, "Fox Ear is dead?"

"Yes, while they were returning to his village after the council." Thunderhead shook his head. "It is a great loss."

"And my nephew attacked the ogres?"

Distracted, the old man appeared not to notice his questions, "As to these," he said waving his hand toward the gathering men, "some are working as warriors, they will defend the refugees, but most of them have other tasks. Other things have happened! Even worse things! They are acting under orders." He paused.

"Whose orders?"

His voice was lower, barely above a whisper. "Mine for now . . ." he looked around him as if to see if anyone were listening in, ". . . the Summer Matron is missing."

—approaching the Twins—

Knowing what to look for, following the tracks was easy now. Pale Falcon moved slow, carefully paralleling them. Looking up, she saw that more snow could come at any time. If she waited, they could be gone. To her, it looked like two or three people, no more than four, and they were dragging or carrying something. They were moving toward the home of the Twins.

Stories told, around winter campfires, recounted the exploits of the hero youngsters. Grandsons of Spider Grandmother they played as mischievous boys until needed by the people. When called thus they emerged from the two boulders as esteemed warriors, ready to vanquish whatever foe threatened the valley. Pale Falcon's favorite story was of how they came to the aid of the Huntress.

As she tracked the strange movements in the snow, she unconsciously thought about that story again.

She had often requested it of her great-grandfather when he was telling stories during the long winter evenings.

She had identified with the young woman who chooses to become a provider of game for her family even though she was but a young girl. Their family had no sons to hunt game, and they needed someone to bring them meat. The girl decided it would be her. Her mother, while unsure of her choices, had never tried to prevent her from pursuing her goals.

Eventually, she becomes a great hunter. But it was her first adventure that concerned Pale Falcon now.

The Huntress story told of how she went out in the dead of winter because her people were starving. After a successful hunt, a female ogre had trapped the young woman in a cave and, after eating all her game, was threatening to devour her too. She prayed to the Warrior Twins to aid her and they heard her prayers. The Twins killed the ogre and slicing her open, returned the rabbits she had swallowed whole to the Huntress.

She took them home to her village to great acclaim for finding game in a time of great need. Pale Falcon longed for such praise.

The only part of the story she didn't like was the conclusion.

At the end of the story, the huntress settles into village life, accepting the domestic role typical of all women. It was a cautionary tale that suggested people should not try to be something they were not and that men and women should keep to their assigned jobs.

Pale Falcon would change the ending.

—at Sky Creek Town—

Fat Badger was feeling dizzy again. "Missing! Was she abducted?"

"No, she went to place prayers at the shrine of the Twins," answered Thunderhead.

"How long ago?"

"More than a day and a half."

Fat Badger felt his panic rising. "What can I do to assist you in the search?" Fat Badger asked as he rose up from the ground.

Turning toward him, Thunderhead paused and nodded his head as if he would need help from wherever he could find it and then he placed his palm on Fat Badger's chest. "Your heart is good esteemed Trader, but I think you are too close to this problem and have had enough to deal with over the last days. You have been very sick and must regain your strength. Go home, rest and wait. We will find her soon, I am certain." The old man made to leave him.

It took Fat Badger a moment to realize what had just happened.

He was being dismissed! This was not right!

He tried to control his anger and thought how to pursue the right line of questioning. Thunderhead's temper was legendary, as his name implied. Still, there were protocols. The Vulture priest aligned with him as a winter servant to the people and he knew Fat Badger well. He must proceed properly.

"What is your plan?" he asked in his calmest voice.

Thunderhead turned to face Fat Badger again, "Plan?"

"How will you go about finding the Summer Matron?"

"Oh yes, that will be taken care of soon. The new Winter Chief will give his orders."

At this revelation Fat Badger was unable to hide his surprise. He sat down again. "The NEW Winter Chief?" he said quietly.

The old priest moved closer to him. "Yes, I am sorry. I see this too comes as a surprise. While you were chasing ghosts at the mine, the council decided to replace you." Fat Badger thought that he detected a tinge of gloating in the old man's voice.

"Who called this council?"

"No one had to call it; it had gathered to appoint a new War Chief and. . ."

Fat Badger had forgotten about the selection of War Chief, how could he not have remembered? Did that have something to do with his demotion? "Was Pale Falcon selected?"

Thunderhead looked away as if exasperated. "No." He turned back, "we arrived at no final decision. Sharp Rocks will assume War Chief duties for the time being. It is a temporary arrangement."

Sharp Rocks had retired from the job of Bow Priest two summers before. While not unqualified, he was old for the position.

"Why was a new War Chief not chosen?"

The old man looked at the ground. "There was disagreement." He looked up, "We will resolve it in the next council."

"Who is the new Winter Chief?"

"Black Smoke . . . for now," the old man said matter-of-factly.

Once more, Fat Badger could not hide his surprise. As Thunderhead walked away, he started to speak to the old man, to ask for more of an explanation for all that had happened and then thought better of it; he would wait. In one conversation Fat Badger had lost all his leverage. With only the position of Trader now, and that was next to useless in the winter, he had to think. There were others he needed to talk to first.

Black Smoke! Fat Badger knew him, he had seen him at certain gatherings, but he had never really spoken at any length to the man. That he had risen to such a position so quickly surprised him. There must be a reason that he was elevated past other candidates. The idea of conspiracy, possibly even an attempt to undermine the strength of the council must be considered. Fat Badger knew that as Valley Trader he could request a meeting to reconsider the selection. The problem with that was the person he might call upon to scrutinize this charge was the one to be investigated, Thunderhead! As Vulture Priest he commanded the investigative resources for the valley during the winter months.

One thing he knew, it was all more than he could sort out. With his War Chief dead, a new one not yet appointed but instead an old man not fit for the rigor of the job filling in; the missing girl, her motives unknown; the fire destroying his childhood home. Then too, there was the appearance of the Red Ants? Were they somehow tied to his illness? Had he been witched by them?" He sat back, his head swimming.

Now his wife was missing!

And his demotion; what did it all mean? Could it all be related to their mining of the Sky stones? Ogres sent to Sky Valley? Were his people damned by the Great Spirit?

Most important in his mind was how he would go about assisting in finding Fire Star? He needed her to help him sort this all out. She was his best sounding board. Only through his talks with her could such a muddle become clear. If she was not available he needed to counsel with someone, but who?

In Fat Badger's mind, there was only one answer. Before he did anything else, he must gain a better understanding of what was occurring. He must seek the counsel of those wiser than he was. To do that he would have to travel to Red Sky Village, he must talk to Yellow Stone.

As the Sun Watcher for Sky Valley, Yellow Stone was widely considered a scion of the valley. Living in Red Sky Village, he was responsible for talking to the Great Spirit and making His wishes known to the Brown Ant People. Each morning at dawn the Watcher or one of his trusted lieutenants waited the approach of the sun, marked it's point of appearance and calculated it's meaning. At certain times he observed the sky all night to divine greater understanding of what occurred. To prepare for life: planting, hunting, migration, and trade; all these things and more hinged upon his interpretations and knowledge. His dreams ruled their lives and now, without his wife's trusted counsel to assist his thoughts, Yellow Stone alone could help Fat Badger.

He coughed. Closing his eyes and leaning back against the post of the shade he felt nothing so much as exhausted. He opened his weary eyes. The plaza had grown quiet again.

Fat Badger looked up. Nearly sunset and a sky full of clouds. If only the ancestors would willingly hold off on their generosity, he might make the trip yet. Fatigue from his trek and recent illness weighed him down. Tomorrow he would join with the others to look for his wife. She must have sought cover somewhere. She would be found in one of the other villages. "Yes," he said aloud, "That is it!"

Then, realizing something, he laughed ruefully! There was one advantage of not being Winter Chief anymore. Tonight he could finally sleep comfortably in the house of his wife again. And yet she would not be there. His mind surged in turmoil.

XXIII

Several young men sat about a small fire beneath a shade in the village. They conversed little. The weather was dampening everyone's spirits. The morning sky still threatened more snow. Clouds obscured the sun.

They heard the sounds of disturbance before seeing who caused it. A young man came around the corner of the house and seeing them there began to talk excitedly, "Red Ants, there are Red Ant people in the valley, the War Chief is mobilizing the warriors!"

Instantly galvanized into action they jumped up and ran off to get ready for battle. Several shouted as they ran through their village, "Enemies in our valley! Gather at the compound! Hurry!"

The alarm was raised! More men came running from all around the village. Sky Creek town, as the most extensive village in the valley, could usually muster over two score warriors, but some were out searching for the Summer matron. Still, there would be plenty.

Asleep in his wife's house Fat Badger was startled by her sudden shaking of his arm. "Husband!" she said, "There is something wrong." Slowly he came awake. He jumped up and eagerly looked for her. Wryly he realized he had dreamed her there. He slept alone. Then he heard the shouts outside. So perhaps the warning had been real. He looked around for the white dog out of habit, but she was nowhere to be seen. "Now I am truly alone," he said ruefully.

Emerging into the plaza, he saw thin flurries had begun to fall. Reaching out, he grabbed the first person he saw running past. It was the same young man he had accosted the day before! "What has happened?" he asked brusquely of the youth.

Pausing only a moment as if considering whether he must respond to Fat Badger's demand, the young man said, "Someone saw Red Ant people near the High Spring, the War Chief musters all the warriors who are not out searching for our matron. He calls them to the compound now!" With that the young warrior shook off Fat Badger's hand and ran off.

Fat Badger watched his slender form receding, and then he realized what it all meant! "No!" he shouted, and he ran after him.

—at the Twins—

Pale Falcon skirted the open area and slowly approached the small rock shelter well behind the looming figures of the Warrior Twins boulders. It was a natural cutout often used by hunters and pilgrims to the area in summer and spring but usually deserted other times of the year. Within it, she knew, was a sacred shrine of the Warrior Twins and she hoped it was here she would find out who had made the tracks in the snow.

The tracks were easy to follow. Rising into the low hills, they appeared to make straight for the Twins. They seemed to be leading her there. She hoped she wasn't charging into a trap. The closer she got to the Twins, the more cautious she became.

Reaching a position where she could easily peer into the rounded crevice of the natural shelter she dropped to one knee and abruptly brought her hand up to her mouth to stifle a sharp intake of breath at what she saw there.

Laying on the ground within the little cave was her mother! She glanced around, but at first, she saw no one else. It was not until Pale Falcon started to run toward her that she saw the other. She ducked behind a lichen-coated boulder. Peering out, she assessed the situation.

Standing slightly above the cave and well hidden from most viewers was a warrior. Though he was turned away from her, she recognized the duty he performed. He held his bow nocked and at the ready. He was carefully scanning all around the area and Pale Falcon was sure that he was there guarding her mother. Fortunately, he looked the other way while she approached.

Studying the guard as best she could from her position slightly above him, she could tell he was not of their valley. By the tattoos on his neck, he was likely a White Ant from the south. Another one! His plain robe fell to his ankles and he had cut places in it for his arms to stick out leaving him free to shoot. That he was standing watch was unmistakable from his position and his nervous scanning of the area approaching the shrine.

She stretched out a little to catch a better glimpse of her mother. Shrinking back behind the rock Pale Falcon was beset by questions. Her mother lay there on the cave floor, unfettered and apparently asleep. Why hadn't her mother tried to escape? Was something wrong with her?

Her father always told Pale Falcon that he liked her decisiveness and so she quickly decided her next course of action.

—at the Warrior's compound—

War Chief for any valley was a prominent position. The holder might be expected to duel the champion of another group in single combat. Sharp Rocks performed tasks like that years before when he was younger, now, he was not so young. It was not that he was afraid of battle. But an experienced warrior knew his limits.

When the council approached him about assuming once again the position of War Chief for the valley they assured him they would not expect him to engage in solo combat. They just wanted an experienced leader. And, the council added, it was temporary.

Sharp Rocks did not relish his first official act as War Chief again. A mature man of more than fifty summers his knees were not what they used to be, and his eyesight was failing. His only consolation was that he assumed the job of War Chief temporarily and all knew that. But he had taken it, so now he must lead.

Looking out over his command he saw twelve inexperienced warriors. The rest were all out searching the western slopes of the valley for the Summer Matron. A runner had been sent to recall them but who knew how long that might take in this weather?

As they left the compound he was surprised by the arrival of Fat Badger.

"Wait!" the Valley Trader said as he got near the War Party. "Sharp Rocks what do you intend?"

Looking at the former Winter Chief the old warrior replied, "We go to ascertain the intentions of the Red Ant party that has been seen in our valley."

"Good," answered Fat Badger, "I will go with you."

"They told me you have been ill." Sharp Rocks said. "Plus your wife is missing, perhaps it would be wise for you to stay here."

"No, I have spoken with these people and I know their intentions."

This remark garnered a raised eyebrow from Sharp Rocks and surprised looks from several of the young men behind him.

"You have spoken with them?" said Sharp Rocks incredulously. "You know their intentions? Has it occurred to you Fat Badger that these people might be holding your wife as a hostage?"

"No, no, I am sure that that is not the case, they are to the eastern side of our land and she went toward the Twins, to the west, if you . . ."

"Enough!" said Sharp Rocks, "I will not stand here and argue with you! Come if you must but we go now!"

—at the Twins—

The guard almost jumped out of his skin when the voice behind him said, "Lower your weapon and lay down flat on the ground!" Though he might not understand the words, he intuited their intent!

He hesitated, it was a woman's voice, and while a woman could still be a warrior, especially here among these barbarians, he was not willing to give up so quickly. Whirling toward the voice, he was surprised by the 'thud' that struck his chest, knocking him back a step and he looked down to see an arrow deeply set into his body. Falling to his knees, he looked up and beheld a tall young woman standing not three body lengths from him. He thought about trying to bring his bow up, but as if divining his intention she pulled back on her weapon and drove another arrow into his chest. He grunted and then fell over. His last thought was the fact that she was left-handed.

How odd, he mused, wasn't the huntress of that one story left handed? Then he collapsed, thinking no more.

Rushing down the hill past the body Pale Falcon arrived at the rock overhang. She saw her mother was injured. Her scalp was crusted with dried blood apparently from a club wound.

"Mother!" she whispered loudly, "We must go! Mother, can you hear me?" Pale Falcon squatted down next to Fire Star.

Finding one of her arms was tethered to a stake, Pale Falcon drew her knife. She slashed the leather thong and pulled her mother up into her lap. Drawing her bow up over her right arm, she looked back over her shoulder to assure herself that the guard was dead and no one else approached. She drew up one leg and sliding her knife into her sash she reached under her mother.

A shadow fell over them. Falcon swiveled her body and drew out her knife again but was relieved to see it was just a thick cloud covering the sun.

Seeing the clouds made her realize what that portended! They were threatening snow, again! She whispered aloud, "Please, Bléssed ancestors, allow me to get her home safely before you begin your blessings anew!"

Picking up her mother, she carried her out into the open and disappeared into sere bushes and shrubs as flurries swirled down around them. They made the sound of whisperings. To Pale Falcon, it seemed as if they were laughing mockingly at her.

—approaching Cloud Spring—

Fat Badger found that he had trouble keeping up with the party, as did their leader, Sharp Rocks. The young warriors ranged ahead of them surely even in the snow. Knowing their inexperience, the War Chief had to counsel their caution more than once.

"Keep to the leeward side and do not emerge atop into the clearing until we are all together," warned the old warrior.

For his part Fat Badger was frustrated. He had been forced to admit that he knew of the Red Ants. Even worse he acknowledged having spoken to them. He was sure that he would have to answer for these admissions before the council upon their return.

Though much taxed by the uphill struggle through the snow toward the spring, he felt he must approach the War Chief again. He redoubled his effort and caught up with the old warrior.

"Sharp Rocks, listen to me," said Fat Badger between breaths, "make sure they do not provoke a battle," he paused to catch his breath, "your young warriors are inexperienced!. This, ah, this misunderstanding can be solved — I am sure of it!"

The old man stopped. Fat Badger saw he too was breathing heavily with the exertions.

"What nonsense is this? Do you question my fitness to lead?"

Fat Badger raised his hands, "No, no it is not that!"

"Then stop worrying. You sound like an old woman! They will listen to me!" he snapped.

"I am certain you are correct but . . ."

"Quiet!" hissed the War Chief, holding up his arm, "we are nigh unto the spring!"

Fat Badger looked and saw it was true. The warriors were spreading out and were finally moving cautiously as their war chief had told them. Now, if only they could prevent bloodshed. Fat Badger again pushed his tortured lungs and rushed up as fast as he could. He reached the level area just as the warriors did, their bows at the ready.

Looking at the spring, he saw it deserted.

XXIV

His people were weak from the wracking coughs and fevers. The oldest of them had died the day before, and they had reluctantly buried him in this strange land. Digging a shallow grave was doubly hard with everyone sick and the ground nearly frozen. He had seen that they piled additional rocks than was expected on the internment to keep animals off.

Now he was torn. He had expected the man from the Brown Ants to have returned yesterday. When he didn't show, he had been disappointed though he was not ready to give up just yet. Something might have happened to delay his return.

He looked about him. They tucked their scant camp into a hollow between three hills as protection from the driving wind and snow. It sheltered them but it was not a defensible position. "Always decisions to be made," he said to himself, "weigh one factor against another." That made him smile ruefully. It was a smile latent with sorrow.

He stared at the figures huddled beneath the junipers around him.

When they had begun their journey it had been sudden, there was no time to prepare decently. The attack on their home village by the White Ants had caught them all unawares, and most barely escaped with their lives, let alone sufficient food and clothing.

Even though his little band had long lived in proximity to several White Ant outposts there had never been any indication that anyone resented their presence. Active trading was always encouraged and briskly maintained between the two divergent groups.

It was the nature of the attack that still puzzled him. Without any warning, a nearby small village was overwhelmed and all the inhabitants slaughtered. They had not even taken any as slaves. His scouts sent to search for survivors had reported that the bodies were left where they fell, and some were attacked even in death and further disfigured.

158

It made no sense, a raid at the beginning of winter was unheard of, let alone one that sought only to kill! Who would do such terrible things?

Then even as his scouts returned with the news of the slaughter, an attack occurred at their main village in such force, that they instantly fled for their lives. Only a few managed to escape, precipitously driven from their homes.

He surveyed their pitiful state.

They numbered only seven now, three men, two women and two boys, one of whom was barely five summers old. Less than half the number of people who had started out with him after the attack on their village late last summer. What kind of defense could they offer against an attack now?

He did not suspect that that question was about to be answered.

—near the Twins—

Mercifully Pale Falcon ran into a small party of the searchers who had seen the tracks and were also heading toward the Twins sanctuary. At first, she saw only three men approaching, and she ducked down and gently lowered her mother to the ground. Peeking over a rock, she saw that Many Fires, a friend of hers and a fellow warrior, led the group.

"Ho!" she shouted when she recognized them, "we are here!" She waved to the startled warriors and watched as they saw who she was and ran up the hill to her.

"Pale Falcon," said her friend as he reached her, "you have found the matron! We are searching for her!"

"It was pure luck on my part," she answered. "She is hurt! Perhaps you can make a platform to carry her back."

"Yes, yes of course," he motioned to the other two who went to gather materials. Turning back, he said, "It is a wonder to find you here and with our matron!" He extended his hand to grasp hers meaning to bring it up to breathe upon it.

She backed off, "No!" she shouted, do not touch me!" He drew back. "I have killed a man!"

"Who?" Many Fires asked confusion showing on his face.

"He was a stranger standing guard over my mother." She looked down at the matron. "I bid him surrender, but he resisted."

"So you had no choice." She nodded. "How did you find the matron?"

"I saw tracks," she answered, "in the snow." She pointed to the marks. "They were old, but I did not know why they were there, so I followed them and came to where they had put her. She lay in the shadow of the Twins, in the shrine."

"They kept her in the shrine of the Twins? That must be how you found her!"

"What do you mean?" she asked as the two other warriors returned.

"The Warrior twins!" he said excitedly, "Obviously, they called you there to help her!"

—near Cloud Spring—

It took them quite a while to locate the camp of the Red Ants. Eventually, a young warrior named Two Roots saw a thin trail of smoke, and he motioned to his partner who brought the others. In the time it took for the sun to travel the breadth of a splayed hand across the sky they were finally in place.

Fat Badger was surprised how easy it was to surround the Red Ants. They were always rumored to be such fearsome warriors.

He heard a muffled cough from the hollow below them and thought back to his recent illness. Maybe they were witched by the same malevolent spirits that had attacked him.

Sharp Rocks grunted like a bear and stood. Simultaneously his warriors rose with him.

Fat Badger saw the Red Ants jump up and scramble for cover, but he knew they had little choice; a superior force surrounded them. They must surrender.

Sharp Rocks shouted at them, "Put down your weapons!"

Fat Badger saw them look all around at the dozen warriors and then they looked at each other. There was a long moment of hesitation.

"Where is the Summer Matron?" Sharp Rocks yelled, and Fat Badger saw the confusion on the Red Ant leader's face. Turning to tell Sharp Rocks that he couldn't understand the question Fat Badger saw another of the young warriors nod at Two Roots who nodded back at him and the two drew back their bowstrings.

Several snowflakes drifted between him and the two warriors. They floated on the air gently, dropping at a leisurely pace as if they could almost stop time. It was as if they sought to separate Fat Badger from what was about to happen; somehow to absolve him of guilt.

"No!" yelled Fat Badger and he struggled past Sharp Rocks toward the nearest of the two. As he did, he felt a sharp pain in his head, and he fell unconscious.

—at High Seat Village—

Coyote Alone did not like verbal confrontation. Either fight or leave but don't argue! Hungry Fly sat across from the man, Digging Squirrel. Coyote Alone had been instructed to stand in the doorway while they talked.

Two Eagles spoke first, "We welcomed you here and provided for you as a brother."

"And I am most grateful," replied Digging Squirrel.

"And yet you repay us by counseling our people to leave this village!" Hungry Fly spoke in anger.

Two Eagles raised a hand toward his war chief and then turned back toward the other man. "Is this true, Digging Squirrel? Have you been encouraging those who have departed from High Village to seek homes elsewhere?"

Digging Squirrel looked uncomfortable, "No, I have only told my story to any who have asked, surely that is no crime. I felt your people had a right to know."

Two Eagles looked at a fourth person who sat next to Hungry Fly. "Counts Deer, you have something to add to this talk?"

Looking first at Hungry Fly and then at Digging Squirrel, the other man began slowly. "My wife, Wings has taken our children and gone to her mother's village. She argued with me about leaving; I did not want them to go in this unpredictable weather." He took a deep breath, "She told me that it was because of this one," he indicated Digging Squirrel with a nod of his chin. "He frightened her so with his stories of ogres grabbing children."

Looking back at the man, Digging Squirrel, Two Eagles asked, "Is this a true statement? Did you tell women of our village that ogres are coming to get their children?"

He shook his head violently, "No I would never do such a thing," Digging Squirrel glanced over his shoulder at the hulking form of Coyote Alone standing grim-faced behind him, "Some women heard why I was here and they asked me if the story was true. I merely told them what I told you, about the missing girls and the footprints."

And," shouted Hungry Fly angrily, "that the same footprints were seen at our spring, and that the man who fell from the sky was proof of the ogres, as was the death of Tall Claw!" The War Chief stood up, "And you repeated stories of human bones found scattered across the land between our valley and yours! Deny that you repeated these stories over and over again!"

"I — I think I accidentally passed through the Haunted Canyon I believe you say it is Forbidden. It was an accident. I saw some bones belonging to the dead women. No one cared for them. They lay scattered in the open. I told my story."

Hungry Fly took one step menacingly toward the cowering man. "You were in the Forbidden Place and didn't tell us?"

Digging Squirrel shrank back against the implied threat, "I tell you now, I meant no harm! I answered questions! I gave my opinions when asked!" He looked at Two Eagles, "I have done nothing wrong!"

The old chief nodded, "That may be. We will counsel on this, Coyote Alone," he raised his eyes to the warrior standing guard, "please escort this man back to the house where he stays. Give him whatever he needs but do not allow him to venture out unattended until we have made our decision."

After they had left the chief turned to Hungry Fly and said, "Please gather all of our leaders that remain."

"I think all of the council is still here," the war chief answered, "it is the people who do not hold office currently that are leaving."

"And some of our office holders stay despite the fact that their families have left!"

Hungry Fly nodded in acknowledgment that his leader spoke of him. "I felt it my duty."

"Yes," said the chief wearily, "I know."

XXV

—at the house of Tall Claw—

He awoke again in the house of Tall Claw. His daughter Butterfly was bathing his head with a warm wet cloth. "Oh father you are awake, thank the ancestors!"

His mind had trouble grasping what had occurred at first. He looked about the room noting its familiarity to him yet he wondered how he had come to be there. "What, what . . ." he winced, "has happened?"

"You are being touted as a hero, father, but why did you do such a dangerous thing?"

Fat Badger shook his head in confusion which caused it to hurt even more. "Butterfly what are you talking about?"

"It is all over the valley, you charged the enemy warriors and were the first to be injured for your bravery!"

He sat up which was a even worse choice. His head exploded with pain and he fell back onto the mat.

"You need to rest, you took a heavy blow to your head."

When his head stopped throbbing and with his vision still swimming he asked her, "Who hit me?"

"You were struck by one of the Red Ant warriors. He threw his club at you." She placed her hands on his chest and looked directly at him. "Your head took a severe blow and it's a wonder you survived. Now you must rest. When you are better we will take you home."

He thought about that. "Home?" he asked weakly.

"Yes, home to my mother's house. Oh, you don't know! She is back!"

That news precipitated another attempt to sit up which also failed miserably. "When, how?" Fat Badger asked in a faint voice when he was again laying down.

"They say our sister found her, thank the ancestors!"

"She is well then?" He managed a smile but kept his eyes closed, "I thrill to hear that news."

Not hearing a response he opened his eyes and saw the doubt reflected in his daughter's face. "What is wrong?"

"Uh-eh, I do not know . . ."

His eyes opened wider, "What do you mean?"

Butterfly hesitated. "She — she was injured. That is all I know. I was told that Pale Falcon carried her home." Fat Badger saw tears forming in her eyes, "I had already come here to nurse you, I — I do not know how badly she is injured."

He struggled to sit up again despite the pain shooting through his head. "I must go to her!"

His daughter pushed against his chest and said, "No father, not now, rest, I promise we will go as soon as you are well enough!" Her tears flowed freely now and he saw the intensity of her emotions in her eyes. He knew she too was torn between duty and wanting to go to the aid of her mother.

He nodded slowly and replied, "Yes, I will wait daughter." He lay back slowly to minimize the pain. Closing his eyes he continued, "But you must do me a favor."

"Of course, father, what is it?" she wiped her eyes with the cloth.

"You must tell anyone who comes that I am no hero!"

—at the Warrior's compound—

Outside the house, several people gathered about in groups and singly in the small plaza of the war chief. The two dogs laid over in the southeast corner eyeing all the people who had invaded their home.

Pale Falcon stood off to one side in the area covered by the shade, waiting. Four other warriors and the War Chief, Sharp Rocks were grouped talking to First Light and Black Smoke.

"What do you think, War Chief?" asked the Winter Chief.

Sharp Rocks considered his answer before speaking slowly, "The Red Ants were to the east, I do not believe they could have traveled across the valley, attack the Summer Matron and then return to that area without anyone seeing them. Too many people have been leaving the valley by the eastern trail, they would have been discovered sooner."

"So we can rule that out," said Black Smoke. "Have we heard from Grandfather Scorpion?" he asked everyone in general.

"We sent a runner," Sharp Rocks answered, "but with all this snow," he leaned out from under the shade to peer at the shrouded sky, "and the fact that our ancestors still gather in great numbers to bring us more." He shrugged.

"Her wound appears to be from a club, does it not?" asked First Light. Sharp Rocks nodded, "In my experience she could not have fallen and caused that wound. It was the one that held her prisoner, I believe, that attacked her," he paused, "as that warrior reported." He motioned over his shoulder with his chin in the general direction of Pale Falcon but no one turned to look at her.

"All we can do then is wait for Grandfather Scorpion," said First Light wearily, "The others have gone into seclusion?"

Sharp Rocks nodded, "There are six that I sent to pray and purify themselves after taking a life and," he glanced back toward Pale Falcon, "only the one warrior awaits my dismissal."

"What about sending for the immigrant's healer?" asked First Light hopefully.

Black Smoke looked at the sky and shook his head, "She is even farther away, you can send a runner but — with the uncertainty about who is in the valley, if they are enemies and considering the limited number of warriors we have still available — I think it would be unwise."

First Light nodded in agreement, and the meeting ended.

As the others left, Sharp Rocks sighed and turned toward where Pale Falcon stood. He took two steps toward her without approaching too close. "Many have died this day," he said peremptorily. "We of Sky Valley are in great danger!" He looked at her finally, "I know you desire to stay and see to your mother but we cannot risk you infecting others with the shadow of death, especially a death in battle, so you must go now as the others have."

Pale Falcon's head dropped to her chest, but she brought it up again and nodded without meeting the War Chief's eyes.

"Pray and fast, purify your heart! Heal yourself. We will welcome you back in four days," the old warrior said gently.

As she left the compound, he looked up at the sky. "Merciful Ancestors!" he said to himself, "No more please!"

XXVI

—in the house of Tall Claw—

Fat Badger struggled to his feet. His head throbbed, though it was not as persistent as it had been. Looking around the room, he found a stout stick and maneuvered his way to the water jar. Shaking it, he was pleased it was half full. He drank long, letting the soothing water roll down his throat and fill his belly.

Then his daughter Butterfly appeared at the top of the ladder leading down into the snug house. "Father! What are you doing?" she asked with concern in her voice.

"I am going to see your mother," he answered and he put the jug down, picked up his mantle and struggled to pull it over his head.

"You are doing no such thing, it is snowing terribly and evening approaches!"

He looked up at her surprised, "Evening! I thought it was morning. Hu-eh! have I slept so long then?"

She finished climbing down the ladder and joined him on the floor of the house. Taking his arm, she led him back to his sleeping mat. "You need your rest and do not worry, I have just come from seeing mother even now. She is well-cared for."

He sat stiffly down on the mat, his head throbbing with pain. "Our ancestors have unleashed Thunderbird within my skull!" he said. She smiled. "So your mother is well?" he asked.

As quickly as her smile had appeared, it was gone. "She rests peacefully. She has not awakened since Falcon found her." Fat Badger heard the worry that was implicit in her voice.

He made to rise again, "All the more reason for me to go!"

She placed her hands gently on his chest as if to restrain him. "All the more reason you should not go!" she said firmly. "Let her rest, and you rest too and when you both have recovered there will be enough time for a happy reunion!"

He thought about protesting further but looking beyond her he saw that flakes of snow were falling through the opening faster and thicker now. "All right my dear," he acquiesced, "but after one more day of your forced indolence, and if this blessing of our ancestors finally subsides then —" he nodded at her, "I will go!"

"Yes, fine, if all that happens I will help you!"

—at Red Sky Village—

Yellow Stone also found it hard to rise from his mat, having seen more than sixty summers, his bones ached and creaked at his every move. Though once he was seen as tall among the various men of the valley, he stooped now when standing. In old age, he was less than physically prepossessing. Still, his visions were intense and his counsel much admired.

Emerging from his warm house, he peered up at the dark sky and saw that indeed the snowfall increased just as his dream prophesied. He walked two steps around the corner of his house to find his intern, Many Cactus warming his hands over the fire under his shade.

"You are here," Yellow Stone said.

"Yes, Watcher, I await your direction."

As Watcher for all of Sky Valley, Yellow Stone served in the revered post of Sun Watcher. His observations of celestial events were critical for the well-being of everyone in the whole valley. As such he set the dates for planting, harvest and many ceremonies according to the placement of the Sun and Moon in the sky.

"My direction is that you hie yourself back to the house of your mother and grandmother and see to their welfare."

"But Watcher, what do you intend to do? Won't you require my assistance?"

"Not nearly as much as the aged of members of your family will. This snow will not let up for some time I fear," he glanced out at the many flakes drifting by in the gathering darkness. "I must prepare a special invocation to ask our ancestors something I have never asked before."

The young man stared at him nervously.

"I must ask them to stop blessing us!"

He saw the young man shiver and Yellow Sky knew it was not from the cold. "But Watcher, the Summer matron attempted such a task, and now I hear she lies near death!"

"Hush!" said the old man quickly and with an edge of anger in his voice that he had not intended. "I know what happened to the Matron and it was not spiritual in nature." He saw that the intern had taken the rebuke hard, so he modified his next statement to soothe the young man's hurt. "It was merely a man who injured our matron. All the more reason we must act. We are tasked with the welfare of all. The spirits know what good is in our hearts."

"But . . ."

The old man held up his hand to shush the response, "We do not know that the appearance of the stranger who attacked the matron was not just some accident or coincidence." He lowered his voice. "To approach the Twins, one must pass near the Canyon of the Dead Women. That is a grave undertaking for a woman."

He noticed that the youngster's eyes betrayed more he wanted to add to his argument, "I did not mean to be harsh. Speak freely." Yellow Stone said.

As if still concerned about speaking out of turn Many Cactus looked in the yellow flames that licked at the dry wood for some time, gathering his thoughts.

Finally, he took a deep breath and began, "Elder, these are very troubling times. A man falls from the sky. A man who appears to be a White Ant. The War Chief is killed. Both of these things happen close to the mine where we take our sky stones. Our blesséd matron is attacked while upon a mission seeking the welfare of all who dwell here in our valley. She is attacked by a strange man, who also appears to belong to the southern White Ant people. And the skies fill with clouds in numbers unheard of before. Snow falls without end. Is this all coincidence or are we being warned and refusing to see the message?"

He finished and sat waiting for the Watcher's response. The old man nodded his head but stared off into the distance as if his eyes could penetrate through the gathering darkness. He smiled at the boy and said, "You have been thoughtful in your argument, and I would be foolish not to heed it. You will make a fine Watcher someday."

Many Cactus allowed a brief glimpse of pride to cross his face.

"But," continued the old Sun Watcher, "I have weighed these same arguments already to myself. My mind is at peace with my decision." Worry reappeared in the eyes of Many Cactus. "I will attempt to contact our ancestors and request that they halt their blessings for now. If in doing so something happens to me, you and all the others will know that your suspicions are correct. It will be time to abandon our valley."

—in the house of Tall Claw—

Thunderhead made his way laboriously down the ladder into the house of Tall Claw where Fat Badger was recuperating. Nodding to Butterfly, he strode over to the mat where the wounded man slept and sat down to wait. He took a bowl of warm tea from Butterfly and smiled his thanks.

"Has he slept long?" he asked her quietly.

"Since late this afternoon."

"I am awake." Fat Badger said, opening his eyes.

"Ah, our hero awakens! Just what were you doing at the camp of the Red Ants? Did you think to become War Chief for your actions? Our temporary War Chief is angry with you!"

"What I was trying to do was to stop the bloodshed from occurring!"

"You have a funny way of doing that by attacking your enemies."

"I did no such thing! They were not enemies!"

"Really? They sneak into our valley and attack your wife, and still, you think them your friends?"

"There is no proof that they attacked Fire Star."

"The one your daughter battled was likely their leader."

"I understood he was thought to be a southern White Ant?" "Exactly so," said Thunderhead triumphantly, "There have been many times when Red Ants aligned themselves with the southern White Ants and were led into battle by them!"

"But I still ask you, what proof do you have that this is the case?"

"And I respond in kind, Fat Badger, what proof do you have that they were not working with the White Ant Man?"

Fat Badger closed his eyes and lay back on his mat.

"It all makes sense," Thunderhead continued, "A man falls from the sky, he is a southern White Ant. We find a similar person where our

Summer Matron is held captive! Our War Chief is killed on an ancient little-used trail leading to the western White Ant's villages! White Ants figure in each of these incidents, don't you agree?"

"No, I do not."

"You are a stubborn man, Fat Badger, that is only one of your problems that often clouds your decision-making skills."

For his part, Fat Badger did not argue this point because he agreed with that assessment of his abilities. Changing tact, he asked Thunderhead, "What happened after I was knocked out?"

"You mean after you started the battle? How did it proceed? Finally, you ask the important question," the old man taunted.

Fat Badger eyed him but did not take the bait.

The Vulture priest sighed and continued, "The Red Ant people were not numerous enough to threaten our warriors. We overwhelmed them with you as our only casualty."

"You took them, prisoner, then?"

Thunderhead looked surprised, "No! We killed them!"

"What?" Fat Badger sat up suddenly, his head pounding in protest. "You killed all of them?"

"Not all, we took two boys and a woman prisoner. We killed three men and a woman who resisted."

Fat Badger covered his eyes with his hands and fell back. "More deaths on my head!" he said quietly.

"What makes you say that?" asked Thunderhead.

Fat Badger did not at once reply. After a time he said only, "I am tired, Vulture priest, please excuse me for now. We can talk more about this later in you like."

"Humph!" said the old man who stood up suddenly and made to leave.

Butterfly, who sat all this time quietly, now spoke up, "The snow increases elder, it may be best not to venture out this evening."

"All the more reason for me to leave at once!" he snapped, and he struggled up the ladder and was gone.

XXVII

—near the Immigrant's village—

She struggled through the rapidly falling snow, slipping in the cold mud and sliding downhill three steps for every four she managed to climb. Exhaustion threatened to overwhelm her and leave her to die amid the swirl of stinging snowflakes upon a bed of ice.

She couldn't see more than two body lengths ahead of her in the blizzard. She seemed to be feeling her way home. Just as her feet slipped out from under her, she recognized a formation looming out of the white blanket that had fallen upon the world as the hulking nob of stone just a quarter of a day's walk from her village!

Hope swelled in her, and she began to think she might escape the enclosing hand of freezing death that hovered above her! Pushing herself up using the bare stump of a tree she took a step, and another and another.

Darkness came, but the snow did not lessen if anything it increased in fury as if determined to defeat her.

She did not remember the final frantic struggle of her climb over the last ridge above her village. She did remember falling though as she rolled down the snow-covered slopes virtually right to her door. Her father jumped up from his mat near the glowing hearth with a yell of surprise as she pushed through the curtain. She came crawling into the room and collapsed at his feet. Her mother asleep in the back room came running out to see what had occurred.

Both her parents were horrified at her condition. Her torn clothes barely covered her against the frigid night and beneath them she displayed many cruel scratches and bruises from her struggles to return home.

Gently picking her up, her father cried at how easy it was. She weighed no more than a young child! Carrying her over to where he had been sitting, he laid her down gently, like a feather falling on water. Her mother hastened to bring blankets. While her father lifted her head to try and pour a little water down her parched throat, her mother put more on to warm so she could bathe her wounds.

"My poor Tree Cliff Sitting!" her mother said, tears streaming from her eyes, "What has happened to you?"

"This proves Wind Killer wrong! She absolutely was not with anyone who cared for her!" her father added. "That is certain!"

Across the plaza of his little village, Wind Killer stood just outside his house and tried to see the sky. It was hopeless. All he could see was a mass of falling white. Behind him, his wife called, "Get in out of the snow you old man! You will catch your death of chills!" Sliding back under the curtain into the dim lit room he muttered something under his breath.

"And stop your muttering," his wife added.

"What was that?" he asked and pulled the thick curtain away again as he stuck his head back out into the night.

His wife looked up from her weaving, "What was what?"

"I heard a noise . . ."

"You will hear a noise of one of my pots breaking against your old skull! You're letting the snow in!" she said sharply.

"I thought I heard something," he spoke over his shoulder, though he knew by her tone she was only half attending as she worked with her deer bone awl threading yucca and making a basket in the faint light offered from the glowing hearth. "It sounded like someone talking or yelling off in the distance," he paused, "though it is hard to tell for sure, this snow muffles sound and fools your ears." He stuck his head outside again.

"I will muffle your sounds if you do not get your foolish old ears inside here this instant!"

Shadows loomed dimly amid the swirls of snow.

"Trees," he spoke in no more than a whisper, "the trees are groaning with the weight of snow."

"What?"

"It is the trees that are talking!" he whispered awestruck.

"Husband, are you going senile?" His wife snapped. "What do you prattle on about?" Looking about outside once more before he released the curtain to fall back in place over the opening, he shook his head and realized there was nothing to be done in this kind of weather.

"Well, what did you see." She looked at him now, interested if amused at his eccentricities.

"Shadows." Smiling, he shook his head again. "There is nothing to be seen in this storm." his voice sounded calm, but his eyes filled with worry.

He might have been even more worried had he noticed that some of those shadows stalked towards them.

—in the house of Tall Claw—

At dawn Fat Badger slowly rose from his bed, worried that his head might still be paining him but to his relief, the throbbing subsided considerably. The willow tea must have worked. Climbing up the ladder, he found that snow continued to fall gently from the clouded sky though not as thickly as the night before.

Seeing the dogs laying beneath a few slanted pieces of wood just to the side of the house he whistled experimentally and was rewarded with their duet of low growls.

"Ah, my heart soars at your tribute!" he said out-loud.

A voice came from behind him, "Talking to dogs? Isn't that said to be tempting fate?"

Fat Badger turned to see that Climbs Hills, Grandfather Scorpion's assistant sat huddled beneath the shade. Though wrapped in a thick robe he was still shivering. A small fire was in the rock-lined hearth at his feet, but it struggled to maintain itself in the swirl of snowflakes blown into it by the wind.

"Good day to you," said Fat Badger, "I did not expect anyone to be here."

"Except those disagreeable dogs."

"Exactly," answered Fat Badger climbing down from the house to join the younger man. "They should have alerted me to your presence."

"Hmm, perhaps they have become lazy in this weather."

"Or they chose to let me be surprised. Why did you not come into the house?"

"Grandfather said I was not to bother you."

"So you have been sent here by Grandfather Scorpion?" Fat Badger surveyed the plaza of the Warrior's compound, "It could not have been easy to get here?"

"No, indeed! I battled deep drifts all along the way, and I am not all that familiar with the trails between your wife's village and this place." He smiled, "I am glad that I came alone because my struggles would have provided much hilarity for those more knowledgeable who might have accompanied me."

"I had heard that you enjoy making people laugh."

"Sometimes," he nodded, "though not always, especially not at my own expense."

"If Grandfather Scorpion instructed you not to bother me and yet here you are, he must have sent you to convey some message to me."

"Perceptive as always, Valley Trader, yes, my tutor has charged me with an important message for you."

"So he is treating my wife then for her injuries?"

"Yes, in fact, that is why he sent me!" Climbs Hills looked at some point beyond Fat Badger, "Your daughter Butterfly said you were eager to go to your wife's aid."

Fat Badger nodded.

"Yes, well, he asks that you not visit her yet."

XXVIII

—at High Seat Village—

Counts Deer pushed aside the curtain and stepped into the dimly lit house. He nodded to Many Elk, the young warrior who stood to one side of the entryway. "Hungry Fly sent you?" The youth nodded. Counts Deer scowled, this boy looked to be no more than fourteen or fifteen summers. "You relieved Coyote Alone then?"

Again the boy nodded.

"See that you stay awake!" he snapped. He saw the boy swallow hard. Turning, he looked at Digging Squirrel, seated on a mat across the room. "And as for you, witch!" he hardened his eyes.

"I am no witch," the other man replied quietly.

"Our counsel will decide that," Counts Deer continued. "If found guilty it will go badly for you. It would be better if you admit your guilt now!"

"One cannot admit to something he has not done."

"You poison the minds of our people with stories of terror and death! You conspire with someone to cause our people to leave their homes during a time of dangerous weather! You bring death! I say you are a witch!"

"Who do I conspire with?" asked Digging Squirrel. "Who would benefit from such an action?"

"I do not know the answer to that question yet, but I am convinced this is all part of a plot to gain control of our village. You can rest assured I will seek this truth until I ferret it out. I will locate the deadly snake in this ground squirrel's burrow yet."

"You have a vivid imagination."

Turning back to the youth who guarded the man, Counts Deer asked him, "Why is this man not bound?"

Looking confused the boy answered, "No one said to bind him, Coyote Alone said only to keep him here." He glanced over at the prisoner. "Is he d-dangerous?" he asked.

"Do you think a witch poses a danger to us?" He saw the boy's eyes widen in alarm. "I will go talk to Hungry Fly, and we will return and bind him. Until then, keep a close watch on him and have your war club at the ready!"

Many Elk nodded and brought his club up to a level with his chest. His face looked stern, but Counts Deer saw the uncertainty in his eyes. He decided he'd better hurry to check with Hungry Fly.

—in Fire Star's house—

Grandfather Scorpion gazed down at his patient. She lay motionless, and her breath came out shallowly and was drawn back in slowly. He placed a long, hexagon-shaped crystal on her chest.

"Well?" asked Thunderhead who stood near the doorway.

"Nothing has changed. Fire Star sleeps, but I do not know that she will wake today, tomorrow or ever. Even if she does, there is a strong likelihood that she will be severely hampered in movement and possibly speech. I cannot heal her any more than I have. It is up to the spirits and her will to live now."

Thunderhead looked at Butterfly who sat on the other side of her mother. "Are you prepared?"

She looked up, a stricken expression twisting her usually placid features. "Me? You mean now?" she stared at her mother. "You expect me to take over while she yet lives?"

"I expect you to do what your mother would have done; I expect you to do your duty in the best interests of our people. We do not have the luxury of hesitation; serious problems are facing us all!"

Butterfly swallowed hard. "What do you suggest?"

"The council meets today to discuss all that has occurred. They will recommend actions; I have no doubt."

Sitting up straighter and composing her expression Butterfly answered, "Bring me their advice and I will — I will act on it."

"Good, that is how your mother would have responded if she were able," the old man said and, pushing aside the curtain, he left.

Hummingbird entered then and, looking at her sister she asked, "Do you want me to go care for father?"

176

Butterfly looked up at her and replied, "No, I need you here, I need you and your sister, Falcon. Where is she?"

"She is in retreat still."

"Oh yes, I'm sorry, I had forgotten." She stole a glance at Grandfather Scorpion who sat off to one side of the room lost in his chanting. "Oh my, I can't be forgetting such things. I fear I am not ready for this."

"What do you mean?"

Butterfly looked up at her sister and said, "Thunderhead wants me to assume the position of Summer Matron, at least until our mother is well again."

"Oh!"

"Yes, and I don't feel I am prepared for such a responsibility! If we are to move it will be up to me! How can I ask people to leave their homes in the dead of winter? Especially a winter like this! Oh, I am not ready for this!"

Hummingbird nodded, "Who could ever be?"

—in the Warrior's compound—

Standing next to the shade with snow flurries falling all about him Fat Badger stared at the man, Climbs Hills, "What do you mean?" he asked.

Climbs Hills paused, he looked down as he answered, "Grandfather Scorpion has concerns. You have been close to passing over to the next world twice now. He fears that your proximity to Fire Star in her current state might have the effect of pushing her from this world into the next. He is very cautious."

"So he forbids me coming to my wife in her time of greatest need?"

"No, Trader, of course not. He does not presume any such thing."

"I see," said Fat Badger though his voice indicated anything but understanding. "He leaves the decision up to me." The other man nodded. Fat Badger snorted a derisive laugh, "He counts upon my sense of duty. How long must I wait?" he asked.

"Not long I hope and yet I also fear."

"So you have doubts as to her recovery?"

"It is beyond my saying. Even the great Scorpion one feels that he has done what he can and we must now wait."

Fat Badger strode around the perimeter of the shade looking off into the snow that still flurried through the air.

"Perhaps the Valley Trader has another task that he might pursue while we await the result of Grandfather Scorpion's efforts? Something to distract his mind from the waiting."

He waved his hand angrily at the snow, "In this?"

"It was merely a suggestion," said Climbs Hills.

Fat Badger stared at the man, then his features softened and he looked down, "Yes, thank you, I appreciate your trying to suggest a distraction. Waiting is hard." He looked up and out toward the north, then to the east, "I intended a visit to Yellow Stone. I could do that I guess, his village is not too far from here."

"Yes," said Climbs Hills, "seeking the counsel of the wise Sun Watcher would be a good idea."

Set high above the valley on a ridge that faced the east, Red Sky village afforded the sun watcher Yellow Stone the best location for his observations. He could watch the sunrise at it's earliest appearance, and he greeted the moon as she rose over the distant peaks.

Fat Badger would still have a long walk ahead of him in this weather. The most natural route to get there would take him past Snow Spring village. That was the village of his sister-in-law. That helped him make up his troubled mind as he had urgent business there too.

"Yes," he said decisively, "I will go to Red Sky, and then I will come back to find my wife much improved." He smiled, "So I hope, and I wish."

"As do we all Valley Trader. Go safely."

Fat Badger nodded and left Climbs Hills beneath the shade. He climbed back onto the roof of the house and thence down the ladder to make preparations to visit Yellow Sky.

But first, he must speak with his nephew, Angry Cloud.

XXIX

—*on the Sky Creek trail*—

When he re-emerged, he saw that the other man had gone. His tracks were evident in the snow leading back towards the big village where Fat Badger's wife lay even now, fighting for her life.

He paused a long moment staring at those receding prints, longing to follow them but at the same time understanding what it was that Grandfather Scorpion feared. Fat Badger was powerfully touched by death now, and his escapes were near things at best. Grandfather Scorpion bore responsibility for having cured him of the sickness. Who better would understand what he should do?

He turned his thoughts toward Red Sky village.

The snow seemed to know that he was trying to go somewhere, it slackened even as he started out. The day promised more cold to come, but for now, it was chilly but tolerable. Stopping after a bit to rest he noticed with surprise that the white dog followed him.

"Am I back in your good graces, you surly beast?" He allowed himself a chuckle.

He went to the home of Angry Cloud's mother in Snow Spring village. She welcomed him, sat him down near a small hearth full of coals and brought him a bowl of broth. She walked back to her flat grinding stone and continued her never-ending task of preparing corn meal.

He drank half the broth and then looking at his wife's sister he said, "Where is everyone? Your village seems almost deserted."

The woman looked around the room before answering, "A girl went missing. People are scared. Some have left."

"The weather may be to blame," Fat Badger said.

His sister-in-law shrugged.

He decided to change the subject to the one that most concerned his visit, "I would speak with my nephew."

She nodded and then looked troubled. "I thought as much. Ee-uh, that may be hard to accomplish."

"Why?"

"He has gone into seclusion and seeks purification."

"Why? Did he kill an enemy?"

"No, no, nothing of the sort. This seclusion is for something different." She grew quiet for several breaths. When she spoke again her voice was soft, hushed, "He feels he has been chosen."

"Chosen?"

She nodded.

"I see," said Fat Badger. "Where has he gone?"

She waited a long time then shrugged, "I cannot say."

The answer surprised him. "You do not know?"

She shrugged again at this question.

"So you do know."

Angry Cloud's mother waited a long time before answering. He sat listening to the scrape of the stone against the flat surface. Finally, she said, "I cannot say."

"He has gone somewhere that you know of and yet you cannot say where?"

He thought about that. Fat Badger brought his hand up to his mouth as sudden recognition of her meaning struck him.

Angry Cloud's mother looked up at him with sad eyes. She gave a very slight nod of her head.

Neither spoke for some time.

Fat Badger broke the strained silence. "So he blames himself for the death of the elder?"

She shrugged, "I cannot say. You must ask my son."

"Then I shall ask my nephew. Has he gone to make his peace with the spirits in the Canyon of the Dead Women?"

His mother looked up and smiled her sad smile. Then she just shrugged again and went back to her grinding.

Fat Badger recognized that she labored within her mind between wanting to secure help for Angry Cloud and trying to protect her child against danger. Her mind had split into two opposing ideas and would, therefore, choose neither. Knowing she was not likely to share any more information with him, even though she hoped for his successful mediation, Fat Badger rose to leave. Sadly quiet, he went from her house. Outside the white dog was laying up against the adobe-plastered walls keeping out of the snow. She got up and shook herself as he emerged.

"Where I am going you may not wish to follow," said Fat Badger to the dog.

She followed him anyway.

—at High Seat Village—

Hungry Fly pushed aside the heavy blanket that screened the warm room from the weather outside and was instantly sorry he had done so. Snow still streaked from the sky like tiny stinging stones striking anyone so foolish as to venture out.

"We are the most blessed here atop the Giant's head," he laughed sardonically. "Down below us, I understand, the snow has stopped falling, while here in our village — " he held his hands out before him in a helpless gesture, " – we continue to be blessed!"

Travel across the plaza was limited to the narrow trails laboriously trampled through the snow which lay upon the ground at a depth higher than a man's knees. His sandals crunched upon the pounded snow surface. The cold seeped through his socks quickly and caused him to hurry. Looking across the plaza to the room where the man from Many Rocks canyon was kept he thought he spied a guard standing outside the doorway, but he was not sure. The snow made visibility murky at best.

Entering a room he saw that several men gathered close upon the glowing coals of the hearth. He squatted and sat down to join them.

"Good you are here," said Counts Deer.

"Going anywhere in this weather is a struggle!" answered Hungry Fly holding out his hands toward the warm glow. Several faces lit in flickering red light looked up at him the rest of their blanket shrouded forms lost in shadow.

"I visited the prisoner some time ago," began Counts Deer.

"Let's call him a guest," corrected Hungry Fly, "he is, as of yet, innocent of any wrong."

Count's Deer looked up at the War Chief and briefly allowed his anger to flash across his red-lit face. "Fine!" he snapped, "Our esteemed guest, then! I found him unbound."

Dark Snake spoke up from across the fire, "Why would a guest be bound?"

"Why indeed!" answered Counts Deer angrily, "Because if he is a witch, as I suspect, then it is dangerous for him to be allowed to go free!"

"You use the word 'suspect' yourself!" answered Dark Snake, "You are speaking your opinion! No facts exist!"

Counts Deer stood up, surprising the entire group all of whom flinched and looked up at him with wonder.

"My 'opinion' is born of these facts! A man comes to our village with a story of strange occurrences and abduction of young women. Then a young woman is apparently abducted in full light of day, and unusual prints found. Subsequently, this stranger who brought the story agrees that this is as it was near his home. Finally, people begin to leave our village, abandoning their homes in the time of the most dreadful winter any of us can remember, and the reason seems to be that this 'visitor' is telling them stories of a place that is damned and of spirits that are murdering people!"

Counts Deer sat back down. Next to him, Hungry Fly grunted derisively. "A great performance, truly."

Long Thorn sitting on the other side of Counts Deer said, "Do not forget, a man fell from the sky!"

"No one can forget that!" said Counts Deer.

Next to Dark Snake, Coyote Alone shifted uneasily. Two Eagles who had thus far maintained silence looked at the young warrior and asked, "You have something to add?"

Looking at each of the others in turn, Coyote Alone said, "He should be bound."

—on the trail to the Forbidden Place—

Fat Badger also found the way forward to be a struggle. It was not only that he worried about his destination; each step took him farther away from where his wife lay struggling to remain among the living. Struggles everywhere! Adding to the forces of his mind that pulled at him and sought to dissuade him from proceeding, the land itself appeared to conspire against him. Snow still shrouded much of the ground though it was easier going along the creek. He picked his way carefully, avoiding the drifts and using logs and stones wherever possible but that, of course, slowed his progress even more and damnably gave Fat Badger more time to think.

His thoughts kept returning to his next destination.

To get there, he must cross the creek as he had a few days before, the memory of which still caused him to shiver uncontrollably. He reached the stones and log that spanned the watercourse. Surveying it, he saw that some of the snow was disturbed. "Probably from my nephew's passing," he said to the dog.

The white dog looked at him as if questioning his judgment in preparing to cross the near-frozen water course yet again. Do you not remember the last time? the dog's look seemed to say.

He stared longingly downstream. If he followed the stream here a few more moments, his wife's village would come into sight on his right. He looked across the rushing water. If he crossed now his way was clear — he would go to the Canyon of Dead Women.

That was where his nephew must be. When his sister-in-law said twice she 'could not say' the message became clear. Angry Cloud had gone to a place people did not speak of usually.

Years before, two women went missing and they had been found in that canyon. They were dead. Both had been strangled and bludgeoned to death. The abductions and attacks had taken place about a moon apart. The body of another was found later, but it had been there too long to determine a cause of death or sex. Most people believed it was another victim of the same attacker.

Subsequently, the people of the small village near there whose people had discovered them abandoned their homes and went elsewhere to live. The canyon had been untrammeled ever since. Stories grew up about how and why the women were killed. Lying a little north of the Twins it was said someone was being punished for improper behavior and the crimes were committed behind the backs of those Warrior twins. Many theories were proposed as to the meaning, but the message was deemed plain. The canyon was ever after a shunned place.

It had become Forbidden. All the inhabitants left the village within the area.

And yet Fat Badger knew instinctively from his discussion with his sister-in-law that that was where his nephew had gone.

XXX

—at High Seat Village—

Hungry Fly and Coyote Alone struggled across the snow-swept plaza. Halfway across Hungry Fly noticed that the guard he had seen earlier must have retreated inside. "It's good he went back in!" he said to his companion.

"Who?" asked the warrior pausing momentarily.

"The guard who stood outside."

They took two more steps then Coyote Alone stopped. Hungry Fly looked back. The younger man stared at him incredulously. "What did you say? The guard?" he asked. "You saw Many Elk outside that room?"

"I could not be sure it was him, but someone was standing just outside the . . ."

Coyote Alone looked ahead suddenly and strode off through the dense snow as fast as he could toward the room, leaving Hungry Fly standing there, his words unfinished. Hungry Fly got over his surprise and struggled to catch up.

The younger man had already entered the room when the War Chief arrived, panting. Inside it was dark and Coyote Alone was searching for kindling to restore the fire from the coals. It flared to life, and Hungry Fly saw the boy's body lying against the wall his skull crushed. Blood pouring down from his wound along his left arm lay in a pool next to his lifeless body. No one else was in the room. Coyote Alone grabbed a torch and lighting it in the sputtering fire he hurried past the dumbfounded War Chief and back outside.

Hungry Fly stood looking at the dead youth for a moment longer and then followed his warrior.

Outside in the swirling wind and stinging ice particles, Coyote Alone was sweeping the area with his wind-tortured light, causing crazy shadows to fly about in the driving snow. He stopped then and crouched down, looking at the prints he found. Coming up to him, Hungry Fly asked, "What do you see?"

The younger man looked at him as if he had forgotten he was not alone then answered, "Not here, come!" the wind grabbing his words and spiriting them away as he took Hungry Fly's arm and led him back into the room.

Inside it was smoky. The fire was dying once again, so Hungry Fly added a few more branches and watched as Coyote Alone covered Many Elk's body with a blanket. Striding the few steps over to the hearth he sat down across from the War Chief. Warm air took the smoke up toward the ceiling as the two men stared at each other in mutual exhaustion and sadness.

It was Coyote Alone who spoke, "Several men came, I think. They surprised Many Elk; he never had a chance. When they left with Squirrel, they scuffed their tracks. It took me some time to discern their trail. It went west."

Alarmed Hungry Fly jumped up, "The guard at the west gate!"

"Stay and martial what warriors you can, I will go. Send two more to assist me, but I fear it will too late to help whoever is on guard there."

Hungry Fly was too disturbed to realize that he should be the one giving orders these orders. "I think it was Acorn Boy," he said wearily. "Another who was not ready to shoulder such responsibility but what can we do? We are too weak. Too many have left."

Coyote Alone looked at him and nodded. Then he left, swallowed up by the seething snow and the shadowed night. Sitting there, keeping watch over the dead, Hungry Fly suddenly felt very old and tired.

—in Dead Women Canyon—

Following the old trail up into Dead Women Canyon was not a simple task. Snow covered everything to the height of his knees except where someone had gone ahead of him. There it was tramped down somewhat. Fat Badger assumed that it was the trail made by Angry Cloud, but even there the snow was thick. Ice had formed beneath the snow and footing remained treacherous.

Worst of all the sky continued to be shrouded in thick gray clouds. More snow would come. How long could this last?

He wondered about his nephew, too. "He is up here alone, in this horrible weather and sick in spirit, perhaps sick in mind." He surveyed the desolate landscape. "I must find him soon!"

Fat Badger often stopped, despite the cold, he was sweating profusely. It occurred to him that perhaps he was not yet as fit as he should be when attempting such an arduous task.

Behind him, the white dog too was hampered. To follow him, it traveled in leaps that were exhausting in this weather. Its tongue lolled from its mouth, and it kept looking all about as if expecting to see a place to rest.

"No one said you had to come with me you know," said Fat Badger, his voice sounding odd in the snow muffled canyon. Hearing no response, he went on, "With any blessings at all we may find him soon." He stared about at the silent hills. "If not we will make a camp up there on that flat space." he pointed with his chin at a point on up ahead of them.

Then Fat Badger laughed, shaking his head in wonder, "Like I need to share my plans with you."

He wondered how long this would take? Finding his nephew in this deserted canyon was not an easy task. He looked at the dog again. "You could help, you know," he said. The dog turned its head sideways to look at him.

"Oh don't play innocent with me! You and your sister always know when people are coming long before I do. I am convinced you could find my nephew much faster than I could.

As if in answer the dog turned around twice and laid down in a relatively clear space under the edge of a tree.

"Fine! Have it your way! You are a stubborn dog; you know that?" He looked at the dog laying there beneath the branches of the cedar. Then he looked top at the sky, and a snowflake dropped into one eye. Rubbing the eye, Fat Badger added, "But perhaps you are smarter than I am."

—at High Seat Village—

Coyote Alone approached the west gate of the compound wall surrounding his village. It was the farthest opening from the central plaza and the small room block nearest there had been unoccupied for the last few years. Guarding that gate was known to be the loneliest of duties.

Coyote Alone proceeded with great caution. While it was unlikely that raiders trespassing at his village would leave anyone behind as a deterrent to pursuit, he couldn't afford to be reckless. They had lost one warrior already, albeit a young one and they could ill afford another loss.

Pausing at the corner of the abandoned rooms, he peered through the gloom to see if the guard stood there. He saw no one. Slowly he slid his body around the corner and moving as fast as he could he ran toward the gate.

He stared at the ground, holding his war club at the ready. Even in the near darkness, he could tell that there were many footprints around the gate. Looking up, he saw that a half moon was peeking out from amidst the dense clouds. He stared at the ground again this time looking for signs that there had been a struggle. He saw none.

"Where is the guard?" He said aloud. A noise behind him had him spinning around and slipping in the mud, stumbling to his knees in the snow. It was Hungry Fly, Counts Deer and two others. Coyote Alone got up sloughing the wet snow off him.

"What happened?" asked Hungry Fly eagerly.

"Nothing as far as I can see," answered Coyote Alone. He spied Acorn Boy with them. "Wait! Who was on guard here?"

"It was Three Ravens." answered the War Chief. "He relieved Acorn Boy just a while ago."

"The Town Crier? Why him?" asked Counts Deer

"We were short-handed, you know that everyone has to help out and assume extra duties."

"Did you say Three Ravens?" asked Fights Hard, one of the other men.

"Yes," answered Hungry Fly, "why?"

"Because I saw him sleeping in his house just before you came to get me."

There was a moment when everyone stood still digesting this bit of news. Then, without a word to anyone, Coyote Alone started running as fast as he could back into the village.

XXXI

—in Dead Women Canyon—

Fat Badger arrived at the flat space seen from the trail and looking around he saw a juniper that offered to make a likely camping spot. "Com'on White Dog I'll show you how to build a winter camp. Even you will be impressed!"

Walking up to the tree, he moved around to the northwest side opposite the prevailing wind and began breaking off branches. Some of the more stubborn ones he cut with his knife. Picking up the branches he wove them into the remaining ones on the tree to thicken the sheltering wall. Employing a stout branch as a broom, he swept the floor beneath the tree clean of snow and debris.

For her part, the dog sat there watching him. She mercifully did not comment on the wisdom of any activity she observed.

Fat Badger then scoured around the area, gathering all the dead wood he could find sticking out above the snow. Bringing it back, he made a pile to the right of the tree. Taking a few rocks he saw peeking out; Fat Badger piled them to the left. Abruptly the white dog stood up and ran over to where he worked. Fearing her bite, Fat Badger instinctively flinched from the dog's approach.

But he needn't of worried. It was not Fat Badger the dog was interested in now. She sniffed about the exposed ground beneath the tree and began digging.

"Ho! Dog what have you found?" Fat Badger fell to his knees and joined the dog scrambling in the loose soil to uncover some treasure. Beneath the dirt, about a hands length down, the earth fell away and exposed a nest of sleepy ground squirrels. The white dog snapped up the quickest one as he attempted to escape and Fat Badger smashed the others with a flat stone from his pile.

Lifting the stone he saw three dead squirrels laying there. Turning to the dog, who sat off to one side happily crunching up the squirrel she caught, Fat Badger smiled and said, "Nice work White Dog! I'm glad you came with me."

He picked up the three squirrels and then he swung himself around and sat down right beside the hole. Using his knife, he skinned the squirrels and threw the skins over to where the dog was still chewing her prize. "You can have those too, dog!"

He shoved a straight stick up into each of the little bodies and set them standing upright next to him. Then he dug a shallow pit in front of him, using the dirt from that to fill in the nest. Lining the hollow with stones, he chose some of the driest wood he had found and then took out his fire-making kit.

Soon he had a small fire going and sitting with his back against the tree trunk, enveloped by the wings of woven branches around him; he found it quite comfortable. He roasted the three squirrels and ate all three whole, crunching their little bones to mush. Their thin flesh had a strong flavor of juniper berries.

—at High Seat Village—

Hungry Fly, Counts Deer and Coyote Alone burst into the house of Three Ravens suddenly causing the sleeping man to jump up startled. "What do you want?" he said.

"Why are you not on duty at the west gate?" Hungry Fly retorted.

"W-What? What do you m-mean?" he stammered.

"Why are you not at the gate where I assigned you to watch?"

"Oh," said Three Ravens yawning, "I switched with One Arm Cactus."

"Who?" asked Counts Deer.

"One Arm Cactus," said Three Ravens getting to his feet. "He saw me there and said I looked tired. I said I was tired and he offered to take my watch."

"He is new to our village," said Coyote Alone.

"He has only been here one moon, he is not fully trained," said Hungry Fly.

"I have seen him standing guard before," answered Three Ravens defensively.

"At the front gate, with another guard, never alone!" Hungry Fly snapped.

"What has happened? Why are you angry with me?" asked Three Ravens looking from one face to another of the two men.

"Many Elk is dead." said the War chief.

"What?" Three Ravens asked shocked, "Who? What? How did he die?"

"We think raiders came through the west gate. I saw a man standing outside the house where we held the man from Many Rocks Piled Canyon, and I assumed it was the guard Many Elk. But it was probably one of the raiders keeping watch."

"Is that man dead too?"

"You mean that witch?" spat out Counts Deer.

"No, he is gone." Hungry Fly said wearily ignoring the other's comment, "Coyote Alone thinks that they came to free him."

"But how would they know that we kept him prisoner?" asked Three Ravens.

"Witches have ways of knowing these things don't they?" said Hungry Fly.

"Yes, that is the question," lamented Hungry Fly, "and it may be so. But I am afraid we don't have time to answer that question or any others right now. Right now, I need you to do your job." "My job?" asked Three Ravens.

"Yes, your job as Town Crier. Go out into the village and tell everyone to prepare to abandon the High Seat Village as soon as possible!"

—in Fire Star's house—

In Fire Star's room, Grandfather Scorpion also packed to leave. He placed individual items one by one into a badger skin bag. He whispered inaudibly to each object as he settled it down within the pouch. Looking at a bearskin pad next to his patient he selected which piece to pick up next.

Butterfly looked at him, her eyes imploring him to give her good news.

At first, she got the impression that he was unwilling to meet her eyes with his. He picked up each item he had spread out and carefully placed them into a bag made from the skin of a badger.

She cleared her throat.

He looked at her and held out his hands. He said softly, "I have done what I can." He looked at the pale form laying at his feet. "She may wake and be fine, or . . . she may not wake."

"But if she wakes she will be better?"

He thought about this. "I do not know this for certain." Kneeling beside Fire Star, he felt her pulse and listened to her breathing. Examining the wound on her head, he continued, "She may wake and be unable to talk. Or she may not be able to take care of herself. She may appear to awaken and yet not respond to anyone who talks to her." He held his hands out palms up. "Her wound was severe and not cared for initially." He sighed, "I have done all I can." He shook his head. "If I had gotten to her sooner, maybe . . ."

He stood and walked to the doorway, pausing with his hand on the curtain he turned back and said, "If she does wake you can send for me again if you like. I will come. It is up to you."

She nodded, biting her lip.

"It may be better if she does not wake," he added.

"I have hope yet!" said Butterfly.

"Hope is good, as are prayers, but still . . ." Grandfather Scorpion shook his head slowly.

She watched wordlessly as he turned and left.

XXXII

—in Dead Women Canyon—

Fat Badger woke with a start, shivering. He had slept sitting up against the tree, his legs extended and his feet on either side of the rocks of the fire pit. The white dog lay up against his left leg. His blanket was stiff, coated in frost. He rose, his entire body shivering violently, jostling the dog who growled at him. Fat Badger ignored such comments; he was too familiar with them by now. Pulling his blanket over his shoulders, he set about to try and start a fire.

Once a bit of flame curled up from his kindling he added the last of his thorny canotia bush and a few sticks. Soon he felt the heat spread out from his little blaze.

He saw that the dog was staring intently at something out away from their camp.

Scanning the surrounding hills in that direction, he was surprised to see his nephew standing not five body lengths away, partially screened by a tree.

Fat Badger raised his hand and waved him over. He was further surprised when his nephew ducked back behind the tree as if hiding from him. "Angry Cloud, come here!" he called to him. His voice came out hoarse and strange sounding.

After a few breaths the young man peeked out again from the other side of the tree and then after looking all around him, he walked down the gentle slope toward Fat Badger's camp. He hesitated several times along the way. Stopping about two body lengths from him, Angry Cloud stood and looked at his uncle as he was kneeling by the fire. It gave Fat Badger a chance in turn to scrutinize the young man's appearance.

He was shocked at what he saw. The boy's hair lay in a matted mess upon his head. He wore a ragged blanket over his shoulders, and he appeared to have lost much weight since his uncle had last seen him. Most shocking was his face. His cheeks were hollowed out and shadowed, his cheekbones stretching against his skin. His eyes were as hollow looking; they held a haunted look like he was afraid of something.

Fat Badger reached into a pouch and drew something out. He held out a bit of dried meat. "Have you eaten, nephew?"

Angry Cloud stared at the offering as if it was something that was entirely unknown to him.

"It's dried meat pounded with berries. It's good. Take it. Eat!" said Fat Badger.

Angry Cloud looked at the dog. She sat quietly beside Fat Badger; her head cocked to one side. He turned his eyes back to his uncle, and suddenly those hollow eyes seemed to brighten. He reached out and took the meat, biting off a small piece and chewing it experimentally. His face broke into a smile as he crouched down and took another bite. He closed his eyes and ate very deliberately.

Fat Badger took another piece out of his pouch and said, "Move closer to the fire, warm yourself." This statement made his nephew jump up and retreat a step to two away from him. The dog barked at the sudden movement but did not rise.

"What is wrong with you?" Fat Badger asked his voice sterner than he meant it to be. Angry Cloud shrank away a little farther. Deciding that he had to find a way to bring his nephew closer, Fat Badger scooted himself a ways back from the fire. "Warm yourself, please," he said as gently as he could while indicating the fire with a wave of his hand.

Watching his uncle all the while, Angry Cloud gradually approached the fire. He still chewed on the last bite of meat he had taken. Fat Badger got the impression of a frightened squirrel approaching a hand that held out a treat it dearly wanted. Looking down at the dog, he handed her a piece of the dried meat, letting his nephew think he was not that interested in him.

Eventually, the young man got near enough to the small fire to feel the warmth, and he held out his hands, the one still holding the piece of meat was closed, but with the other one he splayed out his fingers to draw in the heat. Fat Badger heard him sigh.

He squatted down and knelt near the rocks around the shallow pit. Taking another bite of meat, he leaned toward the fire still watching his uncle all the time.

"Good," said Fat Badger. He reached his hand into another pouch and held it out. "I have corn too."

Angry Cloud leaned closer and peered at the corn kernels. Wonder shone from his eyes. What has occurred to so alter him? thought Fat Badger.

Fat Badger lay them down atop one of the rocks and leaned back. His nephew gathered up the corn kernels and stuffed them into his mouth, continuing to chew.

They sat thus for several breaths, neither speaking. The air was hushed. Sounds only occurred when Fat Badger heard the crunch of the dried kernels his nephew was eating.

Straightaway Angry Cloud began to speak in a low voice that Fat Badger could barely hear. "Greetings. I had to make certain you were human. It was the dog that convinced me. They have no dogs. You could have been one of them but not with a dog. They can assume our aspect you know?"

"What do you mean?" his uncle asked.

The young man looked about himself furtively. Evidently satisfied they were alone, he continued.

"They can move freely between worlds too. Like crossing rocks in a stream. They simply step from one to the other."

"Who are you speaking of now? Who are 'they'?"

Angry Cloud paused in his chewing and looked at him pointedly. He turned his head to one side and rapidly blinked several times.

Fat Badger asked him again, "Angry Cloud, my nephew, who are you talking about?"

The youth shook his head as if to clear his mind of clouded thoughts. He shivered and resumed speaking. "I have seen them change. It is both a blessing and my burden. One moment they are as they are and then they are a man like you or, or, or I. The Great Spirit has sent them here to school us in proper behavior. We must attend!"

"Are we speaking then of the ogres?"

As soon as he uttered the term Fat Badger knew he had made a mistake. His nephew jumped up and ran off to the tree where he had been standing when he first saw him. He watched as the youth crouched there as he looked all about him, keenly surveying the hills that surrounded them.

Fat Badger waited. He ate a piece of the meat, slowly dissolving the smoky fibers in his mouth by chewing it over and over, throughly enjoying the flavor and texture. The chewing seemed to help alleviate his worry over the puzzling behavior his nephew exhibited. Was he insane?

After what seemed to be an eternity, the youth slowly crept back to sit across from Fat Badger.

"I'm sorry," said Fat Badger. He noticed that Angry Cloud looked surprised at this statement. "I didn't mean to alarm you. I came to take you home."

This explanation seemed to relax his nephew. "I am well thank you, and you?" he said formally.

Fat Badger humored him. "I am well, but I think you are perhaps not as well as you might be." responded the elder. "You have suffered long enough for something that was not your doing. Come with me now; your mother will be thrilled to see her son."

He thought he had finally gotten through to him when the young man stood up and held out his hand. Fat Badger took the hand he offered and rose with his help. As soon as he was on his feet, Angry Cloud jerked him forward so that they collided! Fat Badger heard the white dog growl menacingly. "Shah!" he said, not wanting to scare off his nephew.

Angry Cloud did not notice the dog. Placing his lips close to Fat Badger's ear the youth whispered, "Come with me, I will show you."

XXXIII

Kills Rabbits struggled up the last of the steep trail to the broad flat where the High Seat Village stood. "How do those skinny girls manage to climb this twice a day with their full water jars balancing on their heads?"

He slid back a step and caught himself before he lost his own balance. Laughing, he shook his head in wonder. Then he looked ahead at the little village emerging from the light fog that covered the valley. Turning back, he saw the low lying clouds were dense down by the streams and the creek but up here the ancestors slumbered in smaller numbers.

Approaching the gate, he was surprised to see that no guard stood outside. How strange! he thought to himself, and he called out "I am here."

Only silence answered his call. He tried again, yelling louder this time, "I am here!" his voice echoing hollowly. He stood for a few more breaths and then strode up to the gateway, walking through it unchallenged into the plaza.

Inside the walls, he saw no one. The only things moving were a pair of ravens who took flight at his appearance and a small skinny dog that slunk away along one wall.

No warming fires greeted him. No smells of cooking wafted out into the plaza inviting him in. He wandered through the village checking house after house. No one was there. In each, he found evidence that they had departed hastily. There were useful items scattered everywhere, and some clothing lay in disarray. So much was left lying about discarded.

He saw multiple footprints in the dirty snow that coated the plaza floor, but there was no way to decipher them. Some went one way, others another direction. It was all a confused jumble.

Behind one row of houses, he found evidence that someone had been digging. Looking at the size and shape of the area opened up and subsequently recovered Kills Rabbits decided it resembled nothing so much as a quickly dug grave. "How odd," he said to himself.

He carefully examined a couple of the rooms. It looked as if people had only removed what they needed and left behind what they didn't. He noticed during his search that all house fires were extinguished so undeniably they left with full intent. But why?

"And, where could they have all gone?" he wondered aloud.

—in Dead Women Canyon—

His nephew held onto his hand the whole way, leading him forward and into the upper reaches of Dead Women Canyon. The dog followed along quietly but did not get close to either of them. It was almost as if she did not fully trust Angry Cloud.

Then he stopped and released Fat Badger's hand. He indicated a shallow niche in the rock face formed by an overhang.

"They let me sleep there," Angry Cloud said. Fat Badger saw that there were a few handfuls of dried grass lying about on the floor of the enclosed space. It was approximately big enough for a person the size of his nephew to lay down and be more or less out of the elements.

He started to look up above the line of the ridge closest to them when his nephew grabbed him and spun him about roughly. "No!" he hissed. "Don't look for them!" Angry Cloud snuck a quick peek over his shoulder. "They watch us even now. I saw one of them standing up there, just so." He indicated with the barest nod the far ridge behind him where Fat Badger had looked. "They are up there. Just behind those two trees. They're watching us."

Without warning Angry Cloud sat down and pulled his uncle down with him. "They don't like it if you look at them," he said, still in a conspiratorial voice. "If they see you looking they move." He nodded with his eyes big as if telling a story to a child. "Then it is hard to find them again."

Fat Badger decided he must get his nephew away from this place immediately before his madness about the ogres became even worse.

"Thank you for instructing me as to their ways, nephew," said Fat Badger evenly. "You have been very patient and informative. But at this time you must come back with me. We will go to the house of your mother. They won't see you there. You will be safe."

He took hold on Angry Cloud's arm and started to rise. At first, his nephew rose with him docilely, and they struggled two steps back down the trail. Then his nephew yelled, "No!" and jerked his arm free. He pushed Fat Badger violently to the right plunging him over a ledge and down an incline.

The attack surprised Fat Badger completely. He rolled down the muddy, snow-littered slope for several body lengths until he managed to stop himself. Turning over and gaining his balance he looked up. The dog stared down at him reproachfully as if saying, "You fell, again, didn't you?" He scanned the ridge. Angry Cloud was nowhere to be seen.

—at High Seat Village—

Coyote Alone walked back into his village. He had not been satisfied with their precipitous flight. He wanted to scout around the area and try and gain a sense of what had happened that night when Many Elk was killed. First, he wanted to see if he had missed something in the mud and snow around the house where the boy had died.

He could not escape the feeling that he was responsible. He had been on watch before Many Elk. Playing Cat was supposed to come relieve him but he did not show up. He allowed the boy to relieve him even though Coyote Alone felt unsure that he was up to the task. He decided later, too late, that the prisoner should have been bound. Would that have made a difference? Did Digging Squirrel assist whoever it was that attacked the boy?

Coyote Alone could not shake the sense that he should have done more to prevent the ensuing tragedy.

His thoughts so consumed him that he almost missed the sign left near the house. Someone else had been here since their flight!

Instantly the warrior crouched down and surveyed the abandoned village. He studied the prints. They were of one man with sandals of an unusual weave. They looked familiar. Where had he seen them before?

"Coyote Alone!" his name shouted from close behind him made him jump to his feet and spin around ready for battle.

It was Kills Rabbits.

"What are you doing here?" Coyote growled.

"What am I doing here, you ask? Where is everyone, I respond?"

"We left the village yesterday morning, early. Everyone who was left is down at Sky Creek village."

"Why?"

"It was the closest big village —"

"No, why did you leave?"

"Our village was compromised. One warrior was killed, and two others were missing. We didn't feel we had enough men left to defend ourselves."

"You were attacked?" Kills Rabbits laced his voice with undisguised shock.

"Not so much an attack, but an unknown group infiltrated the village, and they killed a guard."

"What was he guarding?"

"What was he guarding?"

"Who," answered Coyote Alone, "he guarded the man from Many Rocks Canyon."

"Who attacked you? Was it the people of that canyon?"

"We don't know."

Kills Rabbits looked at him, his face full of surprise at the news.

"That is why I came back," Coyote continued. "I want to try and find out who it was. I mean to track them."

"There I can help you," said Kills Rabbits.

XXXIV

—in Dead Women Canyon—

Fat Badger found some current tracks of his nephew mixed with old ones, but he didn't want to spend the rest of the day trying to find the boy only to be left in the open another night. He considered having the dog try and locate Angry Cloud, but he had no idea if that would work either within the current conditions or taking the dog's attitude into account.

No, he needed to get to Yellow Stone. Working his way back down the canyon trail he thought about going overland by looping up and over the ridge to his left, but with the melting snow, mud, and lack of an established route he dismissed that idea quickly.

As it turned out it was lucky he had given that plan no credence.

Exiting the canyon Fat Badger was about to turn left and make his way to the next crossing when the dog growled, and he heard someone coming up behind him. He spun around, nearly slipping in the mud and to his surprise, he saw Yellow Stone and his acolyte, Many Cactus struggling along toward him.

"Valley Trader?" said the old man, apparently equally surprised by the chance meeting. "What brings you here?"

"Would it shock you if I said I was looking for you?" He could see skepticism in the eyes of the younger man. Was he put under suspicion by this one for being seen exiting Dead Women canyon? Fat Badger swallowed his flash of anger and answered evenly, "I might the ask the same of you elder!"

"Yes, I would guess so!" the old man laughed. He slid a little on the muddy way, and his intern grabbed his arm protectively. "We have come from a sacred task, the very one that injured your wife in her attempt to contact the ancestor spirits. Speaking of which, how fares the summer matron, your good woman?"

Fat Badger hesitated. "I am not certain. The Scorpion treats her, but last I heard she had not awakened."

"You have our prayers, Valley Trader," said the Sun Watcher.

"And I hope your prayers to the Twins are effective at slowing the multitude of blessings of our ancestors we have received of late," said Fat Badger eyeing the still clouded sky. He looked back at the tall, thin frame of the sun watcher and the slight form of his acolyte.

"So why do we find you here coming from this place?" asked Many Cactus purposely avoiding the canyon's name.

Fat Badger considered telling him it was not his business but he decided there was no use antagonizing the young man. "My nephew has secluded himself within the canyon."

It was evident to Fat Badger that both men were shocked at this news. "No!" said Yellow Stone, "Angry Cloud — here?"

"Why?" asked Many Cactus.

"I wish I understood, but I do not. I spoke to him, and my nephew seems to feel he is compelled to be here." Fat Badger answered looking back up in the canyon.

"You spoke to him?" said Many Cactus "And yet he remains?"

"Yes, I could not persuade him to return to his mother's hearth with me."

"That is a shame," said Yellow Stone. "What will you do now?"

"I will return with help after I see if Scorpion will allow me to visit Fire Star."

That caught Yellow Stone off guard once more. He looked perplexed, "He prevents you from seeing her?" he asked, incredulous.

"He feared that in my recent trials I had approached the margin between this world and the next too closely." Fat Badger answered dourly. "He voiced concern that the taint of near-death might infect my wife."

"Ah, I see." the old man reached out and patted Fat Badger on his shoulder. "As you can see I do not have that same fear," he said chuckling. "I have lived too long already."

His acolyte looked shocked, "Sir, you should not jest about such things."

Yellow Stone looked askance at the young man who held his arm. Staring at him, he directed his response to Fat Badger, "The young lack a sense of humor when faced with such weighty matters. But we know, do we not Fat Badger, that it is all part of life."

"But you can understand his concern Uncle, too many have already perished in this cold season, and we are not half way through its dark blessing," said Fat Badger.

The old sun watcher nodded and responded, "Yes, that is only too true. It is what compels me now to visit with the Vulture Priest and other leaders. We must counsel."

—west of High Seat Village—

Coyote Alone and Kills Rabbits found themselves attempting to follow the trail left by the invaders who had spirited away Digging Squirrel. They reached a point a short distance west of High Place village, and there the track bifurcated, one route going left and one to the right.

"It's possible that they have been traveling this way more than once and we are looking at older movements," offered Kills Rabbits.

"I suppose that could be," said Coyote Alone.

"So which way do we go? Or should we split up?"

Coyote Alone peered off to the left, toward Dead Women Canyon and beyond the mountains north of Sky Sweeping peak. For just a moment he felt a sense of dread of things not of this world. He shook them off and turned back to his companion.

"Split up," answered Coyote Alone. "You go right, and I'll go left."

Kills Rabbits nodded. Secretly Kills Rabbits was pleased because this meant he would be going toward the Immigrant's village and if possible it would give him a chance to check in with them.

He felt some frustration that he had so far been unable to locate the missing girl but the weather had been so unpredictable that no one could fault him much for that. Hopefully, one of two things had occurred. Either she had found her way home, or she was safely waiting out the storm somewhere.

He followed the tracks that remained in the melting snow and soon became convinced that they were part of a cold trail. Nonetheless, he continued as he spied the base of Giant's Head hill ahead of him. It would be a short trip now to reach the little village before he returned to see what Coyote Alone had found.

After all, the young warrior could take care of himself, couldn't he?

Kills Rabbits struggled up the muddy slope, slipping more than once while cursing the fact that the shrouded sky gave so little light. Ultimately, he attained the rise that overlooked the Immigrant's village. Standing there, to catch his breath, he sought to get some measure of the place, sniffing the air for the scents of cooking and listening for the endless sounds of stone crushing corn against stone.

But there came to him none of these senses. Quite unexpectedly he felt himself go cold and fear flowed through his soul. And most troubling, he could not say precisely why this was so.

XXXV

—at Sky Creek Town—

Walking into the plaza of his wife's village the first thing that impressed Fat Badger was that so few rooms showed fires outside. With the weather finally clear of snow, if not clouds, he had expected all of the matrons to be out cooking fresh hot meals for their families. Surprisingly as he passed through the outer precincts of the village, only two families that he could see were so engaged.

Arriving at his wife's rooms, he was again to be surprised.

His daughters Butterfly and Hummingbird were sitting outside a little -used lower floor storage room.

They said, "Father!" virtually simultaneously when they saw him coming.

"What has happened? Why are you two down here instead of upstairs with your mother in her rooms?" He feared what they might reply, but for the moment his worst fears were groundless.

"We have our mother here in this room, father. Grandfather Scorpion said it would be too risky to try and move her up into the second-floor rooms," answered Hummingbird.

"So the Scorpion has left then?"

"Yes," said Hummingbird. "The healer said he had done what he could, though he would return if we wanted him to."

"Did he mention taking any cautions as regards me seeing your mother?"

Hummingbird looked at her sister who shook her head, then said, "No, none that we know of.

Fat Badger nodded, "Good! How long before your other sister can rejoin us?"

"She has one more sunset I believe," Hummingbird answered. "I expect her at first light tomorrow."

He nodded once more and, pushing aside the curtain; he entered the little room where his wife lay. His daughters had done their best to clear it out and adapt the space to the care of Fire Star.

She lay on the other side of the make-shift hearth, her face pale, her breath movements barely perceptible. Someone wrapped her head in a clean cloth. Fat Badger saw the stain of blood upon the white fabric. Sage and other herbs smoldered in several small stone pots set all about her, filling the room with warm, fragrant smoke. Coals glowed in the hearth. Fat Badger knelt beside his wife and taking hold of one of her hands he breathed upon it.

She did not stir.

He began to sing his prayers for her.

—at Sky Creek Town—

Not far from where Fat Badger was caring for his wife, Thunderhead also sat, but instead of praying to the Great Spirit to intercede on a single person's behalf, as did the Trader, he struggled with his own beliefs about the entirety of his people.

He squatted at the edge of his shade outside his house looking off into the clouded sky. He had sat thus for the better part of two days only rising to relieve himself or take a bit of food and drink. He was tired. He had ushered more souls onto the way toward the land of eternal flowers in the last few weeks than he had ever been called upon to serve before. Many were elders who had succumbed as was common in the time of cold and cough. And yet several had been young, in full vitality and robust health one day and all that taken from them the next.

Most had succumbed to a thick liquid cough, persistent fever, and chills.

What did it all mean?

Were the spirits adding this to the ills that already beset their valley? How was he to interpret it all? The old priest felt his age more these days than he had ever before.

Hearing footsteps and a warning cough he turned to see Black Smoke approaching.

Thunderhead rose. He was not a tall man, half a hand's breadth shorter than average and slim to a point nearing emaciation and yet his

205

bearing and awful knowledge magnified his size to all who saw him. "Winter Chief," he said, his voice hoarse from the many chants he had sung recently, "what can I do for you?"

"I do not mean to intrude," Black Smoke began. He was of the same height as the Vulture Priest but much broader of built — square-cut like a building stone. "Visitors arrive and seek to counsel."

"Ah, yes," Thunderhead answered. "I wondered how long it would be before others came to the same conclusions I have arrived at."

"Conclusions, Thunderhead?" asked Black Smoke obviously perplexed at his response.

"No matter," the old man waved off his confusion, "we will counsel here, in my room, if that is adequate."

"Of course," answered the Winter Chief, "I will return with them." and with that, he scurried off.

Thunderhead looked about and spied one of his acolytes bringing some wood. He waved him over.

"Yes, Uncle?" asked the young man.

"We will need all that wood and more, please fetch it and find First Light and any of your brothers. We are to counsel. I fear it will be long and contentious."

—at the Immigrant's village—

Kills Rabbits cautiously walked downslope through the Immigrant's village. He heard no sounds beyond the swirling winds that danced crazily around the walls and huddled in room corners. Occasionally a blanket covering a doorway snapped in the wind. Reaching the second line of rooms, he scanned the open area before him. The fabric covered doorways rippled their mindless greetings at him, but no one emerged from those doors to add to their hollow welcome.

"This is not good," he said aloud.

Smelling a fire on the cold fingered wind, he strode around one corner to find a thin swirl of white smoke rising from beneath a large pot. The pot sat on an outdoor hearth beside a shade.

"Some sign of life at least," he ventured.

He walked up to peer into the pot. It leaned off to one side at an odd angle, up against the wall of the house. In the thin light pervading the shadows, he saw that bones covered the bottom of the pot.

"Well, that's good I guess," he continued aloud, "at least they had a filling meal before they left."

From back somewhere behind him, he heard something strike the floor within a room with a thump.

"Oho! Perhaps I am not so alone here after all!"

He scrambled back the way he had come only moments before. He looked uphill to a lone room that sat at the farthest edge of the hamlet. Seeing a small pot rolling out of that room beneath the doorway's covering he stepped quickly through the mud up to the entry and pulled the blanket aside.

Of course, the room was dark. No fire glowed in the small hearth. Kills Rabbits saw lurking shadows. There was something odd about their shape. They looked like robes hung from the rafters. Things trailed from each one, dangling down to the floor.

He stepped within but kept his hand on the blanket to keep it to one side and allow a bit of dim light to filter in behind him.

Even so, it took him several moments to accustom his eyes to the gloom within the small space. Perhaps his eyes attempted to dissuade him from the vision. Standing there, staring at the shadows, he finally recognized what he was seeing. One hand went to his forehead. He struggled back out of the doorway. His other hand went to his mouth and then his gorge spewed forth from between his splayed fingers. He collapsed retching acid bile into the snow.

XXXVI

—at the Mine village—

Laughing Fox had still not recovered enough to return to the mine. That fact vexed him greatly. He believed that they must continue their work at the mine and what's more redouble those efforts to placate the Ancestors and other spirits who were angry. Only then, he believed, would they have a chance to thwart those who cautioned against remaining in Sky Valley.

Ever since the rock thrown from above the mine killed Fox Ear the clamor from those who were frightened had risen in both volume and frequency. But Laughing Fox still hoped everything could be turned around, and life returned to normal.

Each time he attempted to rise from his pallet his head swam and once standing he felt unsteady. He often stumbled when he walked. He could not overcome these persistent symptoms. It frustrated Laughing Fox.

His wife, Flowers Wilting never failed to chastise him for even trying, and she continually harped on how he should listen to her. She knew best what he could do.

And Laughing Fox knew returning to work would be his only relief.

Adding to his misery, Lazy Tree had taken to visiting him daily to remark on his progress.

He walked into the room where Laughing Fox lay, and on cue, Flowers Wilting rose to leave and allow the men to talk. Striding across the plaza of the village, she felt good that she would now have a chance to catch up on the news of the valley. Not that there had been much to say recently, with all the snow no one ventured out far from their warm hearth.

Today though was to be different.

She saw the usual group standing beneath the shade of the Rain priest wife's house and she also quickly surmised that they were very agitated.

She heard the wife of Old Elk Eating say, "I'm told they found nothing, no tracks in the snow, just disturbed ground and mud!"

Strong Tree's wife, Twittering Bird said, "It is like the other one!"

Rushing up to the group, Flowers Wilting asked the first women she came upon, "What has happened?"

Turning toward her, she saw the other had eyes brimming with tears. "My niece," she said, her voice shaky, "I sent her out to the spring this morning for fresh drinking water. She did not return. We found her jar lying in the mud near the creek. She was taken!"

"That is awful. Are the warriors searching for her?" asked Flowers Wilting.

The woman sniffed, "One party just came back, they found no trace."

"Ogres!" said the wife of Laughing Fox.

—on the trail above the Forbidden Place—

Coyote Alone had no better luck in his search. What he hoped would be a quick scout, and perhaps the discovery of a hidden campsite of raiders became a longer and longer trail of branching footpaths in flowing mud and rapidly melting snow.

Three times he had to decide which way to follow based only on his best guess and now as he saw the trail becoming less clear he realized he had guessed wrong at least once. To his practiced eye, he suspected that someone had purposely doubled back upon old tracks specifically to confuse and mislead a pursuer.

That meant they were expecting pursuit. But who were 'they'?

He couldn't accept that the people from Many Rocks were behind this attack. It made no sense for them to attack Sky Canyon because they traded freely with them and each canyon drew their water from different sources. He knew that sometimes disputes over water had escalated into battles. But he saw no reasons for war.

Last year they had heard of two villages just a few valleys south of them who had gone to war over their shared water source. One large town was eventually attacked and burned to the ground by warriors from the other. But this, this was different.

His frustration grew with every step he took and looking skyward he realized that darkness would come early and he would have nothing to show for his efforts.

He scanned the hills. To his left, south by southwest lay the sheltered area beyond the mine where several warriors were in seclusion, stripping themselves of any taint of death associated with their recent battle. He knew that they would be released after the sunset this evening and Coyote Alone wondered if he could prevail upon them to join with him on his hunt tomorrow?

With four or five other sets of trained eyes and willing feet, they might run down his quarry and bring this to a close in a day or two. Then he could go to the people of his village and tell them it was time to return to High Seat Village.

He set out overland headed to the south-southwest.

—at Sky Creek Town—

Yellow Stone settled himself onto the floor of Thunderbird's house. Across from him, the old vulture priest surveyed the gathering. Next to him was Black Smoke, then First Light, his own clan chief, and Yellow Stone. Next to the sun watcher sat Three Trees, the leader of the Coyote clan and the rain priest, Dark Snake. It was enough. Both clan leaders, two rain priests and the representative of the sun and the nadir. Thunderhead was satisfied with the representation.

"Thank you all for assembling so quickly," he began.

"Should we wait for others?" asked Dark Snake. "I understand the Trader is also here."

"I fear we may have waited too long already," answered Thunderhead.

"What do you mean?" asked Three Trees. "Black Smoke, is this meeting your doing?"

"No, elder, it is not," answered Black Smoke, quickly.

"I am responsible here," Thunderhead said.

"Then please, Vulture Priest," said Yellow Stone slowly, "enlighten us."

Thunderhead paused, looking in turn at each man with his eyes seeking any doubt or undue worry over his leadership. Seeing none, he sighed loudly and began.

"It is not for me to instruct you. You are all men of water with grave responsibilities. You are all cognizant of the events that have here transpired within our land these last score of days and more."

Seeing nods of agreement from a few he felt emboldened, so he continued, "I am as distressed as I know all of us are by the dire portents and unprecedented happenings."

As he spoke, Thunderhead thought too. He thought of how to convince these learned men of the rightness of his intentions and the necessity of immediate implementation. As it turned out, he needn't have concerned himself about this concern. Circumstances dictated that these actions grew out of hand in proportion as rapidly as snow gathers snow in rolling downhill.

—in seclusion—

Pale Falcon waved gray smoke toward her face and inhaled the sweet sage fragrance while intoning a brief invocation to the Great Spirit asking for purification and cleansing. Her stomach growled faintly. She had eaten nothing of substance in three days chewing only some bitter bark and drinking water to maintain her strength. But her trial was nearly at an end.

Unfortunately, while her blesséd soul might attain temporary relief, her mind seethed. What was the identity of the man whose life she had taken? Why was he here in their valley, a place he did not belong? Why had he made her mother a prisoner?

All these and myriad other questions plagued her and swirled up in her mind like the dead leaves of the water tree caught in the winds of early winter; a dance of the dead destined never to know life again.

It was with some surprise and indeed no little shock that she saw a warrior striding toward her. She recognized the young man as being from the village of the Giant's Head. "Now what is he doing here?" she murmured aloud.

She rose to greet him and then held up her hands to forestall his approaching any closer.

"I am not yet fully restored!" she warned. "Please do not come any nearer."

He appeared not to have heard her and continued his approach.

"Stop!" she said sharply.

He stopped a bare body's length away. Even as she shrunk away from contact, Falcon observed he was of her height, well-made and with an odd single-minded look on his open face.

"Where are the others?"

"Others?" she asked. "What others do you speak of?"

He looked annoyed, "The other warriors in seclusion. Where are they?"

She glanced back over her shoulder. Pointing that way with her chin, she asked him, "Why? What do you want? We are not yet ready to rejoin the living."

He took another step toward her. Though it was evident to her that he intended to walk past her in the direction she had indicated. She felt compelled to repeat her warning. She was angry and becoming angrier by the moment.

"Are you deaf or stupid? I told you to stay away! My brothers and I are not yet ready to return!"

He stopped and offered her a half-smile. "We both will have to take our chances."

XXXVII

—at Sky Creek Town—

Perhaps what surprised Fat Badger the most; later, when he had an opportunity to reflect on that day, was how fast it all occurred.

So much joy, wonder, confusion, fear, and pain had all come in the matter of a few breaths.

He knew that there was a council called in the house of Thunderhead's mother. After his wife had passed some years before, the aging Vulture priest had returned to live in his mother's house. Fat Badger thought wryly how that mimicked his own move to his grandmother's house when he became Winter Chief. Is that where he got the idea? Did that make the two of them more similar than he thought?

No, his move to 'the house all alone on a hill' had been presaged many years before by his grandmother. He had merely fulfilled her prophecy for him.

Fat Badger felt no urge to join the assembled elders sitting at Thunderhead's hearth. He would have been within his right to go even though his only official post was of Valley Trader now. But Fat Badger decided his place was beside his wife. He looked down at her. She looked back at him.

Fire Star's eyes were open! He reached down and moved a stray bit of hair out of her face. She smiled at him.

He saw that her smile was not straight. Her mouth drooped slightly to the left.

"Welcome home," he said softly. He patted his wife's hand noticing that it felt cold.

She tried to answer, but her mouth did not move correctly in forming the words. The noise she made was garbled and unintelligible. Her eyes flashed with alarm.

"Later," he said, still patting her. "There will be plenty of time later. Rest now."

Her frantic eyes scanned his face. They calmed, and she closed them slowly. He could tell by her breathing that she was again asleep. Outside he heard a commotion of some kind.

Standing, he turned to walk outside and almost ran into his daughter Hummingbird entering the room.

"What is happening?" he asked.

"I am not sure, father, someone came running into the village, and everyone started talking."

"Stay here please," he said, "your mother woke briefly. I do not want her left alone."

"She woke!" Hummingbird said excitedly. "Butterfly, sister! Come here!" she called out the entry. Butterfly rushed in.

"Mother woke for a brief time!" Hummingbird said.

Fat Badger saw tears form in his other daughter's eyes. He patted her shoulder and smiled, nodding. Then Fat Badger walked out and saw a group gathered around the plaza. Walking up to them, he saw that Kills Rabbits lay upon the ground in the middle of the group. Antlers Piled Up, a village elder crouched next to him.

Fat Badger pushed through the group, excusing himself as he went, but moving determinedly. Reaching Antlers Piled Up's side, he asked, "What has happened?"

Immediately the elder looked at him, not having noticed his approach. Fat Badger was shocked by the look of terror on the older man's face. "What is it?" he asked, more sharply than he meant to.

Looking around at the various people gathered about them Antlers Piled Up stood then and took Fat Badger by the arm. He led him off to one side. Fat Badger stared at the hand placed upon his arm like it had a life of its own.

Reaching a point where he could speak without anyone else hearing, the elder said, "Something terrible has occurred!" He indicated the sprawling Kills Rabbits with his chin. "He told me!" His voice was spectral with awe implicit in his breathy tones.

"What now?" Fat Badger asked.

The elder looked around again to assure himself that they were not overheard. He turned back and stared at Fat Badger for several moments in time.

Grasping the old man by his shoulders, Fat Badger focused on him and said, "Tell me!"

His lower lip quivered. His eyes turned down while he whispered, "I cannot. It is too terrible!"

Embarrassed by his rough treatment of the old man, Fat Badger released him and patted him on his shoulder. "Yes, I see, yes. Go now, Uncle. I apologize."

He watched as the old man, his head bowed, turned and walked away from him. Fat Badger swung around on his heels then and approaching where the people were still ringing the inert form of Kills Rabbits. He used his best command voice and said, "Bring him to my wife's house."

—in Fire Star's house—

Kills Rabbits woke slowly. He looked about, not recognizing where he was.

"I had you brought here." a voice said. Turning then Kills Rabbits saw Fat Badger standing behind his right shoulder looking down at him.

"Where is 'here'?"

"You are in the house of Fire Star, the Summer Matron." That news seemed to relax the man somewhat. He closed his eyes and lay back down on the mat. "We have reversed our roles; it seems," he said. "Where once I brought you to my house when you were suffering, now you have rescued me."

"Kills Rabbits?" asked Fat Badger peremptorily, "Can you tell me what you said to Antlers Piled Up that so upset him?"

Kills Rabbits exhaled, speaking without opening his eyes. "I'm sorry about that. I shouldn't have blurted that out to that poor old man. Is he all right?"

"I'm not certain. What did you tell him?"

He whispered, "Something terrible." The hunter pushed himself up then on one elbow and opening his eyes he said, "Go to the Immigrant's village." Fat Badger noticed that the man's eyes were in shadows. There was a haunted look clinging to him. "See for yourself."

"I am asking you to tell me now exactly what I will see."

He closed his eyes again then, and though he stayed up on his elbow, his body visibly shrank and fell into itself as if the life drained from it.

"You will see what I saw and what I realized is the damnation of all who live here. I mean to leave this accursed valley as soon as possible and I suggest you and all your people do so too."

"Tell me!" Fat Badger shouted, surprised even at himself.

"What is the worst thing that you can find that has happened to people you know?" Kills Rabbits said in a small voice. "What could force people to leave their homes in the dead-time of winter?"

A voice sounded at the doorway, "Just what I have finished saying to the gathered council myself."

Fat Badger turned to see Thunderhead standing behind him, half in the room.

"But I am interested," the old man continued, speaking to Kills Rabbits specifically, "tell me, why do you say that?"

XXXVIII

In the end, they went. As a line of worried men, they passed down along the creek, turned at the trail to Giant's Head and made their way past a small deserted village and the crudely built home of Kills Rabbits. Trudging up the hill trail from the spring, they attained the flat below High Seat Village. No one even looked up to see if anyone was there. Kills Rabbits told them it too was abandoned.

They made their way carefully in the mud, melting ice and dirty snow down into the hollow where lay the village of the immigrants. As he set out Fat Badger was surprised to see that the white dog had remained behind, posting herself just to one side of the entrance to the room where Fire Star lay.

It was just as well, he thought to himself. The dog will watch over my wife.

Winds rose up from the basin, whipping at their robes and stinging their skin wherever they located it. There hung over the narrow valley a pall as if of smoke or thin fog. The wind scattered among the rocks and slapped at the bare trees. Fat Badger thought that it made the valley seem haunted.

It sounded like ghosts wailing.

Reaching the outer wall of the empty Immigrant's village, they looked at each other as if waiting to see who would go first. In the end, they went together. Entering cautiously, Fat Badger noticed the curtains of the living rooms flapping in the wind as if warning them away.

They found the large jar beneath the shade where Kills Rabbits said it would be and Thunderhead shooed the rest of the group all away from it. As Thunderhead reached for the pot, Fat Badger heard rattling and caught just a glimpse of the scatter of shattered, broken bones laying within the cook-pot.

The old priest glanced within the pot and then turned back to the group. "Follow me," he said.

Thunderhead led them back to the wall. "Stay here!" he commanded them. Then he struggled uphill to the last room. They watched as he pulled the curtain aside. Peering in, he quickly turned away. His shoulders slumped as if suddenly weighted down. He walked with uncertain steps back to where the pot sat leaning against the wall. The others could see him shaking his head at what he found within the last room. They waited.

After a long while, he got up and walked back to them.

Sitting down, his back against the wall and shielded from the wind, he said, "Now, listen carefully, you may search the rooms. Stay away from the shade," he indicated the place where the pot was, pointing with his chin. "Search the other rooms but do not go into the last room yet." They moved off, all but Fat Badger. He stayed down by the long retaining wall. After a while, Fat Badger saw the old man laboriously stand and walk back to where the pot stood.

Thunderhead appeared to him to have aged many years in the time they had been in that village.

His head still pounding, as it had all day, Fat Badger contented himself with being an observer.

Thunderbird went to work. The old priest sat, singing. He shook a rattle with his right hand while reaching into the mouth of the vessel with his left. Unhurriedly he lifted each of the individual pieces out, carefully, almost reverently, examining them in turn. He laid them down, side by side on the ground, continuously singing. When finished removing them all, he ended his song with a flourish. He exhaled and then placed them all back in the pot, without a word, also one by one.

Unwilling to go to the rooms, afraid of what he might see, Fat Badger stood off to one side and watched the priest as a curious wren might watch a badger digging through a nest of squirrels.

He heard the crunching steps of the others as they searched the rooms.

Led by Black Smoke, First Light and the other men went into the houses one after another. When they reached the farthest one, where Thunderhead had first gone, they sent one man back to tell him they were ready. Thunderhead nodded and said something to the man that Fat Badger could not hear.

The man rejoined the group at the last room.

First Light pulled aside the blanket and ducking, entered followed by the others bringing a torch. Almost immediately two of them quickly retreated out. One fell to his knees, the other bent at the waist and began retching into the snow, just as Kills Rabbits said he had done.

Black Smoke emerged and gradually walked to where Thunderhead was. They spoke in low tones for a few breaths. The new winter chief returned to the last house and evidently told the others what the priest told him.

They were galvanized into action. Fat Badger watched in amazement as if a disembodied spirit.

He heard the efforts of the four men within the room, tearing at the rafters and pulling down the walls to collapse the house upon itself, leaving its contents within. One man emerged and took up a discarded maul. He reentered. Fat Badger heard pounding.

Finally, they all emerged and began pushing and tearing at the walls to collapse the house inward.

They went then to the other rooms, gathering the net bags and baskets from them. Piling the debris upon the collapsed rooms, they sought out anything that would burn. Placing pitch and wood splinters within each house, they kindled fires and stood watching the flames consume all therein. They added wood, baskets, and blankets as they located them.

By the time they had succeeded in setting it all alight, darkness was gathering throughout the valley, furtively wandering in as shadows slinking on silent feet. Lit in reflected orange, six men stood surrounding the pyres. Their faces, seen in the wavering light, were stern and frozen in determination.

"Now come here!" Thunderhead called out. Other than his unintelligible chanting, they were the first words Fat Badger heard from the old Vulture Priest since they had been instructed to search.

Turning from the fires, Black Smoke and a warrior named Leaping Fish walked over near to the old man. "Here too," he said, pointing at the shade above the pot with his chin. "You do not need to burn this but pull down the house wall upon it to cover it all. Leave nothing showing!"

His face expressionless, he watched, as the task was completed.

—on the trail above the Forbidden Place—

With the approach of darkness Coyote Alone, Pale Falcon and three others in seclusion for having killed an enemy, made a camp on the ridge above Dead Women Canyon, very near where Tall Claw had fallen to his death so long before. They saw the fire rise from the Immigrant's village though they were too far away to ascertain precisely where it was happening.

"That looks like a house on fire," said Falcon as she chewed tough, smoky, jerked rabbit flesh. She brought it along with her when she went into fast against not being able to locate game when her trial ended, knowing that she would be famished. She said a small prayer to her ancestor hunters that her stomach would accept the food after four days without any.

Coyote Alone grunted. "It may be an abandoned house with coals that just caught." He peered through the gloaming, "I see no attempt at extinguishing it."

Thunder Sounding, a young warrior who had agreed to accompany them asked, "Who is it that you think we trail?"

Coyote Alone considered this. "I do not know, but—," he chewed a dried corn pudding and drank water from his gourd. "They are several in number I think."

"More than us?" asked the youth quickly.

The other man considered this. "Perhaps. Yes, I think a few more."

"How far away are they?"

Coyote Alone looked up at the clouded sky that was nearly dark. He drank another swallow of water and lay down rolling himself up in his robe. Looking back over his shoulder, he answered, "Too far for us to catch them tonight." Then snuggling his head down he added, "Take the first watch."

Thunder Sounding looked surprised and threw a glance at Pale Falcon. She nodded to him, and he rose to assume a place to watch over them. The rest of the group rolled into their blankets close around the campfire.

XXXIX

—on the trail to Sky Creek town—

Fat Badger trudged along just behind the Vulture Priest on their way back. He looked across the hills and saw no firelight at Grandfather Scorpion's hill. Had the fearful medicine man abandoned their valley too?

As they came to level land just below Kills Rabbit's house he hurried and caught up with the old vulture priest. The others were down at the spring, filling their gourds. They walked side by side for a few steps and then Fat Badger said, "Tell me," very quietly. Without stopping his plodding pace the old man turned to look at him, both their faces alight with the flickering flames of the small torch Fat Badger carried.

Sighing then, the old man looked back straight ahead, but, he began to intone words as if describing a list of odious chores.

"There were two in the pot. I am quite sure of that. Their skulls were in fragments, teeth scattered through the bone debris. I found a few broken rib bones but not all of them." He sighed again, "The long bones were split and scraped out, just as Kills Rabbits said. There was no flesh anywhere. Just bare bones, broken and split."

"So there can be no doubt?"

"Not for me."

"Could you, I mean, were you able to identify their sex?"

That question evidently did not surprise the old man. He answered very matter of factly, "No, there wasn't enough to be sure, but I had a feeling that there were one of each. A man and a woman, or maybe a man and a girl." The old man's voice sounded tired, and Fat Badger heard something else in his words. He heard shame.

"And in the house?"

"It was as Kills Rabbits said, four bodies, hanging from the rafters, all headless."

Fat Badger thought about this. "So that makes six of the ten people who lived there. Where are the rest?"

221

"I do not know," Thunderhead answered wearily. Then he repeated, "I do not know."

Fat Badger asked him, "Have you ever heard of this before?"

Once again the ancient priest hesitated before replying. "Yes," he began slowly, "I would say twice I have heard of such a thing. Something similar."

Fat Badger said nothing, he waited.

"One time, it was long ago, somewhere far away from here. A small family was trapped by snow, excessive snow, a blizzard." He looked around him. "Perhaps it was like what we have experienced these last days." He paused and slowed his pace so that the people walking in front of them drew a little farther away. "One died and the others were starving. They did what they had to to survive."

Fat Badger said, "We burned food at that village, they had much corn stored away."

Thunderhead nodded, "I noticed." He paused, Fat Badger heard the 'plop' of his walking stick hitting the soft ground. "I have heard other stories too," he went on. "Strange, horrible tales of people far to the south of here. Terrible people who practice the eating of human flesh as intimidation to their enemies. Or maybe as a dreadful ritual."

Fat Badger spoke, "But that is in the far south, where other strange people live. I have heard there are people who make war always. They are the ones you mean?"

"Just so," answered Thunderhead.

"Which means neither example you have heard of applies to this place."

"Yes, that is true. Which means it is someone or — something else."

—in Dead Women Canyon—

Angry Cloud did not think of himself in those terms anymore. He wasn't sure what his name was, but he knew it would come to him before long. Just the proper time spent waiting, and it would be revealed. It meant careful observation and an awareness of his place in the world. It would all become clear to him in time. Of that he was satisfied.

He sat up against the same tree where the man had sat just a day before. Wasn't it? Wasn't it one day before this day? He put his hands up to his head and shivered with the cold. Yes, one sun had come and gone, seen only as a pale glow behind dark clouds. He had talked to that man just one day before.

It had been a man, hadn't it? Yes, he remembered the dog! There couldn't be any doubt if there was a dog with him, of that he was also certain.

That man had said he was Fat Badger, his uncle. Could it be true? He mentioned that Angry Cloud had a mother who was worried about him. But he wasn't Angry Cloud anymore so that couldn't be true.

Now he waited for a sign. He was unsure where or when that sign would come. It might be another human that delivered it. Or perhaps an animal would appear and make the wishes of the Great Spirit known to him. Or maybe a messenger from the sacred others would come and direct him. After all, he alone had seen them and lived.

He felt so blessed that he had been chosen above all others.

He shivered with cold again.

Even if it was those creatures that finally made the facts clear to him it was something to be cherished.

It might even be dark enough to venture a peek at them.

He peered into the darkness trying to see if the sacred one stood behind the oak tree on the second ridge, watching him still. He strained his eyes attempting to separate distinct shades of darkness from each other. It was like taking a tightly woven basket apart, warp and weft.

It was too dark. The blessed one could not make out the distant shadowy form. Maybe the others had gone to sleep. Did they have beds? He smiled. He had so much to learn. He believed they still watched him. From now on he was destined never to be alone. They would always be there, somewhere, just hidden from all but the keenest eyes; watching, always, watching him.

The chosen one!

He pulled his robe tight around his shoulders. Something caught his peripheral vision. A glow rose up high on the hills in the darkness to his left. Something burned, and it was a great fire!

XL

—in Sky Creek town—

Fat Badger stood outside the house watching people argue back and forth. There couldn't be three score left in a village that had once held four times that many people but, nonetheless, the acrimony between them was palpable.

He shared little of what he saw at the Immigrant's village. None of them did. But the rumors fairly flew through the gathered crowd.

Thunderhead stood to the back of the group that was urging immediate abandonment of the valley. Though he took no part in the argument, it was patent that he lent his support to that contingent. Standing against them were those who cautioned that they should wait until they were sure that the weather had cleared.

No one argued for staying any longer than that. It was only a matter of when they would leave. The news of what had happened at the Immigrant's village, sketchy as it might be, ensured that no one would stay in their valley any longer than necessary.

It was too terrible.

Of passing interest to Fat Badger was that the leader of the group wanting to stay for now seemed to be Black Smoke. That fact at least assured him that there had likely been no collusion between the new Winter Chief and Thunderhead in his installation into the position.

Not that it mattered. Fat Badger didn't care anymore. His entire world was turned upside down. Things he had held as truth meant nothing to him. What he had witnessed in the last few days altered every part of his life and thoughts. He felt like a leaf carried along a rushing stream, buffeted by the ripples and bounced from rock to rock. He had lost control.

The thing that most worried him now was the turmoil that had arisen within his family. His daughters, Butterfly, and Hummingbird both wanted to stay to care for their mother. For Butterfly it could be a problem, but in the case of Hummingbird, it amounted to a moral dilemma. If her mother did not recover, she would assume the position of Summer Matron, the only one of their key roles that was hereditary — the ranking female of her clan held the job. That meant if the vote was for leaving now, she must go and leave her mother.

It was worrisome. Yes, he knew that Butterfly was competent to stay and care for her mother, but it would rob Hummingbird of one of her best advisors.

Fat Badger decided he must act on this one last thing.

Entering the room where Fire Star slept he saw that both of the young women looked tired. The care alone was enough to tax them without the added stress of a possible exodus, and their resultant split. He hoped he at least had made the right decision!

"She has not changed?" he asked.

Hummingbird looked up and shook her head. "They argue still?"

He smiled wearily and nodded 'yes'. "But I want no argument."

"What do you mean, father?" asked Butterfly.

"Whenever they decide to leave, both you two will go with them!"

"Both of us?" asked Butterfly. "How?"

Hummingbird looked stricken, "What of mother?"

Fat Badger smiled at them, "I will care for your mother." He saw their eyes go wide at first and then; he saw that they accepted the wisdom of what he decided.

Keeping an ear tuned to the talks in the plaza even as he delivered his decision to his daughters, he realized decision-making was in progress outside their house too.

A man named Curved Claw spoke eloquently for Thunderhead's faction. Fat Badger could hear the process unfold.

"No one ever intended any of this to occur, surely no one wished it. Yet here we stand, faced with irreconcilable facts: a man fell," he glanced around the assembled group, "or was thrown from the sky! This happening alone was an unprecedented event! Then, coincidentally, our War Chief dies, also because of a fall from a high place." He looked to make sure everyone was listening, "More snow than we have ever seen falls upon our valley and . . ." here he waved his hand toward the sky, " . . . our ancestors yet linger in uncountable numbers."

There were nods from many as they looked skyward.

225

"Several women are missing, and that has not happened since — since the terrible things that occurred in that one place." He saw several people look down. Within his wife's house, Fat Badger wondered about this argument. He knew of one woman who was missing, but several?

"Finally an unspeakable act is committed upon innocents." The speaker emphasized his words by deepening his voice and exhaling forcefully. Then Curved Claw paused and looked at all the people gathered around him, taking extra time to observe the members of the other faction before continuing. "I know this is a fateful decision for us all. I cannot help but believe that our path is already marked out for us. Those greater than we are have decreed that we must leave Sky Valley and we must do so now!"

Fat Badger heard a woman ask, "But where will we go?"

"We have relatives, brother and sister Brown Ant people just a few valleys southeast of here," Curved Claw replied. "We can make carriers for the old and the infirm and be there in a few days."

Fat Badger heard another voice, "If it does not snow again!" He left his daughters and went back outside.

"I am done speaking," said Curved Claw. As he sat down, Black Smoke rose as if to speak next but he was interrupted by a shout from someone to the rear of the crowd. "Look!" the woman said.

Most turned their eyes toward her and then they too looked where she pointed. Across the stream from where they gathered, dozens of people were hurrying along the northern trail toward the crossing spot to Sky Creek Village.

Fat Badger picked out two men with a litter amid the mass of people hurrying — walking quickly or running east to the ford. He was closer to the group than the people in the plaza, and he ran to the edge of the stream and hailed them.

"What are you doing?" he shouted. At first, no one stopped to reply, so he cried the challenge again. A young man paused and looked at him. It was Lazy Tree.

He motioned Fat Badger toward the crossing and then made his way there. He stood breathing heavily as the trader crossed over to him. People continued to rush by them as they faced each other on the north bank.

"Lazy Tree what has happened?" Fat Badger asked, noticing as he did that all the people in the group were from the Mine Village. That surprised him.

Mine village had steadfastly refused to consider leaving the valley so far. *What could have caused this stampede?* wondered Fat Badger.

Finally catching his breath the young miner watched as the last of the people from his village passed him. When they were out of earshot, he looked at the former Winter Chief with frightened eyes.

"The Ogres," he said his voice breathy and awed. "They threw terrible things down to within sight of Mine village!"

"What things?" asked Fat Badger his voice sounding tired, desperate and full of his unconcealed exasperation. "What now?"

Lazy Tree leaned toward him; his voice sounded high-pitched and amazed, "Heads! They threw human heads!"

—on the trail above the Forbidden Place—

Pale Falcon walked beside Coyote Alone, each scanning the ground for signs. Their little war group arrived at the fork in the trail above the mine and only at the last moment did they see the indication in some old snow that a party of several men had passed the same way sometime before. Their trail went west.

Since then they had been able to locate enough signs that convinced them they followed the track of an unknown group of people who had passed recently. Coyote Alone felt they were only a day or less behind them. That made him nervous but also encouraged him. If the others they followed did not fear pursuit then by moving as fast as possible might bring them into sight somewhere ahead of them on the trail.

But Pale Falcon felt troubled. Something was not right. Initially, she worried that they were being encouraged to blunder into a trap. But both she and Coyote Alone were practiced and experienced warriors. Surely one of them would notice the tell-tale signs before they fell irrevocably into place.

And it was not just that. Falcon felt that she was missing something important. Some bit of information eluded her. She simply could not ascertain what it was.

Finally, when it became too dark to continue along the high treacherous trail and not wanting to light torches that might give away their pursuit to their quarry, Coyote Alone stopped and looked at Pale Falcon. He said, "We should sleep some at least and start at first light." She nodded her agreement. She held up her hand to the others, and they looked around to find a place to rest.

While they searched, Falcon moved closer to Coyote and asked, "Have you noticed that the trail we are following seems to be heading for Many Rocks Canyon?"

"Yes," answered Coyote Alone. "I am not that surprised."

XLI

—at Hill-All-Alone—

Before the last people left Sky Creek Town, Fat Badger agreed to move Fire Star. He constructed a simple travois and loaded her on it. Fire Star was in and out of consciousness during the trip.

They reached Hill-All-Alone at midday.

Fat Badger remembered clearly when last Fire Star was here. She visited his grandmother's house just before the old woman had passed on, bringing her some soup. Then, he remembered, she had walked up the steep hill and into the house carrying a stew pot with dinner for them effortlessly. Now Fat Badger carried her. He realized she might never walk up here on her own again.

He noticed how easy it was to pick her up. Already much of her once generous flesh had melted away. Had this happened just since she was found in the snow? He thought she weighed no more than an adolescent child.

He positioned her in a corner so she would not have to work too hard to keep herself from falling over. Placing some partially burned nubs of wood in the hearth to warm the room he fanned the fire and was soon rewarded with a swirl of smoke. The stew he left simmering outside was filling the little room with a delicious fragrance, and he hurried back out to fetch her a bowl.

He thought about the leave-taking. The events at the Mine village had swung the vote almost unanimously in favor of those who wanted to abandon the valley immediately. Without any argument everyone set about to prepare for the unprecedented abandonment of their homes in the dead of winter.

Fat Badger hoped that would not be the result, a long remembered winter of death!

Soon after watching another group of people of Sky Creek village walk out of sight that morning he returned to the room to find Fire Star awake again. Fat Badger almost turned to run out to try and catch up with his daughters to let them know. But instead, he sat her upright and saw how it was with his wife.

Her mouth remained crooked, and her left arm hung down useless beside her. Speaking to her, she responded only with garbled noise and hearing that noise, caused fear to show in her eyes, even in her half-closed left eye. She knew things were not right.

He decided it was better that their daughters not see her like this.

Chatting with her he had let pass the fact that they were alone for now but she would see her family later. Her right eye widened in wonder at this information and she waved her right hand at him.

Leaning down, he had brought his ear close to her mouth. She mumbled something.

He looked at her. "I'm sorry," he said, "what?" He leaned back down.

She struggled to say words, but only garbled sounds came out.

Then he had an epiphany. He opened his eyes wide, "Grandmother, my grandmother's house?"

She nodded.

So it was they had come to his grandmother's rebuilt house. Emerging with her from her little storage room he saw the white dog following them up the hill. It now lay by the hearth watching them.

Using a doubled yucca leaf, he fed her by sips. She shook her head 'no' when he offered bits of meat and continued to drink only the rich broth. Her left eye stayed half-closed in the dim room as it had in the morning's bright sunlight while they were outside. Occasionally a bit of the soup dribbled from the left corner of her mouth. Fat Badger patiently caught these drips in a clean cloth. Though she did not try to talk he knew she was embarrassed that she could do so little for herself. To alleviate her embarrassment, he kept up a continuous recounting of the day's news.

"Butterfly collected these herbs for me from her larder. She said they were your favorites with rabbit." Fire Star blinked in agreement. "She also said to simmer some beans with it, but I didn't have any. Hummingbird argued that the beans weren't necessary as long as I had cornmeal."

She closed her eyes and smiled.

"That daughter of yours has taken to her new duties quite well," he gossiped. "I think she means to make sure that no one forgets who her mother is and how the tasks of summer matron are performed. She will make you proud. You will see when we go to visit them."

He caught sight of a ghost of a smile at the corner of her mouth.

"I also hope Falcon has reconciled herself to not having been chosen as War Chief. She would have made a good one, but it is unprecedented. Perhaps one day her daughter will change that." He noticed the unspoken comment in her eyes, "Yes, you are correct in that, I agree, this is only if she ever finds a man who can tolerate her as a mate." He laughed for the both of them. He saw the bowl was near empty. "You have almost finished this serving, would you care for another?"

With some effort, she shook her head, 'no'. He saw little beads of sweat standing out on her forehead from the attempt. Reaching out with her good right hand she patted the floor next to her, and Fat Badger put down the bowl. He slid over to the spot. She leaned against him and put her head on his shoulder. For a time he heard her breathing as if in sleep. He pulled up a blanket to cover her. They stayed thus for half of the allotted light of the short winter day.

Shadows began creeping up to the doorway from outside as she shook herself awake. He leaned in and breathed of her hair. Then Fat Badger roused himself, restored the hearth fire and, turning back to her; he asked if she were hungry. She shook her head 'no' as he suspected she would. She made a motion toward the blanket covering the doorway.

"What do you want?" he asked. She shook her head again and then looking beyond him she again indicated the doorway. "You want to go outside?" he asked. She nodded.

He looked at the curtain covering the opening. The sun was retreating, leaving the sky, cold would become master of their land soon. "It will be chilly," he said. He looked back at her with all the doubt he could muster added to his features, but she was insistent, pointing again. Fat Badger relented and gave in to her wish, stopping first to wrap her securely in a blanket before he picked up her spare form and carried her out into the dusk.

They sat on a row of rocks he had placed for the express purpose of observing the setting sun. She leaned against him, and he said nothing. As the last streak of flame left the western sky, he shivered and smiled at her. "You will catch a chill!" Fat Badger said.

She gave him half a smile; the left side of her mouth grimacing instead. She motioned to her mouth.

"Oh, you are hungry? That's good!"

She shook her head. With her right hand she mimicked bringing a bowl to her mouth to drink.

"Oh thirsty, you are thirsty. Here I have water."

She shook her head again and pointed to the doorway. He looked back and then said, "Do you want tea? Is that it?"

She smiled. He got up and said, "I can brew some. I have warm water on the hearth inside." She nodded and then held up her arm. He looked at her. She motioned him toward her. He understood. He leaned down and hugged her fiercely. He noticed her response was weak, but she lingered in his grasp a long time. Finally, she released him.

"I will get the tea," he said. "Are you certain you are warm enough?"

She gave him her crooked smile. The beads of sweat were back and her eyes were watery.

He disappeared into the house and pulling a bag down he emptied some dried leaves into the jar that sat by the glowing coals. Using a cloth, he moved it to sit close to the heat and waited while it simmered. He looked over his shoulder toward the curtained entry in worry once or twice, but because the water was already warm, it didn't take too long.

Stirring the leaves around he saw that the water had the proper color and smelled delicious. He realized he was famished. Taking up some corn cakes he grasped the pot rim with the cloth and strode back outside. It occurred to him he would have to learn to be a better cook.

The retreating red sun had broken through the clouds. Though it was near the end of the day, he noticed the air had warmed considerably.

"Here is your tea my de . . ." he stopped. She was hunched over, slumped down upon her lap. He took another step and saw the blood.

Dropping what he was carrying Fat Badger hurried to Fire Star. He did not even hear the pot shatter as it hit the ground. He did not feel the warm tea splash against his legs.

Grasping her shoulders, he rolled her back. She held a blade in her right hand. There was a clean wound across her throat. Her blood had spurted out over an arm's length from her body, nearly across the hearth.

Laying by the doorway, the white dog suddenly sat up and howled long and low.

XLII

Pale Falcon and Coyote Alone arrived at one of the outlying villages of Many Rocks Canyon. Not wanting to alarm the inhabitants of the little compound, they left the other three back among the oak and junipers.

They stood in full view of the little hamlet's inhabitants so they could judge how to deal with their visitors properly.

After some time two men walked out of the gate to greet them. One was older, and Pale Falcon assumed he was a man of some prestige. "Ho Uncle," she said tentatively, "we are here."

"Welcome, I am Mouse Climbing, and this," he indicated the man standing next to him, "is Shining Star. It is not often we see visitors in winter. Why have you come?"

Coyote Alone answered, "I am Coyote Alone, my village was attacked by some people unknown, and they took a man from us. We search for the perpetrators of these crimes."

"A man was taken?"

Coyote Alone nodded.

"That is strange," answered Mouse Climbing. "We have had three women disappear from our villages, but no men have been taken."

"Yes," said Pale Falcon, "we spoke with a man from one of your villages. He told about two of the women."

"A man from our village?" said Shining Fish quizzically. "Who was that man?"

"He said his name was Digging Squirrel."

Mouse Climbing looked surprised, "A small man, well-dressed in a white and brown blanket, he had a scar from a bracelet being cut away from his arm?"

"Yes," said Pale Falcon.

"He is not of our valley!" said Mouse. "He came from the west complaining that women were abducted from his village at the edge of the White Ant land!"

"What?" said Coyote Alone.

"He was here some three or four moons ago. He was a troublemaker. He spread rumors and encouraged discontent. We banished him!"

"He also spread rumors among our people?" said Coyote. "It took us some time to discover who was behind them."

"Exactly that, we shunned him and drove him from our villages for just those things!"

Coyote Alone turned to look at Pale Falcon.

"We have been stupid," said Falcon. "We should return now!"

—at Hill-All-Alone—

Fat Badger buried his wife at the west edge of the flat space where his grandmother's house stood. It would give her the best view of the valley she loved.

Like gentle winter rains, his tears fell continuously throughout his labors. He did nothing to try and stem their flow.

The white dog watched him the whole time, laying only a few feet from the new grave.

Finished he gathered up all he felt might be useful and after putting it in a basket to carry on his back, he then set fire to his grandmother's house. He merely watched as it burned this time rather than trying to save things from the conflagration. When the roof collapsed, he turned his back on it and started walking down the hill.

His mind swirled in turmoil for a time, then he stopped. He looked at the distant hills. Fat Badger started off purposefully to the northwest, the white dog following behind him.

Turning his face toward the northeast as evening was approaching he entered Dead Women Canyon. The white dog hung back a few steps behind him as if unsure of why they were returning here again. Fat Badger noticed much of the snow was melting while he plodded steadfastly through the canyon up the trail to where he had met Angry Thunder on a few days before. As he went, he kept his eyes scanning back and forth looking for some signs of where his nephew might have gone.

Fat Badger felt an all-consuming need to find the young man and persuade him to come with him.

As the sun slipped below the horizon, he reached the top walls of the canyon. He walked right past the narrow overhang where his nephew said he slept as he saw no sign that Angry Cloud had been there recently. The air turned purple with approaching night.

Using an agave stalk as a walking stick, he attained the highest ridge of the canyon and huffing and puffing he stopped.

Directly ahead of where he stood he saw an oak tree. Leaning up against that tree was an ogre!

Fat Badger almost turned then and ran away, but he stayed his fears. Cautiously he approached the fearsome creature. It didn't move. Standing taller than any man he knew dark fur covered it from the top of its head to its feet.

And, Fat Badger saw it was not real. It leaned awkwardly against the tree. He walked right up to the ogre and went behind it. Someone had built a wooden frame and then covered it with hairy skins. Most of the fur appeared to be from a black bear. Looking at the ground around the base of the structure, he saw the model had once stood upright. Formerly, it would've been more than half again as tall as a man.

Looking at the ground, he saw an odd-shaped rock. Leaning against the back of the framework, it served as support.

He eyed the rock. Initially, it formed naturally somewhat flat. Someone had reshaped it. It was cut into a rough square with two knobs at one end, opposite each other, like handles. Looking at it closely, Fat Badger realized it was the same pinkish rock he had found in Tall Claw's pocket.

He saw that the end opposite the knobs was fractured. So this might even be the same stone. It was broken and then used to help shore up the base of the fake 'ogre'. What had Wind Killer said the rocks were used for at his old village? Were they weights of some kind?

Turning, he looked back the way he had come. In the rapidly fading light, he could barely see the area where Angry Thunder had his sleeping place. Someone built this mock-up of an ogre and put it here so that the boy could see it standing against the horizon.

The White dog growled.

Fat Badger turned and, looking at the little beast, he said, "It's not real, dog . . ." Then he noticed that the dog was looking past the 'ogre' at something else.

Fat Badger raised his eyes and saw a ghost emerge from the junipers in front of him.

To his surprise, the ghost yelled, "No!" and simultaneously Fat Badger felt a powerful blow against his back followed by a burning pain. He was thrown to the ground. He heard the dog growling and barking. It sounded far away.

Before he lost consciousness, the last thing he heard was a loud yelp.

XLII

—the Forbidden Place—

It was like swimming to the surface from deep underwater. Slowly Fat Badger regained consciousness. At first, he thought he was again lying in the home of Tall Claw then he saw that this structure was of a much cruder construction. Looking around him, he saw he was not alone. A young woman slumped against one wall of the house opposite him. He thought he recognized her as belonging to the Mine village. She was bound both hands and feet and gagged. Another one was to his right, similarly bound. This one he recognized as being from the Immigrant's village. "Hey," he said.

Trying to push himself up Fat Badger realized his hands were also tied behind him.

Then he heard a voice coming through the entry in the roof saying, "Lord, he is awake."

Men scrambled down a notched log. Hands grasped him on either side, and he saw two strange men helping him stand up and pushing him up the ladder toward the roof opening.

Hands reached down to assist him coming out, and he emerged into the bright morning light, blinking rapidly. He was dropped summarily to a sitting position on the ground.

Looking around, he saw he was in the little village of Dead Women Canyon. It was the abandoned one from some years past.

Still blinking in the light, he saw a shadowy figure looming over him. As it sat down, he recognized the ghost he had seen the evening before.

"How are you my brother?" asked the ghost.

"You are dead, aren't you?" asked Fat Badger.

The ghost laughed, "Evidently not, little brother," he answered.

"It is indeed you then, Drinking Bird?"

"Yes, I'm afraid I have been forced to deceive a few people because it served my purpose to do so. I allowed the story to continue that I was dead;

killed in a raid." He looked around and then back at Fat Badger. Lowering his voice, he said, "By the way, I am known as Two Ravens now."

Fat Badger looked around also. He saw three men standing off to one side. Further on he saw Digging Squirrel. Up above them rose the ridge Fat Badger attained the night before. His thoughts were swimming. "How long have you been here?" he asked as he closed his eyes and dropped his head down to his chest.

"Quite some time," answered Two Ravens. He took hold of Fat Badger's arm, "Here let me help you up; I want to show you something."

Even with help, he stood wobbling from side to side. His steps were tentative, placing each foot slowly in front of him, he made his way into a clearing behind some junipers.

His brother let him down carefully, leaning him up against one of the trees. Fat Badger looked in front of him.

About two body lengths away was a framework of logs and ropes. Centered in the middle of the framework a log about two body lengths long leaned at an angle. It was attached unevenly to another set horizontal across the construct. Two-thirds of this log was above the horizontal piece and bear's fur covered it. *Like the fake ogre,* Fat Badger thought to himself. The shorter end lay against the ground. Fat Badger saw that there were four large square rocks tied to the lower end of the log, two on each side at the ends.

"What is that?"

"That is 'the ogre'," his brother answered laughing.

"Where did you — how did you get it?"

"Funny you should ask, you were good friends with the man, Wind Killer were you not?" answered Two Ravens with a question.

"Yes, why?"

"He is the one who gave me the idea for this; I call it the 'throwing beast'." He waved his hand at the tied up logs and stones.

"You knew Wind Killer?"

"Yes. As Two Ravens I came to his village where I saw an ingenious thing he had built to allow him to open and close gates of some canals. By the way, you speak of him as if he is dead. As far as I know, he is still alive."

"But his village!"

"He escaped."

"He escaped that slaughter?" asked Fat Badger tentatively.

Two Ravens smiled. "That was a masterstroke was it not? It assured the valley's abandonment."

"Wait? You did that?" Fat Badger stared at his brother.

"I have to admit my culpability in that action. We needed one final act to convince the people who remained in the villages that the valley was irrevocably damned!"

"But it appeared that those people were slaughtered and eaten!"

Two Ravens shook his head, "You always were a gentle soul. My poor brother, you have lived in this backward land too long. In my travels to great towns far to the south, I learned that nothing frightens poor country folk more than being devoured by their powerful lording enemies!" And then he laughed long and loud.

"So they weren't actually eaten by you? You merely made it look that they were?"

Two Ravens simply smiled in response to this question. Fat Badger decided not to press it. He didn't want to know the answer.

What did his brother want? Fat Badger asked himself. Fat Badger thought about it. He noticed that his shoulder ached. "Why am I bound?" he said.

Two Ravens reached over and slashed the thongs holding Fat Badger's hands together. "That was for your own protection," he said.

Rubbing his wrists, Fat Badger reached around and felt a wound on his back. "What's this?"

"Yes, that was unfortunate," said Two Ravens, "I could not stop my man who sought only to protect me. Fortunately, your basket on your back deflected the arrow, so the wound was not severe."

"What of the women that I saw in the room?"

"What of them?"

"Why are they here?"

Two Ravens thought about this. "Men have needs that women can alleviate."

"So you take women hostage?"

"Hostage?" answered Two Ravens smiling again. "Hostage implies that we would allow them to go back." He shook his head, "No, we take no hostages."

Fat Badger leaned back against the oak. "I am more confused than when you started explaining things to me. What is all this about?"

"Come brother; surely you can see what we want. I will admit it all started quite by accident with that fool who fell to his death! I thought that accident might be our undoing but as time went on it worked to our advantage."

"I'm sorry, I do not see. Are you talking about the falling man?"

"Exactly, brother you do see. The man who 'fell from the sky' or was he 'thrown to his death by ogres'," he laughed. "It was perfect."

"No, I still do not understand. What happened to him?"

Half turning Two Ravens waved his hand at the 'beast' as he called the framework of logs, ropes, and stones.

"My 'Throwing Beast' does just that. We pull the long end down to the ground, prop the stone-lined end up with a log set into the notch. Then we place something on the fur-covered end." He pointed at the bear's fur on it. "Then, knocking the log away, the four rocks fall, the weight of them pulls the other end up very rapidly and whatever is on the end is thrown a great distance."

He turned back to look at Fat Badger sitting against the tree. "Unfortunately as we were setting up one day across from the mine the log slipped while a man was sitting on the end straightening the covering. He was hurled out about two body lengths into the air and down he fell." He shook his head. "It was a mistake but a good one."

"So that's why he appeared to fall from the sky."

"Yes and we were just able to disassemble the beast and hide before your War Chief came up the trail. It was a near thing. Our plan was almost exposed before we even got started."

Fat Badger looked at him, "Your plan?"

"Yes. After that, we realized we could move farther away as the beast was more powerful than we thought so we reassembled it above the mine on the other side and put the plan into action."

"But why?"

XLIV

—on the trail from Many Rocks Piled Up Canyon—

Pale Falcon and Coyote Alone were pushing their men hard; they ran back along the trail they had made as quickly as possible.

Stopping only a short time to sleep in the darkest part of the night they were up again at the first hint of light and back on the trail. Stopping at a small spring to quench their thirst they allowed a brief pause in their headlong flight.

"So you think that this is all part of a plan?" asked Coyote Alone.

"I think it must be," answered Pale Falcon, "there must be men orchestrating this whole charade to their own benefit."

"But why do that?" asked the other.

Pale Falcon thought about this. "I do not know exactly, but I think it must be related to the missing women and the fact that the mine was targeted."

"Those two things do not appear to be related in any way."

"No, they do not."

"And what about the evidence of the ogres, the fact that they were seen by your cousin and the things they threw that could not have been thrown that far by any man."

"Yes, I know. I do not have all the answers yet."

"And how could a group of men hide within the valley, even if they were on the edges. They should have been discovered."

"The Red Ants were not seen for quite some time."

"But eventually they were!" said Coyote Alone.

"But if they had located in Dead Women Canyon or the Forbidden Place? Would they have been found?"

Coyote Alone opened his eyes wide in wonder. "I had not thought of that possibility!"

"Me neither," said Pale Falcon. "It only occurred to me when the man from Many Rocks Piled Up was speaking that they must be hiding somewhere in proximity to both places."

—the Forbidden Place—

Fat Badger and his brother walked back up to where the fake ogre leaned against the tree.

"So you created this whole illusion of the ogres being angry at us and threatening us on purpose?"

"Of course."

"The footprints?"

"Yes, we made those with a wooden form and pounded it into the mud and then flipped it over to do the other foot." He laughed, "Brilliant, is it not?"

"That is not the word I would have chosen," answered Fat Badger. "And my nephew saw just this made-up ogre model and that was his proof?"

"No, what he saw as he came running up the trail was our throwing beast's arm rising over the trees throwing another rock. That sight alone was proof enough for him. This bit," he indicated the fur covered mock ogre, "was just to keep him convinced."

"And the heads?"

"Oh, those were real. My last masterstroke to force any recalcitrant village fools into leaving. The people of Mine village were most stubborn. Once they thought the ogres were killing people and ripping their heads off — well, would you stay in such a place?"

"So why tell me all this now?"

"Isn't obvious my little brother? Why else? I want you to work with me. With your skill at trading, we can become wealthier than our wildest dreams. We will market the 'bits of sky' all over the White ant world and thence even further south to the dog eaters and farther!"

He waved his hands across the sky as if to capture the entirety of it. "Even now I have my workers back in the valley making more of the weight stones. Then I will build another throwing beast and then another! We will control all the sky stone there is! Our miners will extract the stone at a greater pace than has ever been seen. Everyone will come to us! We will have all we want and more."

Fat Badger saw something ahead of them. He walked over to it. It was the white dog. Pierced through its body by an arrow, its eyes were closed as if in sleep. Fat Badger knew at once it was dead.

"Who shot my dog?"

"Oh that!" said his brother. "One of my men put an end to the vile beast. Don't worry you will be able to keep a hundred dogs!" He placed his hand on his shoulder. "What do you think brother? Are you ready to become wealthy?"

Fat Badger did not turn around, "What do I think?" his voice was low and his words were spat out. "I think you are insane!"

Pain screamed through the wound on his back, and Fat Badger fell onto his knees next to where the dog lay. Turning his head back, he saw his brother standing over him with his war club in his hand; his face screwed up in anger.

"You always were the stubborn one. That is why father never took you into his confidence like he did with me."

"Father?" Fat Badger bit off the words through his pain. "What does he have to do with it?"

Two Ravens stepped closer to him, brandishing his war club. "Who do you think created Dead Women Canyon?"

"What are you saying?" Fat Badger asked. "Are you saying our father was a murderer?"

"A murderer? No! He was a man! He took what he wanted! You are such a fool!" Two Ravens stalked around the prone form of Fat Badger. "His greatest mistake was taking the sister of Tall Claw. When he got old enough, Tall Claw figured it out and took his revenge. Now, I have also seen my revenge come to fruition!"

"But our father disappeared on a hunting trip!"

"No! My father was supposedly lost on a hunting trip. Your father, well, let's just say there is some confusion as to your father. But I'm willing to overlook that minor point. We share the same mother!"

"What are you talking about? I don't think I believe you!"

"Believe what you will! Last chance, little brother, are you with me or against me?"

Fat Badger paused. He looked up at a stranger who lorded over him.

This man was not his brother. "I cannot join you," said Fat Badger. "You are totally insane."

Two Ravens rose up raising his arm with the war club threateningly, "Sorry you feel that way, I will make this —"

Fat Badger heard the twang of a bow and saw his brother start as the sound of a 'thump' came to him. He looked down and pulled his robe open. Fat Badger saw an arrow point sticking out of Two Raven's chest. As he lay there watching he heard another 'twang' and the sound of an arrow rushing through the air. A second point emerged suddenly from his brother's chest.

Two Ravens, a surprised look on his face, fell to the earth. More arrows filled the air.

—the Forbidden Place—

Later, as he sat against a log from the "throwing beast", he looked at his daughter. Pale Falcon sat across from him her arm around the still shuddering shoulders of a young girl from the house.

"You are Tree Cliff Sitting," he said gently. 'I have seen you at your — " Fat Badger stopped himself suddenly embarrassed.

She looked up at him and nodded.

"I am sorry for your loss. I will see that you get to wherever you wish to go."

"I have no one," she said. She pointed with her chin at the bodies that lay a little ways away. "They killed my family. They, they-they cut off . . ."

"Do not speak of what they did," Pale Falcon said to her. "It was a vile, inhuman thing and they have paid for it with their miserable lives." She looked up at her father suddenly realizing what she had said.

Fat Badger spoke to his daughter. "Your mother would have been proud of you today."

"She never woke from her deathlike sleep then?"

"No," said Fat Badger quietly looking away. "After we arrived at my grandmother's house she collapsed again. She passed from this world without regaining her consciousness and died quietly." He surprised himself at how easily the lie came from him. "I buried her near my grandmother's house overlooking the valley."

"That was a good choice," his daughter said.

The lie burned in him. He felt the need to change the subject before she questioned him more closely. "What does Coyote Alone propose to do with the two prisoners?"

"He says he will leave the wounded white ant as a slave somewhere far from here. But Digging Squirrel he wants to take back to the people of Many Rocks canyon. He thinks that once they know the entire story of the scheme, they will want to deal with him, especially because of their missing girls."

"He should probably take them both there. And what of you?"

She thought about this a moment. "Coyote Alone and I will go together."

Fat Badger smiled. "Before you go I need you to do something for me."

"What is that?"

He looked at the pieces of the 'throwing beast'. "I want you to burn all the pieces of that thing, all the ropes too." He looked to one side, "You can throw those bodies on the fire too if you like."

Pale Falcon looked over at the three dead men that she and her group had killed. "That one is my uncle — your brother. I remember his face from seeing him years ago. Why was he going to kill you?"

"Listen to me! I tell you this, and it is forever true. He was no one any of us knew. He was a man named Two Ravens, and we have never seen him before."

She nodded. Then she said, "What about those oddly shaped rocks?"

Fat Badger picked up one of the rocks. It was heavy and made from a dense material. Carefully ground by hand into the general shape of a square but with two knobs left on opposite sides of one end, it looked useless unless you knew about the weights. The loops of rope had been fitted over these knobs diagonally to hold the rocks against the log.

He noticed that one of the rocks was another of the same pink material as the fragment Tall Claw had had in his pouch. "Hu-eh!" he said in surprise.

"What is it, father?" Asked Pale Falcon.

"Nothing," he answered. He looked at the rocks. There was some wear on the bottom from them striking the ground when they fell. "Leave the rocks; maybe someone will find a good use for them someday."

XLV

—in the Warrior's compound—

Fat Badger walked into the Warriors' compound carrying the body of the white dog. Looking around, he saw the black dog laying over near the wall of Tall Claw's house. She eyed him curiously but did not move toward him.

Walking over to where Tall Claw was buried, he located a digging stick and began excavating a shallow pit in the ground. After a while, he stood up and grunted, satisfied. He laid the body of the white dog down gently on the ground and walking over to the house he climbed up onto the roof and went down the ladder. The black dog got up from where she was laying as he did so and wandered over to where her sister lay. As he climbed down the ladder, he noticed her sniffing curiously at the body of the white dog.

Rummaging around in the house he found a blanket and carrying it with him he climbed back up out of Tall Claw's house. Returning to the body of the white dog, he watched as the other one wandered in a broad arc away from him back to where she first lay.

Breaking the arrow that transfixed the dog, he pulled it out both ends and flung them away. Gently he wrapped the white dog in the blanket and laid it in the pit. Then, thinking of something else, he jumped up and ran back to step up on the house roof. Fat Badger chuckled as the black dog growled at him as it ran off. He climbed down inside the house again.

Once in the house, Fat Badger searched all through the various baskets and nets suspended from vigas and lying on the floor until he found several bits of bone, dried meat, and animal skin. Returning to the white dog's graveside, he lowered these things down into the pit. Then he scraped dirt in over the covered body, singing a song as he did so. It was a simple song that a child might sing to a pet. It seemed appropriate.

Piling rocks over the top of the grave he stood. Dusting off his hands he looked about for the black dog. He didn't see her anywhere.

Then he turned his eyes to the southwest corner of the compound.

Remembering that this was the one place the dogs would never go, he wondered more about it. What Two Ravens said to him piqued his interest because of what he had said about their father.

Their father? He grunted again. What did that concern?

Walking over to the area he used the digging stick to scrape the hard-packed floor surface back and forth, but nothing of interest showed. He looked at the walls. Walking outside, he went around to the southwest corner. It appeared to him that the wall bulged out somewhat on the south side.

Re-entering the compound, he picked up a handled maul and walking up to the corner he tapped on the wall.

He found what he was looking for barely an arm's length east of the corner. Striking the wall about three hands above the floor he heard a hollow sound. He used the maul to hit the wall harder. Pounding it, again and again, he broke through into a small open space. Pulling aside the stones and dirt debris he looked into the rounded niche.

Inside lay bones, the bones of a human being. Scattered in a pile on the rough floor of the hollow; someone had gathered them up and put them there. What's more, he saw that on a forearm bone of the skeleton was a carved shell bracelet. He reached into the space and sliding it off the bone; he withdrew the bracelet. It depicted a snake that rattles.

Fat Badger knew that bracelet only too well. He had seen it nearly every day of his life as a child. It belonged to his father; the man he knew as his father.

He looked at the remains of the skull. It was crushed by many blows probably from a war club. Its fragments lay scattered about amid the rocks. Standing up, he turned his back on the bones. Fat Badger walked away from his grisly find.

"Time to go," he said aloud. He went back into the house. Gathering a few personal belongings, he climbed the ladder up out of Tall Claw's house for probably the last time.

Leaving the compound, he shouldered a basket he had deposited outside and started down the trail toward the stream. Reaching it, he turned to the right on the path past Sky Creek Town. He passed the village not even bothering to look to see if anyone was there. He knew his daughters Hummingbird and Butterfly left with the rest of the villagers days before.

He hoped they had made it to the neighbors' village safely.

After a while, he reached a point directly across the stream from Dead Women Canyon. Stopping, he gazed across the water, noting that it ran bank to bank, swelled by the melting snows. On the opposite bank, he saw the little stream from the canyon ran strongly to join Sky Creek.

High above that point fires still smoldered at the head of the canyon where Pale Falcon burned the pieces of Two Raven's 'throwing beast'. More dispersed smoke rose above the place where the Immigrant's village was. The canyon looked peaceful. Fat Badger wondered if his nephew still hid somewhere up in that rugged defile?

He looked at the sky, it remained full of clouds, but they were white and less dense than they had been in weeks.

Sniffing the wind, he caught no scent of rain or snow.

Sighing, Fat Badger turned and was about to continue when he heard a 'crack' of wood from somewhere behind him. There followed the sounds of rocks falling. He stood in place holding his breath; feeling the beat of his heart. Finally, just as he was about ready to continue, he detected the distant sound of wood striking stone.

Not again! he thought.

A noise behind him made him gasp! Whirling around, holding his walking stick up in front of him protectively, he stared back the way he had come.

There, padding down the trail toward him, came the black dog.

END

—AUTHOR'S NOTES—

The impetus for this story has its origins in several incidents.

As an archaeology student in the early 1970s I had the opportunity to work on some teams excavating a series of sites in the mountainous valleys of central Arizona. Over two+ seasons we cleared six and a half sites. All of those appear as settings in this novel. For example, what I call 'Cloud Spring' was the first site excavated as part of the project. The museum report on the excavation suggested it may have been a trading site.

The site I call 'the Immigrant's village' was the last site we worked on in the valley. Unfortunately, we ran out of time in our season, and did not finish. We left with plans to return the following summer. In the interim, the contract was cancelled and the remaining thirty plus sites scheduled to be cleared went unexplored. Most, if not all, were destroyed, including the one we did not finish.

In case there is any question, I did find mixed-up, broken human bones of two people beneath the fragments of a large cooking pot outside one of the rooms. It appeared to be a case of cannibalism which is unusual in the prehistoric record (it is the only example I am familiar with in nearly 35 years of work). However, as I said the site was never completed and the final report remains unwritten, so it is all speculation.

The next event that help generate this book occurred about a dozen years after the field work. I led a group of Boy Scouts on a hike down into the valley with the intent of camping overnight on the banks of the creek. Within an hour of setting up camp it began to snow (it was late February). Then it really snowed!

Hastily we broke camp. There was only one pick-up available to ferry boys and stuff back up to the cars so it made three perilous trips on a muddy mountain road that became more treacherous with each run. I was in the last group, fish-tailing up the road in darkness (the headlights failed!) by the light of a flashlight held out the window. By the time we reached the nearest town it was a full blizzard outside and we hunkered down at a motel.

One final inspiration came in the form of an archaeologist friend's reports on a phenomenon known as 'fergoliths'. They are the odd shaped stones I describe in the story as being used as weights on the "throwing beast". No definitive theory of the use for these artifacts has been set forth so I postulated one.

A final note, the prehistoric turquoise mine as I describe it in the valley is authentic and as far as I know, it is still there.

Made in the USA
Coppell, TX
21 May 2021